Where the River Goes

Martha Rodriguez

Cover design by Danielle James

ACKNOWLEDGMENTS

What would I do without those who read my manuscript and tell me how to make it better? I trust these worthy people and their insights and honesty: Pat Blake, Debbie Archer, Brenda Rawls, and my dependable family members, Beth and Zoe, who always help and encourage me. Thank you, ladies.

*[God] said, 'I have found David the son of Jesse, a man after My own heart…*Acts 13:22 NKJV

Jonathan and David made a covenant, because he loved him as his own soul. And Jonathan took off the robe that was on him and gave it to David, with his armor, even to his sword and his bow and his belt. 1 Samuel 18:3-4 NKJV

So everything will live where the river goes. Ezekiel 47:9 NLV

While we meander through our world dealing with present issues and situations, we are ignorant about things going in other places with other people. These events often send out unseen ripples, and at some point, these ripples may intersect with our lives to bring about changes, good and bad.

On the river:

"Ping!" A bullet ricocheted off the Keep Out sign nailed to the tree beside his head. The agent dove behind the tree just as another bullet splintered the wood beside him. He peeped out in time to see two men turn and run through the dense brush along the edge of the river. He followed, running from tree to tree.

He came to the river to catch a few fish, not criminals. He didn't expect to have anyone fire at him. What would provoke them to shoot at a lone fisherman? Like an idiot, he left his gun and badge in his truck.

Agent S worked his way through vines and bushes until he could see the two men sitting on a log. *Good, they think they've lost me.* Because he grew up in the area, he likely knew the territory better than they, but he couldn't take any chances. After all, they were armed. He wasn't.

He watched them a while. One had dark curly hair and a burly physique, and the other looked like a sack of bones with reddish hair and mustache. The dark headed one could be one of the men on the wanted list. In fact, if they weren't on the list already, they would be soon.

He awaited his chance. There was plenty of time. After all, it was his vacation. Sure enough, Red rose and went to the river while Burly slumped against a stump for a nap. Red stooped to wash his face in the edge of the river, and Agent S used the opportunity to take Burly. He slipped up on the drowsing man and put him in a headlock before he could cry out. Agent S slammed the man's head against a stump and positioned his unconscious body the same way he was before, then waited behind a tree.

When Red returned, he leaned over Burly to rouse him. Agent S seized the chance to attack, and before Red knew what happened, Agent S stripped him of his shirt and used it to tie him to a tree. He used the same procedure to tie up Burly before he came to.

Agent S searched the two men and confiscated their weapons. He folded his arms and stood, surveying them. "Who are you and what are you doing here?"

They stood, silent.

Agent S smiled and walked around them. "So, you have nothing to say now. You said plenty with those shots you took at me a while ago." He put his face close to Red and growled. "You'd better talk now, Red."

He looked around for something he could use on them. Ah, there. He picked up a rotten limb covered with big black ants. He held it above Red's head and shook it. Ants covered the red hair and skittered down the man's collar. He yelled and twisted as the ants attacked him. Agent S moved close to Burly with the limb. Burly's eyes widened.

"No, please." His head jerked back and forth. "We're just here to catch some fish."

Agent S laughed. "Yeah, right. You gonna shoot the fish?" He raised the limb.

Burly screamed and tried to dodge the insects falling from the dead wood. "No! We were looking for a place to camp out later. That's all."

Red stomped and twisted his head. The ants moved down his face into his nose and mouth. He spit and sputtered. "Tell him, Snyder. I gotta get these creatures off me."

"Oh, Snyder, is it? You know, you look familiar. I think I've seen a picture of you on a poster. And how about you, Burley? Your picture on a poster with Snyder?" Agent S shook the limb and ants cascaded onto Burley's head.

Burley screamed again and jerked his head back and forth. "Arnold! My name is Silas Arnold. Please untie me so I can get these ants off. They're biting like crazy."

Agent S picked up a second dead limb covered with ants and walked toward the men. He lifted the limb. "What are you doing here? What is your business in these woods?"

The men struggled hard. Concerned they would break loose, Agent S pointed a gun and ordered them to be still. They knew if they revealed their criminal activity, freedom ended for them. Which was worse, going to prison or being eaten alive by ants? Either choice would be painful.

One

"I cannot believe you lost us the Lyndell account!" David's boss, Oliver Crandall, pounded the desk and stalked across the room to stand in front of David. "Son, you're supposed to add clients, not drive them away."

David lifted a hand then dropped it at his side. Scarlet crept up his neck and face, and his Adam's apple bobbed up and down. What could he say? Lyndell owned one of the biggest grain companies around, and David was trying to get him a good deal so he would stay with Crandall Shipping. He thought he'd won the account, but Lyndell hired another company to do his business.

Maybe his dad, Jesse Kingston, was right. Maybe he didn't belong in business. Maybe he should've earned a degree in music like Mom wanted. He could have gone to a trade school to be an electrician like Dad or a plumber. Maybe he would've been better off doing mechanic work or welding.

When they were growing up, he and his best friend Kade often visited Crandall's growing shipping business, and David loved it. He loved watching the river boats and barges coming into the dock. He reveled in watching the men wrestle the huge ropes and chains as they loaded and unloaded cargoes of grain, coal, steel, and fertilizer. He loved sitting outside the door of Oliver's office to listen to him wrangle deals with shipping agents and boat owners. After hearing one of these conversations, David knew what he wanted to do with his life. He wanted to be a businessman just like Oliver.

He couldn't believe it when Oliver offered him a position as a paid apprentice in his shipping company. It would give him an opportunity to learn from the best, and together he and Mr. Crandall would build Crandall Shipping into the biggest in the nation. Now if only he could convince his dad Oliver wasn't a corrupt, double-dealing charlatan.

Jesse Kingston and Oliver Crandall had grown up together on Crandall Island, and Jesse had celebrated when Oliver became an engineer. Then Oliver moved to the city and purchased a shipping company, and Jesse sent clients his way when they needed anything built or shipped. According to Jesse, money became Oliver's most valued possession above his family, friends and clients. The two men grew apart and were more like strangers for the past several years. When Jesse found out about the paid internship Oliver offered his son, he tried to talk David out of taking it.

David reached for a bowl of mashed potatoes. "Dad, working for Oliver Crandall is a great opportunity for me. I can learn from him."

Jesse helped himself to a biscuit. "Son, there are so many other things in life you can do besides work for Oliver Crandall."

"But working for him will give me a head start in the business world. He's one of the best, you know."

"I know that Oliver Crandall handles his business in ways that are unethical. I've seen it myself. I hate to see my son hold such a man up as a role model."

"Just because I work for him doesn't mean he's my role model." David stabbed his fork into his pork steak. "Have you never worked for someone who did wrong things? I know you did, because you told me about one boss you had who was a thief. Did you become a thief because of him?"

"No, of course not."

"Nor will I do wrong things because my boss does." David set down his glass and wiped his mouth with his napkin. "Dad, you've taught me well. You're my role model."

Jesse smiled and handed David a bowl of corn. "Well, okay. I guess you'll be all right. You've got a good head and a good heart."

"Maybe I can be a positive influence on him. You said he was a good guy until he became successful. Maybe now that he's successful he'll be good again. People do change, you know."

Sure, that was it. The old Oliver had to take necessary measures to build his business. Now that he was successful, things would be different, and David would assist him in building the business to a greater level of success. Maybe Oliver would make him a partner.

David shook off the memories as Oliver dismissed him. He would make up the loss to the company. He had to. In his office, he scanned the scene from his window. He loved that river. He had looked forward to working on the Mississippi where Oliver made his millions, the same river which was a playground for him and Kade as they grew up. Even though the two boys were quite opposite—blond David, a music lover with big dreams, and dark-headed Kade who enjoyed nothing more than playing a joke on any unsuspecting victim—they shared a love for their families, for Crandall Island, and for the river. His lips curved into a smile as he thought about the days before he started working for Oliver.

Like he had so often in the past, he stayed in the Crandall home with Kade to avoid the boat ride over from Crandall Island where he and his parents lived. The day he was to start his internship, he awoke in the spacious guest bedroom. As a boy, he and Kade bunked together in Kade's room, but Kade's mom, Melody, insisted he stay in the guest room now that he was grown.

He awoke early, slipped on a pair of jeans, and stretched out on the king-sized bed. Heavy navy curtains framed a large window from which he could see the river bordered by trees and buildings. The expansive home lay far enough from the city to escape the smog and noise of the bustling metropolis. David loved his modest home on the Island but dreamed of having a family in a house like this on the mainland. Oh, to have money. Lots of it.

Before he could answer the loud rapping, the door flew open and a body slammed him onto the bed.

"Argh!" He threw up an arm to shield himself from his attacker and rolled over.

"Dang, David. You're such a wimp." Kade rolled off the bed and onto the floor. "Nothing has changed since we were kids."

"Except one thing." David jumped off the edge of the bed and wrapped a leg around his laughing friend. "Now I'm taller than you. Ha!" The two young men wrestled until another knock on the door drew their attention.

"Come on, guys, breakfast is ready." Sadie, Kade's

younger sister, threw a pillow at the two. "Hurry up or we'll eat without you."

David jumped to his feet and before she could get away, he put her in a headlock.

"Ouch!" Sadie squealed "You big bully! Let me go!"

"Not until you say 'I love you, David. You're the most handsome man who ever lived.'" David loved to tease Sadie even though he knew she would retaliate when he least expected it.

"I don't love you, David, and you are not handsome. Let me go!"

He laughed and scrubbed her head with his knuckles before he let her go. She ran down the hall rubbing her head, then turned. "David, before you leave, would you help me with my algebra?"

"Sure. Just let me get ready." David was the go-to when anyone in the family needed help with math.

A few minutes later he tweaked her hair and plopped beside her at the counter where she bent over an open college textbook. "Your dad already left for the office?"

"Yes. You know how he is. Always the early bird."

Melody enjoyed the camaraderie of the three young people who laughed and teased each other. As a teacher she loved children, but none so much as her own.

"David, I haven't seen your mom and dad in a while. How are they?" Melody asked. The Crandalls and Kingstons had remained friends even though they saw little of each other.

"They're great." David swallowed and wiped his mouth with his napkin. "Just the other day Mom mentioned she'd like to see you again. She misses you, you know."

"I know. I miss her too. Kathleen and I spent a lot of time together, talking, laughing, and enjoying life." Her eyes misted, and she gazed out the window. "Is she still giving music lessons?"

"Yes, when she isn't playing in a symphony or doing a fund-raiser for some cause."

"Come on and I'll drive you to the office. Dad said he would meet you there." Kade downed the last of his coffee, and he and David bounded out the door. They jumped into Kade's black escalade, and visions of a red Porsche flickered across David's brain. As they drove through the heavy traffic, Kade turned the radio down.

"Hey, I like that song." David reached to turn it back up but Kade's solemn expression stopped him. "What's going on, Kade?"

"I need to talk to you before you start working for Dad."

"Yeah? What is it?"

"Dad told me this morning he's giving me the Public Relations job. Of course, I'll work under supervision for a while until I learn the ropes."

"Hey! Congratulations! That's a big deal for you, right?" David extended his fist, but Kade ignored the gesture. "What's wrong? Is there something else?"

Kade shook his head and knitted his brows. "You do realize that means I'll be gone most of the time. Dad's sending me to Europe next week."

"Wow! Europe. You sure you're ready? I mean, you've been there such a short time."

"I'll be going with Scott, one of Dad's employees. He's in PR, but Dad's moving him. He's going to train me." Kade grinned. "I'm sort of an apprentice but a little different."

"I'd say so." Kade had always had it good. Being a Crandall had its perks—fancy cars and expensive clothes. A step up in the world. Working for Oliver Crandall would give David a step up, too.

David shrugged. "You're the boss's son. Won't be long until you'll be the CEO." This time when David extended his fist, Kade gave him a fist bump.

"A word of caution, though, David. Be careful."

"What do you mean? I'm working for your dad."

"I know. Just be careful. Dad can be a little like a Venus fly-trap."

David stared at Kade. "I have no idea what you're talking about."

Kade laughed and shook his head. "Never mind." He parked the black Escalade in the parking garage. "We'd better hurry. Dad hates it when people are late."

On the river

Hoping to catch a few catfish to sell, Bill Bates trolled his boat around a log extending into the river. His livelihood depended on the river, and lately his luck was running short. He liked to fish upriver, but with nothing there, he decided to try a new spot. This looked like a good one.

He set out jugs and checked lines he'd set out the day before. One flat-head catfish flopped when he pulled it in, and he whistled at the size of a channel catfish hooked on a jug. So far, so good, but he needed to do better.

A sparkle in the weeds at the edge of the water caught his eye, and Bill pulled close to investigate. He could see an object under the water. He reached and pulled out a water-soaked doll. The yellow yarn hair was a little dirty, but it still looked in good shape. He might have his wife Lily clean it for their daughter, Emile. He peered over the side of the boat and reached again into the water. He gasped when he pulled out a handgun. The cartridge was missing two shells and the lack of rust suggested it hadn't been there long.

Should he take it to law enforcement? The river police disliked and distrusted the river people. If he turned in a gun tied to a crime, they might try to connect it to him. He could keep it, but he didn't want to take any chances. He put the doll in the boat, wiped the gun clean of his fingerprints, and threw it into the deep water.

$\mathcal{T}wo$

They had not been late. In the two months since he started his internship, he had never been late. In fact, he arrived early every day. He was determined to succeed at this job, and he wanted to make a good impression on his boss. When he and Kade were little Oliver was around a lot, but when they reached adolescence, his work seemed to take him away from home most of the time. David knew Kade craved the kind of relationship he and Jesse had. In his and David's teen years, he seemed to have settled for a closeness with Jesse instead.

On one occasion when Jesse and the two boys were camping, Kade confided in David. "Your dad is great. I hope you don't mind sharing him with me." He didn't mind. Kade was like his brother and the two shared almost everything anyway.

"Stop with the memories, already!" he scolded himself aloud. He opened his computer and scanned his files. What could he do to regain the trust of his boss? He opened a file and looked at the columns of numbers. Simpson was picking up a load down river and would be docking in a few hours to unload. But wait. He didn't have a full load.

David dialed a number, spoke briefly, and then dialed again. "Simpson, where are you? Could you stop at Porters and pick up a load from there? Yeah, they have a boat delayed and need a load of grain gone today. Great."

He grabbed a tablet and ran to the dock where a

tugboat loaded with fertilizer was pulling in. He jumped onto the boat and spoke with the captain who nodded as he listened. David smiled and waved as he headed back to his office. One more victory. He would show Oliver he could handle the business, and Kade would be proud for him.

Back at the office he spoke with Ms. Emma Clancy, Oliver's secretary. She had been instrumental in teaching him the business. From her he learned to file, to enter data into the computer, which clients were the most important, which clients were new, and what the clients wanted and needed from the business.

"Dear sweet boy, you're working so hard." Her eyes twinkled as she handed him a glass of iced sweet tea. "Don't let Mr. Crandall get to you. He can be cantankerous sometimes, but he knows shipping. He'll teach you well if you can take his ill-tempered stubbornness."

David laughed and shrugged. "I can take it—at least, I hope. I want to learn everything, you know? I want to run my own business someday."

"And you will. I just know it." She winked and patted his arm. "I'll do what I can to help you."

A few weeks later, Oliver asked David to accompany him to meet a client. David was surprised to see Kade waiting in the restaurant parking lot.

"Lunch with my two favorite men. Doesn't get any better than this." Oliver walked between the two young men into the building and guided them to a table.

Kade laughed. "Dad, you sound like a beer commercial."

Oliver insisted they order the largest steak on the menu and joked with the waitress.

"These young men are the handsomest, smartest and most available young men in the city," he bragged. "You'd do well to snatch one of them up if you aren't already attached."

David and Kade rolled their eyes as they ordered. When they were kids, Oliver had teased them incessantly about girls until they asked Melody to make him stop.

"This steak is really good." David took another bite. "Thanks, Mr. Crandall."

"Yeah, thanks, Dad. Glad you invited me."

"Save your thanks for later, guys. This meal is on you." Oliver laughed when they stared at him, then excused himself. They watched as he spoke to various people and poked his head through the kitchen doors to compliment the chef.

"Dad really likes you working for him." Kade took a swig of sweet tea and forked another piece of steak. "He brags on you all the time to Mom and me."

A smile spread across David's face. "Whew! I thought he'd fire me for a while. I lost a big account and he was plenty mad. But I made it up to him, I think. Anyway, I'm trying."

"From what he tells us, you're doing great. Oh, here he comes."

Oliver slipped into his seat. "I thought for a minute I was at the wrong table. You two look like a cute couple sitting there together. But then I saw the way you're stuffing your faces. That doesn't look so cute."

Back at the company, Oliver called David into his office. "David," he said, "I'm going out of town for a few days, and I'm trusting you to take care of things around here. You seem to be doing better. At least you haven't cost me any more clients in a while." He laughed and handed David a stack of files. "Go through these files and see if you can sort out a schedule for these guys. I'm counting on you, son."

"Mr. Crandall, there's something I've been wanting to ask you."

"Well, what is it, Son? Spit it out."

David moved to the computer. "There's this new software I think would really help our...I mean, your company. It would make scheduling shipping a whole lot easier."

"Ah, we don't need any new computer stuff. I can't keep up now. We're fine with doing it the old-fashioned way."

"But, sir, if you want the business to grow, you need to be current in all the aspects of the business. I've researched it, and most all shipping companies are starting to use it. It would make our scheduling so much more effective. I really think it would help grow our business."

Oliver stared at David and then nodded. "Well, okay, son. If you think it would help us, then go ahead and get it. Ms. Emma will help you if it costs, which I'm sure it does." He grinned as he picked up his briefcase. "A little progress never hurt anyone."

David's chin lifted and his chest swelled. His boss was depending on him, and he wouldn't let him down. He and Ms. Emma purchased the software and before long, he was transferring all the schedules to the program. He loved the new program. He was concentrating on a file when Ms. Emma knocked on his door.

"David, this is Silas Hebron. He has a question about his account. Mr. Hebron, David is Mr. Crandall's intern. He's learning the business around here and right now he's in charge of things." Ms. Emma patted David's arm. "Mr. Crandall is hoping David will one day be ready to help him with shipping."

"Well, David, maybe you can help me with my problem." Mr. Hebron followed David into the office.

"I don't know if I'll be able to help you, sir, but I will if I can."

He opened the files while Mr. Hebron explained that his schedule was all in a mess. "Where was the last load you picked up?"

"A week ago, I picked up a load of fertilizer at New Orleans. I unloaded it in Baton Rouge and picked up a load of seed. My contract says I will be supplied with a load every time I make the trip. I can't see that I'll have a load to carry back south."

"Okay, let's check. Ummm, you can pick up a load of beans in the morning and head south for Natchez. There'll be a load ready for you there to take to New Orleans. That should get you where you need to be. I will contact you when another load is ready for your return trip."

"That sounds great, son." Mr. Hebron slapped David on the back. "You sure know how to make my schedule on that computer."

David smiled. "It's a new program and it really helps us keep things running smoothly."

"I don't know anything about computers, but I'm glad you do."

Soon, another client came in and David helped him work out a shipping schedule. Before long other clients were requesting David's help with their schedules. Oliver returned to find his clients excited about David's assistance.

"David, my boy, I've been hearing good things about you from my clients." His eyebrows raised. "I guess you're learning how things are run around here."

"I've learned a lot, with the help of Ms. Emma." David shoved the folder into the file cabinet. "I want to learn everything possible, so I won't mess up again. And that new scheduling software is great."

Oliver led him into his office. "Is that right?" He turned on his computer. "I'll teach you more about the business and later you'll have to show me how to use the software. How does that sound?"

"Sounds great. I look forward to learning from you." David glanced at Ms. Emma and grinned. If Oliver surpassed Ms. Emma as a teacher, he would be unbelievable.

He was. Unbelievable. Every day Oliver spent time showing David how to run the business. Using his knowledge of the new software, he impressed Oliver when he brought in three new clients in the first three weeks.

"Are you ready for me to show you the scheduling software?" David approached Oliver after lunch one day.

Oliver shook his head. "Did you finish these contracts for the new clients?"

"Yes, I finished them this morning. They're ready for your signature."

David watched as Oliver flipped through the files, reading and signing the papers. He took longer on one file, reading through parts multiple times and making marks on the paper. When David looked over his shoulder, Oliver closed the file.

"Did I do it wrong?" David asked. "I was careful to do it the way you showed me."

"Oh, no." Oliver shook his head. "A couple of things needed tweaked. Nothing important." He buzzed the secretary. "Ms. Emma, these are ready to file." He checked his watch and headed for the door. "Come on, let's go grab a bite."

At the restaurant, the waitresses knew Oliver, as did several other people sitting at tables. Pleasant conversation filled the room as the discussion moved from business to family and memories of David and Kade growing up. They were leaving when a man patted David' shoulder.

"Here's the guy who's been taking the business world by storm." He shook David's hand. "Crandall, where did you find this young man? I heard he's a whiz on the computer."

Oliver beamed and put his arm around David's shoulders. "Hey, Johnson. This is David Kingston, my intern."

"Glad to meet you, David. People around here have been raving about the job you're doing for old Crandall here." Johnson chortled and slapped Oliver on the back. "Won't be long until you'll be taking over the business."

Oliver's smile widened. "He still has quite a lot to learn, but he's quick. I'll make him a top shipper in no time."

"I do have a lot to remember," David said. "I could never take over Crandall Shipping, but maybe one day I'll have my own business. Think Mr. Crandall will help me?"

"Sure, he will." Johnson grinned at Oliver. "Who knows, maybe one day you'll come to work for me." He turned to speak to a waitress.

"Come on, David. We need to get back to work." Oliver tossed up a hand to Johnson and guided David out the door.

On the river

Hands clapped and feet stomped to the sound of fiddle and guitar music. The river people needed a reprieve from the struggles to put food on the table and clothes on the backs of their growing families, and music gave them that needed relief. Like a strong magnet, the new casino boats that docked nearby pulled at those who dreamed of riches. Others were constantly tempted by whispered voices from along the river, voices that urged them to make choices that would change their lives forever—choices that could destroy them.

Three

"Hey, let's get out of here, man!" Kade had returned from Europe the day before and talked David into taking a fun trip on the river for old time's sake. Duffle bags were packed with a box of chips, and three big coolers full of cold-cuts, hot dogs, drinks, and Kade's favorite snack, celery and peanut butter. To be inconspicuous, Kade took his dad's outboard motorboat. They wanted their trip to be lazy and uneventful. One time they traveled the river in one of Oliver's cabin cruisers, and everywhere they stopped or even slowed, they were approached by people asking for money, for food, for drug deals, for anything and everything.

In a short time, they were loaded and motoring down the big river. They visited their favorite fishing holes, icing the fish they caught in a large cooler. They would donate their catch to a luckless fisherman who needed them for his dinner. They camped on the bank, a spot where they spent many nights, and reminisced about their childhood adventures on the river and on Crandall Island.

Jesse often told David and Kade stories about the fun he and Oliver spent exploring every nook and cranny of the Island and the hard work they endured in the cotton fields. Oliver's family ran a ranch at the head of the five-mile long, three-mile wide piece of land in the middle of the Mississippi River, and cotton fields covered the rest. Families often moved to the Island to work in the fields and some called

Crandall Island home, but mostly Crandall's hired hands lived there.

The two boys knew every good fishing hole, every backwater pool, and every snag for miles on either side of the wide expanse of water. They explored every dip and rise of the sandy island. They also knew the favorite runs of bootleggers and drug suppliers who got rich on poor citizens who eked out a living fishing from the banks, from rickety wooden piers, and from john boats. These people lived hard lives, and profiteers who cared for nothing but making another buck off them abounded.

"I wonder, who helped us the night we got caught in that big storm?" David poked the campfire with a stick. "We would've been in trouble if he hadn't come along when he did."

"Yeah." Kade sighed. "I wish I knew. I'd like to thank him for saving us." Silence fell as each young man was lost in his own thoughts as he recalled the night they almost drowned.

They had worked for weeks tying ropes and vines around logs to build a raft, trying to emulate Huckleberry Finn and Tom Sawyer. They pushed the heavy raft into the water on the chute side of the Island and pushed off the bank. The river was already high from recent rains, and when the long poles they used to guide the vessel no longer touched the bottom, they guided it with crude paddles they made from boards. In their excitement, they failed to notice the descending darkness and the gathering clouds. The storm came when they were in the middle of the river. They paddled hard, fighting the current which kept them away from the shore until they came to a bend where the current pushed them to a tree-lined bank.

"David, grab the limb!" A bolt of lightning lit up the night as rain pelted the water around the two boys. The homemade raft bobbed and spun in the raging water as David and Kade clung to the ropes holding it together.

"I can't reach it." David grasped the edge of the raft. "Look out for the root wad, Kade." Kade tried to grab a low hanging branch but couldn't hold on to it. In desperation, the boys waited for another bolt of lightning and another chance to get to the bank and escape the rising water.

Chain lightning lit the sky, revealing a log bobbing beside them. "Can you reach it?" David grabbed a paddle and rowed hard toward the log while Kade extended his hand toward it. "Be careful, Kade. Don't fall."

The warning came too late. Kade fell headfirst into the muddy water. His swimming ability held strong, but the swift water kept pulling him under until David managed to row the raft close enough to grab his shirt and pull him aboard. The exhausted, cold, and terrified boys lay gasping on the spinning raft.

A man in a hooded jacket ran along the banks peering into the groves of trees growing there. A figure darted from behind a tree in front of him, and slid on the muddy banks, almost falling into the raging water. As his hand reached to close on the figure, Shepherd heard yelling coming from under a tree that jutted out over the water. A rickety raft was shoved against a low-hanging branch and two drenched kids hung on.

"Cripes!" He grabbed the branch and hauled one boy out by the shirt and grabbed for the other one. His hand slipped, but he managed to grab the waist band of the jeans before the raft whirled and spun down the river. He pulled both boys away from the river and deposited them under a cypress tree where he knew they would be safe. When he turned, lightning lit the sky and he saw the figure disappear in the darkness.

"Cripes!" He smacked a fist into his other hand and headed back in the direction he had come.

Kade shuddered at the memory. "Who pulled us ashore?"

"That's the mystery." David shifted in his sleeping bag. "All I remember is hands pulling us off the raft and up the bank."

As they traveled further the next day, they caught several more fish, a turtle, and a large cotton-mouth snake, which almost landed in the boat with them.

"Dang, you scream like a girl," Kade teased David. "You've been away from the river too long."

"You'd scream too if a cotton-mouth almost wrapped around your neck." David threw an empty Pepsi can at Kade. "Besides, those people over there heard you yell when that snapping turtle went after your toe."

The bantering stopped when a large, red speed boat came around the bend, turning in time to avoid crashing into them. The wake shoved them into the bushes along the bank, and David, who stood to untangle his fishing line, fell into the bottom of the boat to avoid going over the side.

"Whoa! He could hurt someone. Did you know him?" Kade held on to keep from falling as the waves rocked the small boat. "I know most of the boats in this area, but I haven't seen that one."

"Me either." David righted the bait can and retrieved his pole from the water. "We may need to check with the River Port Authority to find out if he's licensed. He's driving like an idiot."

"David! Look!" Kade pointed upriver to a boat capsized in the middle of the water. He started the engine and sped toward the accident, and when they were near, they could see two figures bobbing among the debris scattered on the water. David pulled close so Kade could pull the soaked fishermen aboard.

Once the man ensured the safety of his young companion, he shook his fist and called the man in the red boat every ugly name he could think of.

"The lousy idiot!" His toothless mouth dripped with tobacco juice. "If I could catch him, I'd beat him within an inch of his life. He should be horse whipped. He has no business owning a boat. We could've been killed." He ranted and raved while David and Kade waited for him to finish. After a while he seemed to run out of steam, and for the first time, he noticed his rescuers.

Red-faced, he stuck out his hand. "Say, thanks, guys. We sure do appreciate your help. Maybe we could have made it, but it's pretty far from the bank."

"Hey, no problem." David picked up a paddle floating beside the boat. "We're glad we were close by and saw you. This is Kade and I'm David."

"Pete Jenkins here. Pleased to meet ya. Hank, will you grab that bait can? This here's my grandson, Hank. Here, pull over so I can get that paddle." The men gathered floating boat cushions, paddles, and other debris from the water. "Do you guys know the maniac driving that red boat?" David and Kade shook their heads and offered Pete and Hank a Pepsi.

"Pull close, Kade. I think I can reach the rope. We'll pull the boat over to the bank." They worked together to get the boat out and to upright it. David and Kade helped dip out the water.

"Hey, Pete!" A johnboat with a trolling motor pulled up beside them. "Got trouble?"

"Oh, hi Tom. That idiot came flying around the bend and knocked us over. These guys came to help us." In colorful words he described the incident, and Tom nodded.

"Man, we been gittin' more of them lately. We gotta do something about those guys before they take over the river."

"Yeah, you're right there. The river's been buzzing with speed boats driven by crazies. Ain't no respect for us fishermen."

Tom glanced at David and Kade. "You guys from around here? Don't recall seein' you before."

"Sure," Kade said. "We grew up on this river, but we've been gone a while. College, you know."

"Say, ain't you Crandall's kid?"

"Sure am." Kade laughed. "Thought I knew you, Tom. You remember Jesse Kingston? This is his son, David."

"Why yeah, I know ole Jesse. Good man he is. Lives on the Island, right?" Tom looked at their gear. "You boys doing a little fishing?"

"Yep, reliving the old days and catching one or two." David jumped to the bank and turned to help Hank who already stepped out on a log to help Pete. "We have a pretty good catch in the cooler. Any of you want them?" He dragged the cooler to the end of the boat and pulled out a large flathead catfish.

"Sure." Tom gave a toothless grin. "We ain't had any luck, and Mama is counting on us to bring home supper." He opened a large cooler in his boat and Kade filled it with fish.

"Thanks, Bud. You've made Mama a happy woman."

The men turned when a motorboat came roaring up and a man jumped out into the water before the driver docked the boat.

"Tom! It's Molly. She's missing."

"What do ya mean she's missing, Zeb?"

"Sharon says she's been gone since yesterday 'bout noon. We can't find her anywhere. You know that girl wouldn't jus' take off." Zeb wiped his face and shook his head. "It's jus' like the other girl who disappeared last week. They still ain't found her."

Tom turned to David. "This is the third girl gone missing in as many weeks. Ain't found none of them yet."

David frowned. "Do you have any idea what's happened to them?"

"Nope." Tom clenched his jaw. "And they're just kids. All 'bout thirteen or even younger. The sheriff is looking into it but found nothing yet. We don't understand what's going on." He turned to Zeb who headed back to the boat. "I'll get help and we'll come help you look. Maybe she's staying with a friend or something."

"Done checked it out. Sharon's beside herself with fear. Jess and Rick are lookin' on the other side of the river. Be glad to have your help." The boat roared back down the river.

On the river

A brown and white beagle sniffed the willow branches hanging low along the banks of the river. A blond-headed boy about six years old threw rocks into the water, and a girl about the same age sat close, playing with a rag doll. The two children were oblivious to a boat creeping toward the bank a little way upriver.

A man stepped ashore approached the children. He looked around and stepped behind a tree so they couldn't see him. He gave a low whistle and snapped his fingers. The dog raised its head and wagged its tail.

"Come here, dog," the man whispered. The dog trotted to him. The man held out his hand and gave the dog something.

The boy looked toward the dog. "Daisy! Come 'ere, girl." The dog looked at him and wagged its tail but stayed near the man. The boy moved toward the dog and saw the man. "Who are you?"

"Daisy is a really nice dog." The man scratched Daisy's ears. "Is she yours?"

"Yeah. Mine and Addie's. That's her over there." He pointed to the girl.

"What's your name?" The man squatted to pet Daisy. Another man, unseen by the children, hid behind a bush.

"I'm Will. What's your name?"

"Will, it's nice to meet you. Is Addie your sister?"

"Yes. She's my twin sister."

"How would you like to go for a ride on my boat? It's right over there."

Will shook his head. "Nah. Me and Addie gotta go home.

Come on, Daisy." He patted his leg and Daisy went to him, wagging her whole body. Will walked over to Addie, and the man followed. "Come on, Addie. It's time to go."

"Addie, would you like to take a little boat ride with me?" The man stooped to eye level with the little girl. She nodded.

Will frowned and shook his head. "No, Addie. We gotta go home."

The man grabbed Addie, and the other man grabbed Will. They loaded the kicking, screaming children into the boat and sped up the river.

Four

"Tom, what do you think's going on?" David watched as Tom gazed across the river. All his life, this river was his home, and the changes he saw had to be hard for him.

"David, there're things going on around here that's got me baffled." He rubbed his stubbled chin. "I'm seeing water vehicles and people goin' up and down this river I ain't never seen, and something ain't feelin' right. I just caint put my finger on it."

David and Kade glanced at each other. They were to be back at the office in the morning, and they had a long way to go.

Kade cocked his head. "What can we do to help?"

"Well," Tom shifted from one foot to the other, "there could be one thing you can do." He ran his thick tongue over dry lips. "Maybe you could get your dad to talk to the River Port Authority about the situation. He's an important man, and they'd listen to him."

"Sure," Kade said. "I'll talk to him. Maybe he'll get something done."

Oliver would be angry if they were late to work the next morning, so they headed toward home. It was starting to get dark. They had gone only a short way when an old speedboat pulled up beside them and with a spotlight, motioned for them to pull over.

"Wonder what they want." Kade shaded his eyes from

the bright light. "Think we should pull over?"

"I don't know." David pivoted toward the boat. "With all the things going on around here we'd better be careful." Kade pulled the throttle but the motorboat could not keep ahead of the speedboat.

"Hey, there! Pull over! Now!" A gruff voice bellowed. They slowed and pulled to the side.

Kade cupped his hand to his mouth to make himself heard over the motor. "What's going on? Something wrong?"

The men held a lantern close to their faces so Kade and David could see them, and a bearded man spoke. "You guys from 'round here?"

"Yes." David nodded. "We've been gone a while, but we grew up on this river. What seems to be the problem?"

The man motioned to the boat driver. "Pull a little closer." He shone a light and peered at David and Kade a moment, and his jaw dropped. "Well, I'll be a horned toad! If it ain't ole Crandall's kid! And the Kingston kid! What're you guys doin' on the river? Heard you was goin' to a high-flutin' college or somethin'."

Kade laughed and turned off the motor. "How are you, Josiah? Haven't seen you in a while."

"We've been taking a few days to relive old times," David said. "Just heading back. Gotta be back to work tomorrow. What's up?"

Another man in the boat stood. "We're watching out for strangers 'round here. There've been some goings-on that ain't right, and we gotta look out for ourselves since the law don't seem concerned."

David looked past the man. "What's going on, Josiah?"

"Well, for one thing we've noticed things missing."

The other man clenched and unclenched his fists. "Yeah, things and folks."

Josiah glanced at the man and agreed. "It's true, David. We've called the authorities to report missing kids, and they come out here and poke around, but nothing ever happens. They accuse us of being bad parents, saying the kids ran away. But it ain't so."

A third man spoke. "And when we report missing property, they don't even bother to come check it out."

Josiah took his cap off and rubbed his gray hair. "We decided we've got to be our own law and protect ourselves, so we're runnin' our boats to keep an eye out for anyone who ain't from these parts."

"Say you've had a lot of property missing lately?" Kade asked. "Do you have any idea where it's going?"

"What kind of property?" David asked.

"Like fishing gear and even boats." The face of the third man contorted. "That's how we make our living 'round here."

"And it ain't just the stealin'." Josiah pointed downriver. "It ain't enough they have a river boat for gambling. Now, they's taking the gamblin' to the banks where we live, and a lot of our folks are being taken-in by these gangsters, especially the younguns."

"Folks along this river are poor, and it's easy for 'em to be fooled into a get-rich-quick scheme." The second man spoke in a quiet, clipped voice. "It ain't right for these strangers to take advantage of 'em."

David frowned. "I don't know what we can do, Josiah. I hate the changes we've seen on the river. I hate to see the good people who live here hurt." He turned to the other two men. "Do you ever see any of the River Port Authorities come around?"

The men glanced at each other and at Josiah. "You might say that." The first man lifted one shoulder.

"Yeah," the third man said. "They come around once in a while. We think they're part of the problem."

"Really?" Kade scratched his chin. "How's that?"

"Hard to put my finger on. Much as anything, it's who they associate with, and they seem to be hangin' 'round more'n usual. Seems when there's a situation, they're always there. I don't know. Just a gut feeling, I think." The man sat and cranked the motor.

"Have you ever heard the name Shepherd?" Josiah asked.

"No." David shook his head. "Who is he?"

"Well, I don't rightly know who he is or what he is. I know he seems to be around a lot. Kind of a quiet actin' man."

"What does he look like?" Kade asked.

The third man spoke again. "He's kinda smallish. Gettin' bald on top. Gray beard. Otherwise a regular guy."

Josiah changed the subject. "Hey, you still strum on a guitar, David? I'd like to hear a little of your music. Got time? My house is close on the foot of the island."

David grinned. Before long, they were sitting in the yard lit only by a campfire with a whole band of musicians playing tunes David hadn't heard since childhood. The mobile home behind them was probably one of the first built and had housed several generations of river kids. Bushes and vines sheltered it from the eyes of those who traveled the river in up-scale speed boats, fishing boats, and yachts.

"Ever hear this 'un?" A gray-haired, toothless man

fiddled a happy tune and the river people joined in. David and Kade sang along. A kid handed David a guitar, and if he didn't know a tune, he strummed along with the others.

"Help me do this song." David's fingers played along the guitar neck until he found his chord.

"Oh, I've heard that one." One of the teenagers jumped to his feet. "One of my favorite songs." He helped David teach his audience the words, and those who weren't playing instruments clapped and danced to the music.

Darkness settled in when David handed the guitar back, and he and Kade bid their farewells. Josiah and the other men walked with them back to their boat, and they headed back toward the city.

Kade guided the boat as they sat in silence. "Think there's anything to the River Port Authorities being involved in the trouble?"

"I don't know." David held on as Kade turned the boat around a curve. "Dad always talked about the honesty of Josiah. I don't believe he'd accuse a person if he didn't have good reason."

"Maybe we can find out what's going on tomorrow when we get back to the office." Kade looked at the moon. "Man, we'd better make time if we want to get any sleep tonight." He revved the motor. They sped upstream, arriving at the pier about midnight.

The next morning Oliver stalked through the door and motioned for David to follow him into his office.

"Want me to show you how the new scheduling program works?" David started toward the computer, but Oliver stopped him.

"No, not today. I'm meeting with Ted Stringer and I want you to sit in." Oliver sat at his desk. "I want to show you how I handle this account. It's important, and I can't afford to lose it."

David listened so he could understand the unusual traits of this client. He owned a large riverboat he used for hauling freight for various clients up and down the river.

"I don't know anything about such stuff," Mr. Stringer grumbled when he came into the office. "And I don't need it. There's nothing wrong with the way I've always done it."

"But Stringer, things are different now." Oliver turned the computer screen toward him. "David knows this computer program well. Yes, it's new, but it's better. We can't afford to lag in our business. You'll lose customers if you aren't careful."

"All this stuff will go away." Stringer waved his hand toward the computer. "You know it's just a fad. I want my business done in a way that's sure and stable, and we'll do it my way."

Oliver stood and walked around his desk. "Ted, I don't understand this computer stuff either, but I know it works. If it didn't, do you think successful businessmen would use it?"

Stringer laughed. "Ah, Oliver, you and I are old school. We could care less about what these other guys do. They come and go, but my business has been here for decades and will be around for decades more. You can take that to the bank." He shoved his chair back and stood. "And if you don't want to do it my way, I'll find someone who will."

"Oh, no, Mr. Stringer. We'll work it out." Oliver buzzed Ms. Emma. "Emma, would you bring in Mr. Stringer's file?" Oliver walked around his desk and looked out the window. "Mr. Stringer, is that your boat by the barge?"

When Stringer walked over to look, David moved to the computer. In a moment, he turned the monitor around facing Mr. Stringer's chair and waited until the two men returned to the desk.

"Look at this, Mr. Stringer." David moved the curser over the screen while he explained the process step by step to the older man. "Here is your boat, and over here is the Brooster boat. See it?"

"That's my boat? Why, it sure is." He scooted closer to the desk for a better view. "Look at that!"

"See this?" David moved the curser around. "Here is your schedule of shipments. And here is a list of your customers and all their information."

Mr. Stringer looked at David and confirmed he understood. David continued. "Now Abel Grizzely needs his freight to leave the dock Thursday at 10 o'clock. But over here Jack Nolen needs his to leave Thursday at two." David moved the cursor and a map of the river appeared along with a chart. "Here, if you leave the dock at seven, you can pick up Grizzely's load at ten then move right over to get Nolen's load at two with plenty of time to spare. If you want, you'll be able to schedule another load going in the same direction, then schedule return shipments. This program can do it for you. It will prevent your shipments from overlapping and you won't waste time."

Mr. Stringer sat silent a moment before he leaned toward the monitor. "Will you show me that again—the picture with the chart?"

"Sure." David opened the chart and the customer list. "This what you want?"

"Yes. So, I can view all my customers at the same time? And schedule shipments just like that?"

"Just like that." David grinned at the man's excitement. "It's easy."

"But I don't know anything about the computer."

"You don't have to worry about it, Mr. Stringer. I'll handle all of it for you. You will provide your client and shipment list, and we'll do the rest. Then you reap the benefits and watch your business grow."

"You have a deal!" Mr. Stringer clapped David on the back. "And young man, I want you to personally handle everything."

"Oh, I'm just an intern." David glanced sideways at Oliver. "Mr. Crandall will give your business the best of care."

"No, I want you to handle it." Mr. Stringer leaned forward with his hand on one knee. "Mr. Crandall will give my account to you." He turned to Oliver. "Right, Crandall?"

Oliver flushed. "Sure, David may handle your account." His mouth twitched, and one side turned up. "He's capable."

"Great. When you get everything ready, give me a call and I'll come over for my approval." Mr. Stringer rose. "I'll bring the information you need to keep me running. Young man, I'm expecting great things."

Oliver showed Stringer out the door and David turned toward the window, a smile on his face.

On the river

Logan and Terry sauntered down a path bordering the river, stopping now and then to throw a rock at a turtle or to chase a snake into the water.

Logan picked up a dead limb and broke it on a tree. "Man, Ms. Thomas made me so mad today. I tried to tell her I lost my geometry homework, but she put me in detention anyway."

"Did you really lose it?" Terry stomped a puffball mushroom and laughed when the brown dust covered Logan's shoe.

"No, stupid. I didn't do it. But she should have listened to me anyway."

"How many times have you told her you lost your homework? She knows you never do it." Terry picked at a zit. "Why don't you just do it for once?"

"I ain't like you. I hate math. I'd rather be out fishing or working on my old truck. Man, I'm hoping to get that thing going before summer. You need to come help me with it."

"Ah, you know I don't know anything about cars."

"Oh yeah, you'd rather be sittin' 'round readin' a book or something. Mister College Prep!" Logan threw his backpack on the ground and walked over to look at a water bug whirling around on top of a puddle. "Hey, Terry. Look!" Logan pointed to an approaching boat.

They watched as the boat docked and two men came ashore. "Hey, guys." A tall, thin man introduced himself as Miles and the other, a red headed man, as Larson. "You boys live around here?"

"Sure do." Terry shifted his gaze to Larson. "Do you?"

Larson laughed. "No. We live up the river a ways."

"Why do you want to know? You got business down here?" Logan lifted his chin.

"Actually, we're looking for someone like you. You guys like to make a little money?" Miles pulled a wad of bills from his pocket, and the boys' eyes bugged out.

"What do we have to do to earn money?" Logan nudged Terry.

"We have a specific need and we think you guys can deliver." Miles stuffed the money into his pocket. "What we need is information."

Terry threw his backpack over his shoulder. "Nah, we don't know anything. Come on, Logan."

"Wait, Terry." Logan grabbed Terry's arm. "What kind of information? We might know something. For a price, of course."

"There we go." Miles lowered his voice. "We need to know who around here would be favorable to move some materials for us. That's all."

Logan jerked his arm away from Terry. "And what kind of material would cause two grown men to slip around asking kids for help? You guys selling drugs? We want no part of anything illegal."

He started down the path, but Logan hung back. He glanced at Terry's departing figure and turned to Miles. "Maybe I'll help you. What do you need moved? I can handle almost anything."

Miles lifted a thumb to Larson who smirked and nodded.

Five

Oliver stomped out of the office and disappeared until after lunch. When he returned, he went straight to his office and closed the door.

"What's got a burr under his saddle?" Ms. Emma and David finished lunch and were chatting at her desk.

"I guess he's upset because Mr. Stringer asked that his account be given to me." David leaned over and watched Ms. Emma. "Think I can do it?"

"I know you can." Ms. Emma laughed. "You can do whatever you want to do. You learn fast, and I'm here if you have any questions."

"I don't want Mr. Crandall to be angry with me."

"Give him time. He'll get over it. Deflated his ego a little, that's all."

The door opened and a brown duck waddled in. A white duck wearing a red cape came in next, followed by a colorful wood duck. David and Ms. Emma watched wide-eyed as the quacking ducks strutted around the office, leaving poop everywhere.

"Where is he? Where is that stinker?" Ms. Emma ran to the door and looked out. "David, you find that boy and bring him to me. He'll clean this mess, or my name isn't Emma Clancy."

When David stopped laughing long enough to regain his posture, he went to the door and yelled. "Kade Crandall, get your butt in here now."

Kade's grinning face came around the door followed by the rest of his lanky body. "Anybody want to adopt a duck?"

"You goof! Where'd you get these creatures?" David herded the ducks into a corner.

Kade stepped into the hall and returned with a cage. "Help me catch them, David. Dang, these things are messy." They put the ducks into the cage and Kade went to get cleaning supplies while Ms. Emma covered her mouth and laughed.

Kade explained after he cleaned the mess. "When I came in a while ago, a little boy stood by the sidewalk trying to sell these ducks. So, I bought them from him. Said he needed the money to buy new basketball shoes."

"Why didn't you just give him the money and let him keep the ducks?" David jerked his finger back when the wood duck pecked him.

"Ah, he needed to feel independent. Keep his dignity, you know."

"Now what are you going to do with them?" Ms. Emma asked. "You can't keep them here."

"I don't know. If I take them home, Mom will kill me." Kade looked at the ducks. "Look how cute they are." He picked up one wearing a little red coat. "You gotta admit this one looks pretty cool."

"Yeah. He looks better than you when you wear a coat." David held his nose. "Why don't you take them to the park down by the river?"

"I can't. There are already too many ducks there. Too much competition for food and attention."

"Then turn them loose on the river."

"Uh uh. The boy said he raised them from babies, and they wouldn't know how to take care of themselves. They might get lost."

Ms. Emma giggled. "Or drown."

"Why don't you take them to the zoo?" David asked. "I'll bet they would take them."

"Sounds like a plan." Kade grabbed the cage. "I'll do that." He turned to leave, then looked back. "When I get back, we've got to talk to Dad about the problem on the river."

When Kade returned, they found Oliver napping in his chair. David slammed the door, and Kade shook Oliver's shoulder.

"Dad! Wake up. We need to talk to you. It's important."

Oliver rubbed his face and stretched. "What's so important you have to wake up a working man?"

"Yeah, right." Kade laughed. "You were working hard."

David walked to the big window and looked out. "Mr. Crandall, have you heard about any trouble on the river?"

"Trouble? What trouble?"

"This weekend when we went down the river, people were telling us about kids going missing," Kade sat on the edge of the desk. "They said they've told authorities, but no one seems to be doing anything about it."

"Ah, you can't believe half what those people say." Oliver sneered. "If kids are missing it's because they want to get away from the mess at home."

"No, Dad. It's serious. Kids are missing. They've looked everywhere. It's more than them running away."

"Oh yeah? How do you know they haven't run away? Those river rats shouldn't even have kids. They're trash."

David whirled around and stared at Oliver. *Seriously?* He'd never heard Oliver put down these people before.

"Dad, there are good, honest people on the river. And a lot of the trouble is on the Island. Did you know that? They need help. Think you could speak to the River Port Authority on their behalf?"

David struggled to hold his temper. "Mr. Crandall, that isn't the only issues they have. Sounds like a ring of thieves and gamblers are taking over down there. It's causing them major problems."

"Son, you may be smart about computers, and you may have learned things about this business, but there's a lot of things you don't know." Oliver smirked at David. "You boys let me handle this. I'll get to the bottom of it."

Kade pulled David into the hall when they left Oliver's office. "What's he mad at you about?"

"Ah, I think he's irritated about an account." David pulled at his shirt collar. "I don't know how he'll get to the bottom of anything when he doesn't believe in the integrity of the river people."

"Yeah, that bothers me. I've never heard him talk about them that way."

"What are you guys doing out here whispering in the hall?" Kade turned around and put his arm around his sister Sadie.

"Look what the cats dragged up. You looking for a job?"

"No, I don't want a job. I had to come in to run a few errands and thought I'd drop by to find out how working people live." Sadie laughed. "Doesn't look like much work is getting done. Looks more like a conspiracy."

David stood grinning at his two friends. He looked at Sadie, admiring the thick, auburn hair and green eyes. Funny, he hadn't noticed how much she changed since he left for college.

"What do you think, David?" Sadie's eyes twinkled.

"Uh, what?" David blushed. "Think about what?"

"You weren't even listening." Sadie pinched David's arm. "I want to have a birthday party at the house, but Kade says we should have it at the Lemon Club. What do you think?"

"Who's having a birthday? I'm not." David laughed. "Oh, I guess I forgot! Sadie is turning sixteen."

"Smart-aleck." Sadie socked his arm. "You know I'll be twenty and I'm planning the best party ever." She hugged herself. "Mom is helping me, and it will be a doozy."

"There's plenty of room at the Club plus a huge pool, and they will cater so you don't have to worry about the food. Having it there will make it easier on Mom, and you too, Sadie." Kade tweaked her nose. "There won't be much decorating necessary."

"Maybe flowers and nice center pieces for the tables." Sadie hugged Kade. "I can't wait. I have a long guest list, and I believe everyone will come."

"Does Dad know about this?" Kade asked. "He'll faint when he sees the bills."

"Ah, Mr. Crandall would do anything for his little girl." David pulled a strand of Sadie's hair. "You know she's his pet."

"You know I am!" Sadie grabbed David's arm. "David,

you're to find a live band, and a good one. You have contacts, and you can pull strings to make it happen."

"Well, I guess." David laughed at Sadie's excitement. "I know a band of guys who might be willing to help out. Right now, I have to get back to work." He turned and glanced again at the slim figure. He had known her all her life, but she seemed different. Kade's little sister was now a grown, beautiful woman.

On the river

Guided by a short, stocky man, the driver backed a blue Dodge truck up to a rickety pier.

"Come on back." The man motioned to the driver, and then waved toward a grove of trees. From there, two men hurried toward the truck, looking upriver.

"Hurry, we don't have much time." The driver looked on both sides and out the back window. "Come on. Hurry, man."

"Ah, don't worry, Fred. We got plenty of time." He turned to the men coming from the trees. "Did you find some good stuff?"

"We sure did." The two men laughed. "Wait till you see."

They disappeared a moment behind a tree that leaned over the water and pushed out a boat covered with a dark green tarp. Holding onto a rope tied to the boat, they walked along the bank, guiding it to the pier. One stepped into the boat and removed the tarp, revealing gas cans, toolboxes, fishing tackle, and garden tools among other things. The men formed a line to empty the boat and load the back of the truck.

"Look at this." One opened an old toolbox filled with antique tools. "This stuff is worth a fortune, and I know the man who'll buy it."

"We hit the jackpot, all right. Those old people have all kinds of antiques laying around," another said.

The stocky man snickered. "Yeah, just waiting on us to find them."

The truck driver whistled. "Gotta go, guys. I'll be back tomorrow about the same time."

"Okay. We'll have another load." The other three men piled into the boat and paddled back into the river.

Six

"David, come into my office." Oliver's behavior had been distant and cool since David took over Mr. Stringer's account. David tried to keep clear of him when he could. Oliver was his boss and his mentor, so it was hard to stay away from him. What could he want now? David swallowed hard as he opened the door.

"Come on in, Son. Don't be shy." Oliver swiveled his chair around and stood. "Sit." David sat on the edge of the chair and waited.

Oliver sat and turned to look at his computer screen. He tapped on the keyboard and turned again to David. "You're doing a great job on the Stringer account."

"Thank you." David sat up straighter in the chair.

Oliver stood. "As of now you are no longer an apprentice here."

David sucked in his breath. *Is this for real? Now? But he just said I'm doing good.* He stood and turned to leave.

Oliver came around the desk. "Where are you going? I'm not finished yet."

"Oh…"

"Look, Son, I'm pleased with your progress. You've proved you can do the work, and my clients like you. You are no longer an intern; you are an employee. Wouldn't you like to have your own office?"

David's eyes widened. "Yes! I mean, of course, I

would." His face reddened as he stuck out his hand. "Thank you, Mr. Crandall. Thank you so much."

"Now go ask Ms. Emma for the Royce and Nance files. I need to go over those with you."

David's hands shook as he opened the door and saw Ms. Emma's smile spread all the way to her eyes.

"Did you already know?" David asked.

"Yes, he told me." Ms. Emma wrapped her arms around her young friend. "I'm proud of you. You're such an asset to this business." She retrieved the files and he stared at the large sign out the window. One day it would be "Crandall and Kingston Shipping". He smiled as he carried the files into the office.

He looked around in awe at the spacious room. The windows stretched from floor to ceiling with a view of the wide river that wound its way through the city and disappeared into the country beyond. A large oak desk sat in the center with leather chairs on either side. Armchairs sat around the room, and a large bookshelf filled one wall. His own office. Now he could buy the red Porsche.

Sadie helped him decorate the office, and Oliver donated books to go along with David's own collection. Ms. Emma contributed a large painting which reminded David of a place on the river he and Kade frequented as kids.

After a few weeks of working with Oliver and Ms. Emma both supervising his work, David was sure of his ability to handle the clients' files. Oliver started allowing him to make decisions which would affect the accounts of important clients. David hummed to himself as he signed his name to contracts and handed them to Ms. Emma to file.

Sadie visited the office, and David blushed when she asked his advice about her choice for a party dress. She brushed against him when she held up two dress selections to show him before she touched his cheek and laughed.

"Why, David! Your face is red. You're not sick, are you?"

"No," David stammered. "I'm fine." He moved to the other side of the room. *What's wrong with me?* Sadie had been like a little sister to him. He spent almost as much time at the Crandall house as he did at home and watched her grow from a snaggled-tooth brat to a flighty teenager and now, a grown woman. *So, what's with the self-conscious crap?*

Ms. Emma and Sadie discussed the dresses and the party plans while David dug in the file cabinet. He needed to finish a contract on a new client but found concentration difficult with Sadie around.

"David." Sadie poked him in the ribs. "Take me to lunch. I'm hungry."

"Ah, uh, I have to get this file done."

Ms. Emma stepped in. "Go on, take her to lunch. I'll find the file and have it ready when you get back."

Sadie picked a nearby restaurant and party plans dominated their conversation. "Mom is great," she said. "She's the best party planner ever. I told her she should get a job planning events for people."

David smiled and agreed. Sadie continued. "Dad's being a grouch, though. 'Too much money' is all he contributes to the conversation about my big day."

"Well, it does cost a lot to rent the Club, doesn't it? And to have food catered, a live band ...."

Sadie cut him off. "The band. Have you found a band

yet?"

David pulled out his phone and showed her a video. "Do you like this group? They're new but they're good. And cheap. And if you get them, they promised I could play with them."

"Oh, I do like them. Who are they? I've never heard of them."

"They call themselves 'Wild Assumption'."

"Yes, they'll be perfect. And I like to hear you play the guitar. I haven't heard you play and sing since...."

"Since I played in church before I started college."

"I miss those days, David. I miss you coming to the house and eating everything in sight." Sadie giggled. "I miss you teasing Mom and making her laugh until she cried." She sobered. "Mom misses you too, you know."

"Yeah. We had good times together. How is your mom?"

"She's sad. And lonely. Dad is gone all the time."

"I'll try to get over to visit her soon." David stood and held out his hand. "Come on, girl. I have to get back to the office."

She entwined her fingers in his as they walked back to the office, and the smile on his face remained the rest of the day.

"David?"

David turned from the computer to see who spoke to him. "Hello Mr. Sapine. What brings you to the office today?"

"David, something isn't right about my account. I wanted to talk to Crandall, but Ms. Emma says he's out. Could you look at it for me?"

"Sure. Come on into the office. Ms. Emma, could you get me Mr. Sapine's file?"

The two men poured over the contents of the file, going over each item with care. David opened information on the computer and shook his head.

"I see there's a problem, but I'm not sure what it is. This column doesn't come out right."

Mr. Sapine checked the file on the desk with the one on the computer. "This item doesn't belong here." He pointed to the screen. "And this number isn't right."

"I can't change anything without checking with Mr. Crandall first," David turned from the computer. "I'll have him check it in the morning when he comes in. We'll get it straightened out."

When Mr. Sapine left, David showed the figures to Ms. Emma.

She stooped to look at the screen. "This isn't right. It seems the numbers have been changed. This amount is wrong. See, the numbers in this column are more than the ones in this column. But here ..."

"Yeah, I see it. An honest mistake, I guess." David rubbed his arm and looked around. "I'll show it to Mr. Crandall tomorrow."

A long night faced David. He couldn't get the error in Sapine's file off his mind. How could it be an honest mistake? It seemed too easy. Oliver paid close attention to his business dealings.

"David, Sapine called this morning. Said he talked to you yesterday about his account. What's going on?" Oliver slammed the door as he entered and stalked to his desk.

David followed.

"Mr. Crandall, there seems to be an error in his account, and he's concerned about it."

"What error? There's no error. I handled his account myself. Sapine is a dunce who thinks too much about his business when he should let me handle it."

"But, sir, it is his business. And I saw the error." David turned on the computer. "Here, I'll show you."

"You'll show me nothing. You take care of your accounts and leave the rest to me."

"Yes sir." Red crept up David's neck and over his face as he left Oliver's office.

If anyone could make him feel stupid, Oliver could. On the other hand, Oliver could make him feel smart. David stopped short and stared at a photo of the river hanging on the wall in front of him. His dad always loved the river and used it to teach his son about life.

He could hear his dad saying, "A river changes when a storm or heavy rain causes it to flood. It can even change its course. It's never the same."

Sounds like Oliver and his moods. What storm made him change this time?

On the river

Intoxicated with happiness, Jeffery and Lisa Snyder moved into a little cabin by the river. Doting family members and friends had given them a nice reception after a small, private wedding. They'd loved each other since kindergarten. They came from poor folks who struggled to make ends meet, and their hard work and dedication to each other proved there was no lack of love on either side. The excitement of having their own home and eventually a family showed as they signed a mortgage to the little house.

"Jeffery, what's this?" Lisa held out a lottery ticket she found in his jacket pocket. He blushed and snatched the receipt from her hand.

"It's nothing. I bought a lottery ticket. So what?"

"You know we agreed not to waste money on things like this."

"Now, Lisa, it won't hurt to play the lottery now and then. We might win something."

"We might not. When you give money and get nothing in return, it's foolish. We need everything we make to pay the bills. We talked about this."

Jeffery stomped into the bathroom and slammed the door. Lisa frowned. He never acted this way. She went to the kitchen to make supper and he slumped in front of the TV. They talked little the rest of the night.

Working on a river boat supplied Jeffery with a good income and good friends. He'd worked on the same boat since high school and his boss mentored him for a promotion. Jeffery was amiable and well liked, and each time a new employee came aboard, he helped him learn the ropes and feel welcome. One such employee warmed up to Jeffery and the two became best friends.

"Hey, Jeff. Let's go to Gold Boat after work." Jay's conversation had begun to center around the gambling boat.

Jeffery picked up his lunch pail. "Nah, man, I'd better not. I gotta save my money."

Jay didn't quit. Every day he begged Jeffery. "You only live once, man. Come on."

Jeffery gave in and it became a nightly thing. He dreaded the confrontation he met when he got home late every night.

"What have you done with your paycheck?" Lisa tried not to sound angry, but for the last two months she didn't have enough to pay all the bills.

"I gave you all my check." Once again, he clammed up and slammed doors. She crossed her arms as she observed the same attitude she'd witnessed every night for the past month. This wasn't like the Jeffery she knew and loved.

Seven

When he was at work, David stayed in his office to avoid interaction with Oliver. He met with clients and updated his files during office hours. He and Sadie went out in the evenings.

"David, what's wrong? You're not yourself today. In fact, you haven't been yourself all week." She watched him as she twirled the cherry in the whipped cream atop her strawberry milkshake.

David shrugged and looked out the window of the restaurant. "I don't know. The other day I found an error in a client's file and tried to show it to Oliver, but he got mad."

"Maybe he fixed it already."

"No, I saw it late yesterday. He won't even admit he made a mistake."

Sadie slurped her shake and scrunched her nose. "Let's not talk about it. Let's go to the park for a walk." She grabbed his hand and pulled him to his feet. They both laughed when she stumbled and landed against him. He drew her into his arms.

He leaned down and kissed her forehead. "Come on, let's get out of here."

The shady park welcomed them, and a cool breeze blew across the water as they walked along the banks of the river. The smell of a lilac bush mixed with the scent of pink and yellow honeysuckle growing nearby to add sweetness to the air. David smiled when Sadie ran to feed a flock of geese the sunflower seeds she found in her pocket. He laughed when she emptied her bag of seeds, and the hungry birds chased her. He rescued her from a park bench where she fled to escape the squawking geese. He carried her to a grassy spot under an oak and sat beside her on the ground.

"Sadie, I know we've known each other all our lives, but it's like I'm getting to know you for the first time." David picked up a strand of her hair and tickled her nose with it, causing her to giggle. She moved closer and laid her head on his shoulder with her hand on his chest.

"I know." She pursed her lips. "I never thought I'd feel this way about you. You've always seemed more like a brother, but now I don't want you for a brother." She touched his lips and ran her finger over the cleft in his chin and down his neck.

"Uh, uh, no brother stuff," he murmured as his lips touched hers.

"Mr. Crandall, would you look at this entry on Zeke Maxwell's account? Something is wrong, and I can't figure out what it is." David moved behind Oliver's desk to open the account on his computer.

Oliver studied the information on the screen a moment and whistled. "Son, your problem is right here. You have switched the shipment date with the delivery date to throw off the whole calendar."

"Oh, yeah! I see it now." David clicked the mouse to fix the problem. "Thanks, Mr. Crandall." He exited the account and turned to leave, but Oliver motioned for him to sit in the leather office chair opposite the desk.

"David, I want to show you how to increase your earnings. Watch this. If you take this off...." he clicked the mouse on a column, "and move it over here, look what happens. Just like that, you've gained two percent which would put you in a higher bracket for your commission."

David stared at Oliver. "But isn't that cheating this client?"

"Not really." Oliver shook his head. "It's just manipulating the numbers, but they're not much different. See? These clients don't pay close attention and won't notice the difference. But you will when you get your paycheck."

David ran his fingers through his hair. "I don't know."

Oliver gave a lopsided grin. "Well, of course it's up to you. It's your account. I'm trying to help you out." He turned in his chair and rolled it to the side of the desk. "You serious about my daughter?"

David blushed and stammered. "I...I'm not sure...I...."

Oliver laughed and waved his hand. "Never mind. I'm thinking of Sadie's welfare. She's used to having nice things, you know."

The blush on David's face deepened, and his jaw tightened. Oliver turned, and David knew he was dismissed. He returned to his office. He opened the Maxwell file and looked at it, closed it, and pulled it up again. He changed a few numbers and calculated the totals. He changed it back to its previous status and closed it. It sure would help him pay for that Porsche. He would need to make good money to give Sadie the lifestyle she wanted. He reopened the file and changed the numbers back. He would do anything for his Sadie.

He sat staring at the file when Kade jerked the door open, ran in, and body-slammed himself into an armchair. David jumped and jerked his head around.

"What are you doing?"

"Checking on you." Kade leaned forward and looked at the computer screen. "You looking at the Maxwell file?"

"Yeah." David nodded and closed the file. "I talked to Maxwell the other day, and he told me how he has been struggling to make ends meet. His daughter has cancer, you know."

David raised his head. "Cancer?"

"He moved here to be close to the hospital because of her treatments. He left a great job up north and found a job on Ted Stringer's boat."

David frowned. "He owns his own boat."

"Sure, now. Stringer liked him and helped him get his own boat. Sounds just like him, doesn't it?" Kade grabbed a handful of Skittles from a candy dish on David's desk.

"Don't eat all my Skittles. Get your own."

"Don't be such a grouch." Kade grabbed another handful and left. David sat staring at the screen. Wow. Guess he should use the account of someone else to help him get ahead. But what if the client found out? He checked his list of files.

"Hi, Ms. Emma." He jumped at the sound of Sadie's voice. Oh, of course. They had a lunch date. He closed the computer and grabbed his jacket. He couldn't keep his girl waiting.

He stopped outside the door of his office and watched as Sadie and Ms. Emma chatted. A ray of sunlight from the window gave her hair a copper glow and her green eyes sparkled as she turned to smile at him, causing him to fumble when he started to close the door. How could this girl he had known forever suddenly turn him into a bumbling bonehead?

Kade and David walked along the river talking to the workers loading and unloading the boats along the dock. Some of these guys had been around a long time and the two men from the office laughed and joked with them, enjoying the spirited conversation.

"Kingston!" One of David's best clients, Abe Sanders, hurried across the dock. "I was headed to your office." He puffed out his cheeks. "I got a question for you."

"Okay," David directed Sanders to a quieter place to talk. "What's your question, Mr. Sanders?"

Sanders removed his hat and scratched his head. "I talked to Crandall the other day, and he told me there's a way I could get a lower rate on my cargo. I'm ready to load and I need to know what the deal is. You're my agent, Kingston, but if I can get it cheaper, I'll have to take another route."

"Hummm, I'll check it out, Sanders. Mr. Crandall is in his office. I'll head over there to find out what he's talking about." He wanted to keep Abe Sanders, one of his major clients.

"Yes, David, I did talk to Abe the other day." Oliver rubbed his hands together. "He's one of our best clients and we don't want to lose him. And we don't have to. We'll offer him a rebate on this load and the next load to reduce his costs. That should make him happy."

"It should, but what about the other clients? Won't they want the same?"

"We'll keep it under wraps. There are ways to help

people out, and not everyone needs to know about it. Abe won't talk." Oliver watched David a moment. "We don't need to lose Sanders, David. He's your client. Do what you think is best."

"Okay, I will." David went to his office. He checked the account, did some figuring, and headed back to the dock. He would make this deal with Sanders if the man would promise to keep mum about it.

In a week, everything imploded. Abe Sanders talked, and client after client came forward wanting rebates. Crap! What a big mess. *That's what I get for listening to Oliver.*

"What am I going to do?" David paced the floor of Kade's office. "I can't give rebates to every client. Mr. Crandall would kill me."

"I thought you said Dad suggested it." Kade sat at his desk flipping a pen through his fingers.

"He did. I shouldn't have listened to him."

"Well, if it was his idea and he assured you Sanders wouldn't talk, this is on him, right?"

David fumed and paced harder. "That may be right, but I don't dare go in there and tell him it's his fault. Do I?"

Kade laughed. "Dang, that'd be risky. But you're right, you can't accuse Dad of being wrong. We'll have to figure out how to fix this." He turned to his computer and back around. "Let's go to your office and look at the schedules."

They worked together an hour, and then sent a messenger to the docks. In a little while, two of David's clients were standing in his office.

"I can't give you a rebate," David said, "but I do have something." Kade turned the computer around to allow them to view the monitor, and David talked as Kade scrolled around the screen. "Look, Samuels has a load ready for delivery and his tug quit on him. If you get that load, you'll make double with no extra time since you're going south anyway. And Baker, you can go north for a load of fertilizer from Lonoke. The barge that's due there is broken down. That'll be a bonus for you. Will that work?"

"Sure. Thanks, David." The men left, satisfied.

"Thanks, Kade." David pushed his chair back and ran his fingers through his hair. "I'd better get back to work. I've still got some scheduling to do."

"Yeah, better find more loads for those guys." Kade jumped to his feet. "Yikes! I have a date and I'm going to be late. See ya."

"Oh, I've got to run, too. Promised Sadie we'd go shopping tonight."

"Shopping? She's dragging you shopping? Better stay away from jewelry stores."

"As a matter of fact…"

Kade whirled around. "You're not thinking of proposing to my sister, are you?"

"I am. Why do you sound surprised?"

Kade rubbed the back of his neck. "You may need to wait, David. At least a while."

"Why? What's wrong?"

"Uh, Dad, that's what."

"What does your Dad have anything to do with it?"

"You do remember my dad is also Sadie's dad."

David raised his hands. "Kade, what are you saying? What's going on?"

"I can't say for sure, but I heard Dad talking to Sadie a couple of nights ago. He's trying to fix her up with a competitor's son."

"You're kidding!"

"Nope. He told her it would help his business if she would connect with him. He's trying to manipulate her. Talking to her about the importance of networking in the business world and how she could help him out. Stuff like that."

"And she's listening?" David fell back into an armchair. "I can't believe this."

"I don't know. I'm warning you to be careful, that's all." Kade waved and backed out the door.

Sadie waited in front of a dress shop when David arrived. "Where have you been?" she asked. "I've been waiting thirty minutes. I'm about to leave."

"I'm sorry. I needed to finish a job at the office."

"Well, come on. We have a lot of shopping to do." Her good humor won, and David waited to approve or disapprove her choice of dresses, shoes and purses, and then he carried bags for her.

"Why are you quiet tonight?" Sadie took her bags from his overloaded arms and piled them into the back seat of the car.

"Hard day at work." David drove in silence, and Sadie giggled as she scrolled through social media on her phone.

"Well, go home and rest. Thanks for bringing my bags in." She pulled him to the door, pecked him on the cheek and shut the door behind him.

On the river

Floyd Neely stepped out of the door of the wood-framed house he built for his family. He could no longer stand the wailing of his wife Elsa since Suzie disappeared two days ago. He looked across the stump-covered yard where his small children, Bobby, Nita, and Alex, played. He pictured the golden curls of three-year-old Suzie, his little angel. She was daddy's girl. Tears filled his eyes as he remembered how she raised her arms for him to hold her.

With the help of neighbors, they searched every acre of the woods and river around their home. The children were playing in the fenced-in yard when Suzie disappeared. Six-year-old Bobby said he saw a man come from the river. Five-year-old Nita said she saw a man talking to Suzie.

He reported the missing girl to the authorities who said they would investigate it, but he heard nothing from them. He worked hard to provide for his family, and then this happened. How could he feel like a man when he couldn't protect his own children?

Eight

Sadie breezed in and out of the office preparing for her birthday party the next day. With her constant interference, David worked little as did most of the staff. Sadie had spent much of her life around the office, and everyone wanted to be part of her excitement. She brought in decorations for their approval. She requested advice about songs and food, and her enthusiasm proved to be contagious.

"Come on, David. You have to help me at the club." She pulled him toward the door, and he shrugged to a laughing Ms. Emma who waved him on.

At the club they watched as workers hung lanterns, placed center pieces, and arranged flowers. A crew constructed a stage for the band and allotted an area for dancing. High society people from all over would attend the party, one of the biggest social events of the year. What a great opportunity to meet important people—rich people! This party could be a plus for his career.

The evening of the party, David looked at himself in the mirror before he left to pick up Sadie. He had worn a tuxedo only once and that was to his senior prom. Like most of the guys in his class, he rented one from a formal wear shop in a small nearby town. It made him feel like a million bucks, like a whole different person. At that time, he had no idea he would have a career in the Crandall Shipping business and be dating the Sadie Crandall.

He and Sadie arrived at the club early to make sure everything was perfect. While she talked to the caterers, David discussed song selections with the band. Sadie gave him a list of songs she wanted, and he chose ones he liked. One of the band members handed him a guitar and asked him to practice with them on a selection he would play for Sadie's birthday.

He stood with Sadie in the reception line, smiling and making small talk with guests as she introduced him to those he did not know. It was a great night for making new friends, and when Sadie pointed out important businessmen, he took every opportunity to get to know them.

Sadie led David around the room to mingle with her guests. He was relieved when she led him to a table to await the food. He mouthed a thank you to Melody who sat next to him and murmured directions to help him use the proper utensils at the proper time.

Sadie danced the first dance with David and a line formed of handsome young men asking for their turn. David danced with Sadie's friends but then excused himself and stood by the punch bowl, watching her. She smiled into the eyes of the men twirling her around the dance floor and flirted with them all. She seemed to favor one man dressed in an expensive looking tux which accentuated his tall, dark figure. David remembered him from the reception line. He flirted with Sadie when he came in, kissed her hand and demanded her attention. David's dislike for him grew as he watched them together.

"So, Crandall, this is the young man I've been hearing about." An older gentleman turned to Oliver when David approached them. Oliver put his hand on David's shoulder and nodded.

"Moore, this young man has been an asset to Crandall Shipping since he joined the company. He brings in new business about every week."

David beamed. Moore laughed and turned to speak to someone on his right. David turned to watch Sadie still dancing with the tall guest.

He talked with a few of the other men, and then waited until the band ended a song. He stalked onto the dance floor and pulled her into his arms before another guy could get to her. She laughed up at him, like she had with every man she danced with. She was by nature a friendly, outgoing person. Perhaps he over-reacted to her flirting, but they should know she was his girl.

"I thought you were ignoring me." David knew he sounded petty, but he couldn't help it. "You've danced with every man in this place."

She looked at him and puckered her lips. "Now, don't you get jealous, David Kingston. I have to dance with my guests, don't I?"

"I know. I guess I assumed you'd dance every dance with me." He twirled her and she laughed when he dipped her and pretended to drop her.

At the end of the song, they went to the punch bowl where Kade grabbed his sister for a dance. David smiled as he watched them laugh. What was Kade telling her? Sadie caught his eye and motioned for him to ask a woman to dance. He found the woman easy to talk to, and the lights and the music captivated him. He danced with several women while Sadie enjoyed her guests.

"David! Up here." The leader of the band raised a

guitar and motioned to David. Sadie seated herself right in front of the band and waited for her birthday song. Red crept up his neck as he took the instrument and sat on the edge of the stage. He gazed at her as he strummed the guitar. Everyone stopped to listen as David's rendition of 'Can't Help Falling in Love' filled the room.

In the middle of the song, he noticed Oliver and Melody dancing. Oliver held her close and she whispered something in his ear before resting her head on his chest. David remembered one time he was spending the night with Kade and saw them together. He'd gone to the kitchen for a drink in the middle of the night and noticed a movement outside. They were dancing in the moonlight. No music, just the two of them floating around on the patio among the roses and lilies. Oliver had a red rose in his lapel and one adorned Melody's dark hair just above her ear. It was a good memory.

When he finished, Sadie wiped her eyes and threw her arms around him. "Oh, David, your song was beautiful! I loved it." David turned to thank everyone for the applause as the crimson on his face deepened. Oliver shook his hand and Melody came over to give him a hug.

"I'd forgotten how well you sing, David. Such a beautiful and romantic song." She sighed. "Made me wish for youth again."

When Sadie saw the last guest out, she and David walked to his truck. "Let's drive to the river. I don't want this night to end."

"Aren't you tired? It's really late." David stooped to kiss her before he closed her door.

"No, I'm not tired. I could dance all night. I want to watch the moon for a while." She looked through the sunroof.

"Isn't it beautiful?"

He maneuvered the truck through the river park down to the river and turned off the motor. He pulled her close and pushed back the seat to better see the full moon above.

"Do you see Venus?" Sadie pointed. "And there's Jupiter." David stroked her cheek, and she continued. "See the bright star over there? That's Sirius. And over there you can see Polaris."

David ran his hand over the back of her neck and through her hair. "All I want to see is my Sadie."

"Don't you think the moon and stars are romantic?" Sadie lifted her face and he kissed her lightly starting with her forehead, moving to the tip of her nose, and settling on her lips. The moonlight gave her hair a copper sheen and he buried his face in the silkiness, drawing in the heavy scent of Gucci. Her fingers threaded through his hair and she pulled his face down to meet hers. His heart rate quickened as the warmth of her breath spread across his cheek and down his neck. He gathered her into his arms and pulled her closer. Blue eyes gazed into green, and their lips met. A firefly blinked on the dash of the truck, and they failed to notice the stars shining brighter as the moon hid behind a white, fluffy cloud.

David's phone dinged with a text from Sadie. "David, I'm going shopping with Mom in New York. I won't be gone long."

He slumped in his chair. He looked forward to being with her after work, and now he would have to spend the evening alone. Oh, well. At least he could finish his work early and go for a run. He had neglected the track and he could sense his muscles relaxing. He had to keep them tight.

He texted her every day, but her answers were short and blunt. One time she texted 'I love you' with a heart. That's it. He asked Oliver what day she would return.

Oliver gave a half smile. "Now, son, you need to give her a little space. She'll tell you when she's back." He snapped his fingers. "Say, do you have your guitar here? Will you do my favorite song for me?"

David went into his office and returned with his Gibson. Oliver sat staring out the window silent while David played 'How Great Thou Art' for him. When David played the last note, Oliver turned, smiling.

"Thank you, son. I've always loved to hear you do that song."

A week passed and still nothing. Unanswered phone calls, texts, and messages plagued him until he couldn't concentrate on his work. Several times, he had to revisit files and fix mistakes he made. After another week, he'd had enough. Time to find that woman and win her back. Maybe she and her mom had returned from New York.

When he drove to the Crandall home, Melody rose from her flower bed and pushed her graying bobbed hair from her face. Her smile welcomed him as he stepped out of the car. He hadn't seen her in a while, and a sense of emptiness filled his heart as he pictured her and his mom chatting together while they worked on some project. A trip home would do him good.

A glass of sweet tea and a piece of Melody's blackberry cobbler topped with vanilla ice cream satisfied his pallet while cheerful conversation warmed his soul. They discussed

David's work, Kade's latest prank, and finally Sadie.

"I hoped she might be here." David tried to sound nonchalant, but he knew she could see right through him. "She won't answer my calls or messages. I haven't seen her since she got back."

Melody tilted her head. "Got back from where?"

"She texted me that you and she were shopping in New York."

"I'm sorry, David. I haven't heard from her in two weeks." She played with her fork. "I thought you guys were getting serious. What happened?"

"Nothing has happened. At least if it has, I don't know it." David's shoulders slumped as he turned on the barstool. "I hate to mention it, but Kade thinks Mr. Crandall is pushing her to dump me for another guy."

Melody pressed her lips together. "I'm not sure, but he may be right. I heard him mention merging with Harris Shipping and how Jasper Harris would be a good connection to make it happen."

David's nostrils flared. "It's bad enough Oliver would use his own daughter to make a deal, but it's even worse if she agrees to it." He jumped to his feet and threw his hands in the air. "Guess I know where I stand."

Melody put a hand on his arm. "Listen, I could be completely wrong." A half sob, half laugh escaped her lips. "I see so little of Oliver, how could I possibly know what he's doing, much less thinking."

"What do you mean?" David asked. "Why don't you see him?"

She smirked. "Well, according to him, he's working all the time." She mocked his tone. "'I run a successful business, you know.'"

David didn't know what to say. "I'm sorry, Mrs. Crandall." The apology sounded lame. "He does work a lot. I try to help him as much as possible, but he still has a lot of clients to deal with."

"I guess." She signed. "It gets lonely around here. I miss Kade and Sadie." She smiled. "And you."

"You and Mr. Crandall need to take a vacation. Go away, just the two of you. Go on a cruise. Swim in the ocean. Climb a mountain."

"Now that sounds like a good idea. I wish I'd thought of it myself." She brightened. "I'll try to talk Oliver into it."

When David went to the car to leave, Melody stood smiling and waving. "Now promise me, David, you'll go visit your mom."

"I will. Soon." He would make sure he kept that promise.

On the river

Harvey Stockton jumped behind a tree when he heard crunching leaves and breaking twigs. Someone was coming. He glanced behind him where a makeshift tent sheltered his shotgun. Maybe he could get to it before whoever was coming saw him. He dove under the tarp he had hung from tree limbs and grabbed his gun. He had to protect his precious goods at all cost.

Containers of various shapes and sizes covered the ground under the tent. No matter what anyone thought or said, this was his living. And it was a good one. It didn't hurt anyone. Besides, what's wrong with giving people what they want? And they sure did want his product. His work provided his wife and kids with a home, clothes, and food. It sure beat working in a factory or in construction where a man put in two days' work in one to have a couple of dollars left after the government took what it wanted.

He waited, hoping that government agent wasn't snooping around again. He dealt with him once and it wasn't pleasant. He ended up spending six months in jail and having to rebuild his establishment from scratch in a different location. This time he found a spot in a ravine so secluded and thick with trees and bushes only squirrels and birds could find it.

The sound of movement stopped, started, then stopped again, and he grinned and lowered his gun when a large buck followed by a doe broke through the thicket. He was safe for now. He set the shotgun against the tree and turned. The grin disappeared as he stared into the barrel of a rifle.

Nine

"Mom? Dad?" David walked through the house looking for his parents. He'd lived in this house since birth and knew every creaking board and squeaky door. Where could they be? Hoping to surprise them, he hadn't let them know he planned to come. He would be the one surprised if they weren't home.

He walked out the kitchen door into the back yard and found them wielding tools, climbing a ladder, putting a roof on a gazebo.

"David! You're home." Kathleen dropped the hammer and threw her arms around her son. Jesse grinned as he climbed down the ladder.

"Son, you should have come earlier so you could have helped us with this project."

"Looks like you're doing a pretty good job without me." David laughed. He and his dad always enjoyed building things together while Mom supervised. They joked about her input in their projects, calling her the boss when she pointed out things they needed to change or improve. Truth was, though, she was a good engineer. She built a chicken coup once all by herself, much to the pride of her doting husband.

Kathleen pinched David's chin. "A beard, huh? When did that happen?"

David rubbed his face and grinned. "Trying to look

grown-up, I guess. Kade and I decided it's time to ditch the baby faces and look like men."

"I like it. Well groomed." She smiled. "My handsome son." She turned to go. "Now while you boys finish out here, I'll make lunch."

As they measured, sawed, and hammered, David and Jesse rehashed old times and talked about David's activities in the business world. When David mentioned his trouble with Oliver, Jesse sat and watched while David nailed another board to complete the bench he worked on.

"You know, Oliver used to say he detested dishonest people. He told me about his high school math teacher who gave special privileges to ball players. He didn't even hide it from the rest of the students. He said ball players were required to keep good grades, and he had to do his part to make sure the school had a winning team."

"Sounds like he may have learned more from that teacher than math." David pounded the nail into the board.

"Son, don't be too hard on him. You keep the right perspective on things, you'll be okay. Everything you learn in life makes you who you are. The rocks and boulders in a riverbed may seem like obstacles, but they may be stepping-stones. They'll teach you some things about life and people."

"I sure don't look at life the same. Nor people. I don't see Mr. Crandall the same way I did before." A corner of his mouth lifted. "I guess I've been wrong. Looks like he hasn't improved any."

"Just be sure to maintain your integrity. You don't have to follow his example."

"I can't believe he used Sadie to try to influence me to cheat a client." He plopped down beside Jesse. "If I took his advice, I'd be a crook." He massaged his temples. "I want my clients to trust me."

"I know you'll do right by those who depend on you. I've told you this before, but I'm going to tell you again. You're like that river over there. You can carry life-giving water or death." Jesse leaned back and chewed on a piece of grass. "You can carry compassion and integrity, or you can carry hurtful things, like deceit and irresponsibility. You must make choices that will give life wherever you go."

"Yeah, I remember." David lifted his head. "Make life choices, not death choices."

"Yep. Now let's go see if lunch is ready."

After his visit home, David bounded up the steps to his office, ready to face anything. But he hadn't prepared for what awaited him in the city. Kade left for a business trip abroad, Oliver was out of the office all week, and Ms. Emma stayed home sick. Messages from agitated clients who needed help filled his machine. In the middle of all the others, he heard one from Sadie. He ignored the others and listened to it.

"David, I need to talk to you when you get back. It's important." He dialed her number but got a voice message. He listened and redialed, but she didn't answer. He had to get his mind off her and deal with these other problems. One at a time he returned calls and dealt with issues, most of which were simple with a quick solution. A couple of problems required him to go down to the dock to deal with them in person.

When he walked back to the office, his phone rang; the sound of Sadie's voice stopped him in his tracks.

"Where have you been, David? I've been trying to call you." She sounded impatient.

"I'm sorry, Sadie, but I just got back to the office. I tried to call you several times."

She cut him short. "Meet me at Roscos. I'm hungry."

When he arrived, she gave him a peck on the cheek and led him to a booth in the back. "How are your parents?" she asked. "I just love them."

Before he had time to reply the waitress came for their order, and Sadie chattered on about her busy life and social problems. He tried to interject a word a time or two but gave up and listened to her prattle.

His burger tasted as heavy as his heart felt, and his drink tasted as bitter as the conversation. What happened to his sweet, amiable, gentle Sadie? Who was this girl sitting across from him? Except for the thick auburn hair and sparkling green eyes, she seemed like a stranger.

Finally, the hammer fell, driving the nail deep within his soul.

"David, I've found a man who will make my dreams come true. You've been such a good friend I know you'll understand. I'm getting married soon, and you're invited to my wedding." Her nose crinkled as she gave the final blow and rose to leave.

David's heart fell to his feet. "What do you mean, you're getting married? I thought there was something between us."

"Of course. There's friendship between us." She patted his shoulder. "We've known each other forever." She kissed his forehead and left.

David sat still. A good friend? The waitress came to

refill his drink, but he didn't notice. People came and went, but everything around him was a blur. His shoulders quivered. He remained silent. When he rose to leave, he barely remembered to throw a tip on the table and nod to the waitress.

He drove down a narrow dirt road leading to a branch of the river he and Kade often used for fishing. He pushed through the thick branches, vines and brambles until he reached the river. He walked out on a log extending over the water and gazed at the blue depth below him. A large fish swam by and minnows played at the edge of the bank. A bullfrog leaped, startling a bird from its perch on a limb hanging over the water. Life as usual. Except his life. *Why did she leave? How can I go on without her?*

A splashing noise a short distance away drew his attention. A blue heron rose from the water with a fish in its beak. The long wings flapped hard as it carried its prey to feed its young in a nest high in a tree. An otter swam close to look at the intruder, and then it dove to join its mate waiting under a willow tree. Only last year a flood caused many of the inhabitants of the riverbanks to move, and birds and animals were found dead on shore. These creatures, God's creation, continued with life no matter what disturbed them. His life would also continue. But not without Sadie.

By the time he made his way back to his truck, he had a plan. He would go to her apartment and convince her to forget the other guy and marry him. Maybe the problem was because he hadn't proposed to her. He would go to the best jewelry store in town and buy her a diamond engagement ring. A big one.

Before he knocked on the apartment door, he felt his

pocket. Yes, the black velvet box was still there. No way could she turn down this stone. A groggy Sadie answered the door. Uh, oh. Not in a good mood.

"Oh, it's you." She turned and started back inside, motioning him to follow.

"Are you okay? Did I wake you?"

"Yeah. I was out late last night." She pulled a shirt over her low-cut tank top and yawned. "I gotta have some coffee. Want some?"

"No, thanks." He watched her stumble around the cluttered kitchen. Dirty dishes filled the sink and trash spilled out onto the floor. She sniffed a coffee mug she pulled from the sink, wrinkled her nose, and rinsed it out. She uncovered a coffee maker and filled it with water and ground coffee. Soon the smell of coffee filled the room.

The velvet box in his pocket would have to wait. He turned toward the door.

"Did you want something?" She wiped her eyes and sat on a stool.

"No, not really." He started to leave, then turned back. "Thought maybe you'd like to go to a movie or something tonight."

She laughed. "I would, but Jasper is taking me to New York to see a Broadway play. He's all about that kind of stuff, you know."

"Oh. Well, guess I'll go." He leaned forward to kiss her but drew back. "See you later, I guess."

Would he have to learn to like Broadway and opera to win her back? He scratched his head. Could a guy who grew up on the river fishing and hunting learn to like those things? A picture of her yawning in the middle of a messy room filled his brain. She was still beautiful. Yes, he could. Sadie was worth it.

The next day David left the office late and stopped at the market to purchase groceries when he heard someone call him. Tom Wade, one of the river people, stood behind him.

"Kingston, have you found out anything about the trouble we're having down our way?"

David shook his head. "Kade and I told Mr. Crandall, and he said he would look into it. We haven't heard anything else. You still having trouble there?"

"Why yeah, it's even worse." Tom sounded agitated. "I seen Crandall on the river the other day. In fact, I've seen him there a couple of times. Caint figure out if he's investigating the matter or involved in it."

"He's been out of the office a lot." David chose a loaf of bread but returned it to the shelf. "What do you think he's doing?"

"I don't know, but he's driving a snazzy red speedboat. Looks new. Doesn't appear to be shipping business he's up to." Tom shrugged. "Thought you ought to know. See you later, Kingston."

David finished his shopping and decided to run back by the office to grab a file he wanted to complete. When he turned the key to enter the office, he heard a noise inside. Who would be here this time of the night? He waited a moment and eased the door open. He could see lights in Oliver's office and two figures moved about. Not wanting to infringe on Oliver's privacy, David moved against the wall to his office, picked up the file and turned to leave.

But before he could get out, a woman's squeal cut

through the quiet. "Oh, Oliver, darling, you're the best. You know just what I like. Thank you."

The silhouette of a slender woman with long hair embracing Oliver was visible through the door of Oliver's office. David eased the door closed behind him and ran to his truck, wishing he had gone straight home from the market.

On the river

Sitting in the cabin of the large river boat, Captain Ben Kerns rubbed the back of his neck and stretched his legs. Why did Amelia have to get sick now? His wife had always been a healthy, independent woman, and he found it hard to watch her sitting in a dark room day after day in obvious pain. The doctors said the cancer spread to her lungs. They could do nothing else

The hospital bills were astronomical. He took a third mortgage on the house and their life savings were gone. Not only would he lose his beloved wife, but he would lose his home. Rather than lose everything, he took the money.

Early this morning, a man approached him with an offer. If he would carry a load of unauthorized cargo, the man would pay him one hundred thousand dollars. What kind of cargo would be so valuable? The man wouldn't say. He said it would be loaded at midnight and unloaded at dawn several miles down the river. He told Kerns to keep it mum. Not even the crew could know. The men would not ask questions of their trusted captain. If he said it was okay, it was okay.

Ten

Kade breezed through the door, back from his trip and eager to talk about what he learned at the convention he attended while abroad.

"David, look at this!" He opened an app on his iPad and swiped it. "This will help me keep up with my scheduling and my clients."

"Yeah, you need all the help you can get with your schedule. Did you remember to call Austin about going with us down river this weekend? Or did you forget we're going?"

"Oh, I did forget." Kade entered the information on his app and grinned. "There. I'll call him today."

"Wait. Don't call him. I have an idea. Have you ever attended an opera? Or a Broadway play?"

Kade gawked and outstretched his hands, palms up. "You want to go to an opera? Seriously?"

"Yes. I've been thinking about it. I think it would be good to broaden my knowledge of finer things."

"Finer things? What makes you think the opera is a finer thing?"

"It wouldn't hurt us to experience some more elegant things, like caviar and Broadway plays."

"Don't get me wrong—if you want to go, I'm game. I've never been to an opera or a Broadway play. But I think the finer things in my life are sailing down the river in my boat, spending time with my family and friends, and eating celery and peanut butter. Can't get any better than that."

"Yeah, I get that. But I want to go. Just to see if it's something I'd like."

"Okay. You make reservations, and we'll go."

Kade went into his office, closed the door, then jerked it open and stuck out his head. "David, you've got to get this app. It's great."

David worked in his office all morning, avoiding any contact with Oliver. He had a meeting with him in the afternoon. He dreaded it. He checked Silas Hebron's files and noticed something different. Closer inspection revealed the file was altered, and David knew he did not make the change. The totals on the spreadsheet were fixed to cause the client to pay more shipping for the freight. He started going through the files of all his clients, and several of them were altered the same way. The changes were slight enough to bypass the notice of the client but enough to bring extra dollars into Crandall Shipping.

He buzzed Ms. Emma to come to his office and showed her the files. "Ms. Emma, what should I do? I didn't make these changes."

"This is bad, David." Ms. Emma cringed. "Does anyone else have access to your files?"

"Mr. Crandall." David covered his eyes with his hand and groaned. He couldn't believe Oliver would do this to make a buck.

"Ms. Emma, what should I do? I can't confront Mr. Crandall. He'd fire me for sure."

Ms. Emma rested a hand on her hip and studied his face. "Tell you what. You fix what you can, and whatever happens, happens. You have to take care of your clients. They trust you. Keep that trust no matter what."

David jumped up and hugged her. "Thanks, Ms. Emma. You don't know how much I appreciate you." He worked on the files the rest of the morning and through lunch, fixing the ones he could. Those already submitted could not be changed. He would have to amend the difference on future shipments for them.

"What in the world are you doing?" Kade came in eating a stalk of celery with peanut butter. "Didn't you go to lunch?"

"No." David lifted his hands as he completed the last file. "I had to finish some work. You have peanut butter on your chin."

Kade snatched a tissue and wiped his chin. "What's so important you can't eat?"

"Nothing. I just want to finish up. I have a meeting this afternoon with Mr. Crandall and I want to be ready."

"A meeting about what?"

"It's a quarterly evaluation. He's checking my work to find out if I'm doing okay. It'll be all right."

"Well, don't let the old man get to you." Kade laughed. "I know how he is."

When David went into Oliver's office for the meeting, he knew from Oliver's black expression trouble was brewing. He tried to make eye contact, but every time he did, he saw the scene from the night before.

"Have a seat, David." A stack of files lay on Oliver's desk, and one was open on his computer. "I've been looking at your work, and for the most part you're doing a good job."

"Thank you, sir."

"There's one thing, and it's a big thing. I see here where

you've given a rebate to Abe Sanders. I also see where you've lowered the shipping costs for other clients. Will you please explain why?"

David stared at him, mouth open. "Well, sir, I gave Abe Sanders a rebate because you advised me to do so. Then several of my clients found out about it and demanded a rebate. I couldn't see my way clear to do a rebate, so I offered them lower rates. I didn't want to lose them."

Oliver's face turned crimson and he rose from his chair. "Look, boy, don't you pin your mistakes on me. I never advised you to do any such thing."

David straightened in his seat. "But Mr. Crandall..."

"Don't you Mr. Crandall me, David. I built this company from the ground up, and I know how to run it." He leaned over with both hands on the desk in front of David. "I'll tell you what. You do your work and leave the dealing to me. I'll take care of the shipping costs. Understand?"

"Yes, sir." Oliver stalked across the room to stare out the windows, and David rose to leave. Oliver stopped him.

"Oh, one more thing." Oliver's countenance changed. "Are you coming to Sadie's wedding?"

David stared at him. "Uh, I don't know."

"You'll get an invitation, I'm sure. You've been such a good friend to her, I know she'll want you there. She's marrying Jasper Harris, you know, from Harris Shipping."

"Yes, I know." David clenched and unclenched his fists and waited.

"Well, son, you're considered part of our family. Melody loves you, and so do Kade and Sadie."

"Thank you."

Oliver smiled. "I'll give Melody your regards and tell

her you expect an invitation." He waved his hand in dismissal and turned back to the window. David stood there a moment, stunned. Then he left.

"What's wrong, David? You look like you've seen a ghost." Kade slapped his friend on the back.

David blew out his cheeks. "At this rate I may be a ghost before long."

"How'd the eval go? I told you not to let him get to you. Looks like you didn't listen."

"Do you know he expects me to attend Sadie's wedding? Doesn't he know she dumped me? Oh, that's right. He planned the whole thing." David jumped up and walked out the door. Kade quickened his gait to keep in step.

"I'm sorry, David. My old man is losing it. I'll have a talk with him."

"No, it's okay. He did tell me I'm doing a good job. Then he turned around and blasted me for reducing the shipping for my clients. Said he never advised me to do anything."

"Yeah, sounds like him. Do it, then say you didn't. That's his motto." Kade turned to leave. "Don't worry about the wedding thing. I'll take care of it with Mom, and Sadie doesn't deserve for you to be there."

On the river

A small motorboat trolled down the east side of the canal that cut off Crandall Island from the mainland. Max Shepherd peered through the trees along the shore. Once or twice he slowed and pulled closer to the bank and turned back down river to repeat the process. After half a mile, he moved to the west side of the canal to look through the trees on the Island. This went on from late morning to the middle of the afternoon when Shepherd docked and went ashore.

He went along a narrow path to a house built on stilts, climbed the steps, and knocked on the door. No one answered.

He started back down the path and met an older man with a young woman carrying a baby. He shook the man's hand and put his arms around the woman's shoulder. She smiled at him as he talked to the child.

"Have you found out anything yet?" she asked.

"No, but I'm working on it. Did you do what I told you to do? This can't work if you don't follow my directions exactly."

The man nodded. "We did what you said. What do we need to do now? How long is this gonna take?"

Shepherd spread his hands. "I don't know how long, but right now all you need to do is wait. I know it's hard, but we have to be patient."

He escorted the couple to the house and returned to continue the search.

Eleven

David and Kade headed down the river for a two-day trip, hoping to relax and catch some fish. Things were going well until Kade's line snagged under a log.

"Dang! Pull closer, David. I have to get my hook loose."

David eased the boat closer to the log, and Kade jerked the pole. The hook broke loose and flew right at Kade who threw up his arms to guard his face. He yelped and raised his hand with the hook imbedded and blood flowing.

"Hand me the pliers so I can pull this thing out," Kade flung blood all over the boat. David found an old towel in the tackle box, and when they wiped Kade's hand and saw the hook, Kade turned white and sat down.

"Don't you pass out." David looked at Kade's pale face. "We should take you to the ER."

"No, you pull it out." Kade leaned back, and David took the pliers, but he couldn't do it. He revved the motor and headed to the other side of the river where buildings lined the banks.

"There's an Urgent Care over here in this town. We'll take you there."

It took a while, but the doctor pulled out the hook and bandaged the wound, admonishing Kade to be more careful with his fishing gear. They could tell it wasn't the first hook he'd removed.

As they left the building, they heard their names called. Turning, they saw Josiah Burney headed their direction.

"What in the world happened to you, Crandall? Using your hand for fishing bait?" His belly jiggled as he laughed at his own joke. "Must'a been a big'un to do all that damage."

"Yeah, well it wouldn't work for you, Josiah." Kade retorted. "Stick your nasty hand in the water and the fish would all jump out."

"That may be true," Josiah teased. "Everyone ain't sweet as you with your purty beard and sweet smelling parfume."

The men laughed at the joke, then Josiah sobered. "We still ain't heard from the river police 'bout our troubles on the river. You told Oliver yet?"

Kade nodded. "Yes, we spoke to Dad about it. He said he would check it out. You still having trouble? Have you found the missing kids yet?"

"Nope, not a sign. Still havin' problems. Only change is they's worse than before."

David frowned. "I don't understand it. I thought Mr. Crandall would have talked to an agent before now. Have you seen him down there?"

"Yeah, a time or two. Drivin' a nice red speedboat. Saw him once talkin' to a feller at one of the gambling boats."

"He's friends with a lot of people on the river." Kade shrugged. "He never sees a stranger." Josiah's lip curled, but he said nothing.

They returned to their boat, traveled down the river, and then pulled aside to fish near the bank. They snagged a couple of catfish and a mess of perch before they went ashore. They gathered dry leaves and twigs and built a campfire.

They enjoyed the campfire cooked fish complete with a salad of wild berries.

"Remember when Leroy caught a bunch of carp and his mom canned them? I visited his house one time and she made fish cakes for lunch. Man, they were good." Kade stretched out under a tree with a twig of grass in his mouth.

David yawned. "Yeah, she gave Mom jars of those. She fixed fish patties with fried potatoes, brown beans and cornbread. Mmm! Boy wouldn't I like to have a plate of those now."

Kade leaped to his feet. "Hey, let's go find Leroy and see if he still catches them. I'll bet he gets his wife to can them. If we can't talk her into making us a meal, we can take a jar home and fix it ourselves. He lives a little way from here."

It didn't take long to clean up their campsite. Then they walked along a narrow dirt path to a small, neat house built high above the ground.

"Hello!" Kade called out. A woman appeared at the door surrounded by three blonde children, and a man stuck his head around beside her.

"Kade! Kade Crandall, you ole cuss! And David Kingston?" His deep voice resounded, and his laughter boomed, almost shaking the building. "Man, you look all spiffy with those nice-looking beards." He bounded down the steps and shook hands with the young men.

"Hey Leroy! How's it going, man?"

"What in the world you guys doin' way out here? Are you lost?"

Kade laughed. "No, we're not lost."

"Have you caught any fish lately, Leroy? Carp to be exact?" David asked.

Leroy slapped his leg and laughed. "I shoulda known you wanted something. Fish, eh?" He looked around at his wife. "Clara, got any carp you canned last month?"

"Sure do." Clara disappeared in the house and returned carrying two jars of canned fish.

"Come on in, guys. Sit a spell. We ain't got much, but we ain't ashamed to share it with friends."

Clara fixed a lunch of beans, cornbread, fried fish, and coleslaw, and laughter filled the home as they recalled old times. The tone became serious when Leroy talked about the trouble brewing on the river.

"The casinos and bars are bringing more crime into this area. People's lives are being disrupted." He struck his fist against his knee. "All we want is to know our families are safe."

"Have they found the kids who went missing a while back?" asked Kade.

"No." Leroy's forehead furrowed. "The last I heard there's another one missing. No one seems to know anything about what's happening to them."

"Is law enforcement involved? I haven't heard anything about it." David knew the river people were clannish and liked to solve their own problems without involving outsiders. He was sure they would seek help if their children were in danger.

"We've reported it, but you know the attitude about river people." Leroy pressed his lips together "We're second-rate citizens. They don't consider us part of this country."

"Maybe you guys could talk to the authorities for us?" Clara pressed her hand to her throat. "You know the right people."

David's jaw tightened. "You've got to be kidding! I can't believe the attitude of the law enforcement around here."

Kade swung his leg over the porch railing where he sat. "We'll see what we can do as soon as we get back. And David," he jumped to the ground. "We need to get on down the river. It's getting late."

They bade goodbye to their friends and walked a narrow path to the river. Before long, they trolled toward one of their favorite fishing holes where they would set out lines and do a little night fishing. Maybe they would catch a few catfish to take home.

They reached the spot and baited their hooks when they heard a splashing sound in the grass at the bank. They paddled the boat closer and saw a girl stooped over the water. She dipped water from the river and sloshed it onto a bundle she held. When she heard them, she looked up with wide eyes and backed into the brush.

"She's going to run," Kade muttered. He raised his hand. "It's okay, Miss. We just want to help you."

The men stepped out of the boat into the shallow water and approached the girl who watched them through dark hair. She crouched down, clutching a tiny baby against her blood-covered dress.

Kade looked around the area and David walked over to the girl. "Are you all right? Do you need help?"

She shook her head and pulled back. He lifted his hands, palms up, and made his voice soft. "We won't hurt you. We just want to help. What is your name?"

"Maggie," she whispered. "Are you here to get my baby?"

"No, we're not going to take your baby. Is it okay?" David touched her arm, and she jerked away. "May I see it?"

She shook her head and backed further behind a bush.

"It's okay. We want to help you."

She looked at David and back to Kade. "I…They said they'd come when my baby's here. I didn't know she'd be born today. I was walkin' home from a neighbor's house when it happened real fast. I hurt too bad to walk the rest of the way home."

"Where is your mom?" Kade tried to move closer but stopped when she backed away.

"I…I ain't got no mom." Her frightened eyes darted from the men to the river.

"Do you have any family? A dad? Sisters? Anyone?" David asked.

"Nah, nobody but my grandpa. He went to the city to do his business."

"Who is coming for your baby?"

"The people. They said they'd take my baby when she's born. They come almost every day to check on me. I have to have her ready when they come. I figured you was them."

David looked at Kade's blazing eyes and shook his head. "Maggie, we didn't come for your baby. We don't know those people. But we want to help you. Will you let us? We won't hurt you or your baby."

Maggie swiped her white face and swayed. Kade rushed to catch her before she fell. He lay her on a bed of moss under a tree, careful to hold the baby steady.

"I'll get the first aid kit." Kade headed for the boat.

David hovered near the girl. "May I see the baby?" She relaxed her hold on the bundle. He leaned over, and a red little thing with dark hair wiggled in her arms.

The umbilical cord remained attached to the placenta. He thanked God he and Kade had taken First Aid classes. They would need to cleanse her from the polluted river water. Kade brought paper towels they carried in the cooler.

"I done already washed her," Maggie said.

"She's very pretty." David looked into her face. "What's her name?"

"She ain't got a name yet." Maggie closed her eyes and sighed. "I guess they'll name 'er."

Kade opened a bottle of water and used a paper towel to wipe Maggie's face. "We need to get you to a hospital so they can take care of you and your baby."

Maggie stiffened and pulled the baby close. "No. I caint go to the hospital."

Kade straightened. "It'll be okay. We'll take care of you. You both need medical attention to make sure you won't get an infection."

"You don't understand." Her voice pleaded. "They'll be here in a little while looking for the baby." Tears filled her eyes.

"Do you know these people? How did you meet them?"

She shoved her hair back from her face and stared at them. Then she brushed the tears away with the back of her trembling hand. "No, I don't know them. They came to the house a while back. Said they're our friends and want to help us so's we won't be poor no more."

She shivered. "When they saw me standing there all big and fixin' to have a baby, they asked if I was married, and who was the daddy of my baby. When I told them he left me, they said they could take my baby out of here so it won't grow up poor like me. Said they'd give me money to help me do better for myself."

Kade's eyes flashed. "Do you know the names of these people?"

"No." Maggie touched her neck. "I heard one call the other one Mack. I never heard anything else."

"What did they look like? How many were there?" Was Mack a name or just a slang term?

"There was three. One was bald-headed. One was kinda fat and loud. The other was younger and good lookin'." Maggie blushed.

"Do you know if anyone else on the river has talked to them? Maybe they've helped other girls so they won't be poor?"

"Yeah." Maggie picked at a fingernail. "A girl I know gave them her new baby, and I heard she's moved to an apartment in town."

"Is that what you want, Maggie?" David peered into her face.

She cringed. "Sure, I'd like to have a nice place in town, but I want my baby more."

Kade patted her on the back. "Good, Maggie. You can keep your baby." He pointed toward the boat. "Now don't you worry about anything. We'll take care of you. First we have to get you and the little one to the hospital."

"Yes." David nodded. "We'll keep those people from getting your baby, and we'll get you help. Does that sound okay?"

Maggie consented, and they fastened a life jacket around her. They tucked her and the baby into the bottom of the boat. Before long, they pulled the boat into the pier of a river town large enough to have a hospital. Kade called an ambulance to meet them and assured Maggie they would see her at the hospital. First, they found a law enforcement agency to file a report. The officer offered little help.

"These river people are nothing but trouble," he said when they told him about the girl. "I wish they'd disappear."

Kade jumped to his feet, but David laid a calming hand on his arm. He knew anger would accomplish nothing and Kade needed to keep a cool head. They filled out the report and left. They would have to find a source of help from a person who would sympathize with the folks on the river.

Back at the hospital, David found a social worker who promised to help Maggie and her baby. "I know this is happening." She slammed a stack of papers on the desk. "I'm from the river myself, and I know what these people suffer at the hands of crooks and con men. I go back often and try to educate them about these issues, but because of their poverty, they often do desperate things. And they get little help from people who don't even want to admit they're around." She grimaced. "I guess you could call it the culture of the river. It constantly changes but never changes."

On the river

Maisie threw the report card on the table and covered her face with her hands. Again, three Ds and one F. The B last nine weeks in history had now fallen to a C, and Logan's grade in computer class dropped. She scoffed. Of course, he had an A in PE. He was a star basketball player. Or was. With grades like these, he would be benched.

Logan had always been a good boy, but he had changed. He became defiant and belligerent. What changed? The challenging job of a single mom made her weary. She couldn't give him everything he wanted, but she worked hard to provide him with everything he needed. When special shoes were required for basketball, she sacrificed and purchased them. She never wanted him to do without because of her bad decisions.

Another thing bothered her. The other day she saw him playing with a new electronic game, and when she asked where he got it, he mumbled that a friend loaned it to him. He also wore a pair of expensive shoes she didn't buy for him. He explained that, too. But she didn't believe him. Where were these things coming from? She bit her lip. If only she had someone to share parenting responsibilities, life would be easier.

Twelve

David made reservations, and he and Kade went to New York to watch an opera. He had researched options and had chosen the *Barber of Seville* at the Metropolitan Opera House. After a light meal, they arrived early to look around. David found the orchestra pit interesting, while Kade was fascinated by the set. David had reserved box seats, and next to them two middle age women spent the first intermission flirting with the handsome young men. When Kade went to the concession, one of the ladies came into David's box and sat in Kade's chair.

"You handsome devil, I'd sure like to get to know you." The woman put her hand on his knee, and David gently removed it. "Are you from here?"

"No, ma'am. I'm just here to attend the opera."

She gestured toward her friend. "The two of us have been watching you all night. Would you and your friend be interested in dinner after the program?"

"Uh...no...uh...we already have plans. I'm sorry."

"Oh, poo! Plans can be changed."

Kade returned and stood next to her. She gazed up at him. "What about it, gorgeous? Dinner with two lonely ladies?"

Kade picked up her hand and kissed it. She swooned. "Ms...?

"Laine. Marcenilla Laine." She batted her eyelashes up at him. "Nilla."

"Well, my lovely Nilla, we would be happy to take you to dinner, but you see, we already have ladies and don't need anymore. You understand, don't you? Yes, I knew you would." He took her elbow and, ignoring her protests, led her to her seat.

He returned to the box and David grinned. "I'm glad you handled that."

Kade snickered. "If I'd left it up to you, we'd be having veal cutlets, Crème Brulee and who knows what else with those women. Now shush, Barber is back on."

David glanced over at Nilla and watched as she whispered and pointed at their box.

He whispered to Kade, "I don't think it's over yet." Sure enough, during the next intermission, Nilla's friend came over.

"Hi. I'm Mable." She squeezed her large frame between them, pushing David into the floor. "Oh, I'm sorry." She pulled on his arm to help him up and elbowed Kade in the process. Kade stood and leaned over the side of the box. Below, he could see people moving about and realized the intermission was about over. When he turned to reclaim his seat, Mable rose, knocking him over the side of the box. He grabbed the side and hung there, dangling over the crowd that watched from below.

Mable wrung her hands and sputtered her apologies. David tried to get around her to pull Kade back over the side, but in her frustration, she seemed to take up the whole box.

"Mable, please, move over. I've got to help Kade."

"Oh, I'm sorry. Here, let me help." She leaned over to

help and smashed Kade's fingers. He yelled until David managed to get her out of the way. He grabbed Kade's hands and pulled him back into the box. The audience applauded Kade's rescue, and the show continued. The red-faced women left them alone after that, and the young men had an opera story when they returned home.

David had errands to do before he went to work mid-morning. He waved to Ms. Emma and headed to his office when he heard loud voices coming from behind Kade's door.

"I've heard enough about David. He has trifled with my clients, and I won't have it."

"Dad, he's helping you, and you don't even know it. He kept you from losing Amos Cole, and since he's been here, he's added a lot of clients to grow your business. You should be thankful for him."

David stood still. Wow. Kade defended him against his own father. The next words cut.

"Son, I know you've been friends with that country bumpkin all your life, but you may need to rethink your friendship. I'm through talking." Oliver slammed the door and moved across the room without a glance in David's direction. David looked at Ms. Emma. She lifted one shoulder and forced a sympathetic smile before he hurried to his office.

Kade came in and sat on the edge of David's desk. He watched as David worked, flipped through a stack of papers, and fiddled with the phone.

"Hey, let's go grab lunch." Kade poked David's arm, and David rose.

"Sure, I'm hungry." He treasured a friendship even a powerful man like Oliver Crandall couldn't destroy.

It rained three days straight, and the weatherman predicted another week of downpour. The saturated ground couldn't absorb more water, so it poured into the river from the many tributaries, causing the river to rise. It didn't look good.

David shuffled shipping times and dates to accommodate his clients, and clients were in and out of the office, worried the flood would cost them money.

"Of course, it will affect you." David assured them. "But that's why you have insurance." One of Oliver's clients came into his office for help because Oliver failed to increase his coverage when his shipping increased. David put his account into a different category to have better coverage, and the man insisted Oliver move his account to David.

"Now, Artie, you've been with me a long time." Oliver tried to soothe the man. "David is a beginner. You don't want him to be responsible for your business."

"Sure, I do." Artie waved his hand. "He knows his stuff. He can handle my business any day."

Oliver stormed around the office, becoming more agitated when several other clients asked for him to put David in charge of their accounts. David kept a low profile and tried to avoid Oliver's anger, but when he heard a reporter on the small TV in his office talking about a burst levy, he forgot his own troubles. Lives and property in a large community below it would be endangered

David ran into Kade's office to tell him the news. "We've got to help the river people," he said. "They're in trouble."

Kade whirled around and flipped on the TV to a

reporter standing by a marker showing the river flood stage. The wind whipped his umbrella and the rain splashed the water where he stood knee-deep. "The river continues to rise, endangering the lives of those along the banks," he shouted into the camera. "People down river have been told to leave, but for many it's too late. Crandall Island has already been evacuated." A tree floated behind him, and the camera zoomed in on a submerged building. The reporter adjusted his earpiece. "I've just got word another levy has broken. A mandatory evacuation has been issued for those living on the river. People, get out before it's too late."

Kade grabbed his raincoat. "Let's go." They ran for the door, planning as they ran. They would gather as many guys with motorboats as they could find. It would be dangerous, but the river people needed them.

"You take my boat, and I'll take Dad's," Kade yelled when they got to the dock. A couple of guys were standing close, and Kade motioned to them. "Got a boat?" The men shook their heads. "Come on and help us. Frank, you go with David, and Jim with me."

They cranked the motors and headed downstream, dodging floating debris and logs. They faced a different river than the one they traveled a couple of days before. That river flowed calm and inviting; this river roared, swollen and angry.

They kept toward the middle of the stream, watching for movement along the sides. The waters covered the banks, making them invisible. When they arrived at the area where the river people lived, they slowed, one boat on each side of the chute, searching for anyone or anything needing help. Before long they saw a boy with a dog hanging on to a piece of board. Frank helped him and his dog into the boat, and he pointed to a small cabin floating along. They pulled alongside the building, where a woman held on to a rafter sticking from the roof. Her weakened arms gave way before they could get to her.

"Grab her!" shouted Frank to Jim. David gunned the motor. Jim missed her as she sunk into the muddy water. Kade tried to maneuver his boat to get in front of her, but she once again disappeared in the murky water. Jim jumped into the water and came up with her. Kade pulled her into the boat and Jim held onto the side. She vomited a lot of water and lay gasping for breath. Kade grabbed the back of Jim's jacket just as a large log slammed into the boat, knocking it sideways. Jim slipped from his jacket and sank.

"Where is he? I can't see him." Kade yelled at David.

"There! He's there." Frank pointed to a log Jim was holding with all his might. Kade pulled close to him and hauled him spitting and sputtering into the boat.

They worked for hours, carrying people with their possessions and animals to a high place where they could find shelter. Help in the way of boats and supplies flooded in from all over. As Kade and David carried a boat load to higher ground, another boat pulled alongside them. A balding man with a gray beard steered the boat.

"Hey!" he shouted. "We need help on the east side. When you empty this load, will you help us?"

David lifted a thumb and they rushed to unload and sped off to help. They found the man down river and saw the predicament. A tree jammed against a house, blocking a family inside. As the water rose, those inside stood in danger of drowning.

"If we could get the tree away from the house, we could get to them."

"Look out, Shepherd." The passenger in the boat pushed away a large piece of debris with his paddle.

The balding man who steered the boat ducked, barely dodging a limb. He yelled to his passenger. "Jake, if you could jump on the tree, maybe it would give. Be careful."

Jake jumped on the tree and bounced, holding on to the branches. The tree moved, but not enough. Kade jumped up beside him and they bounced it while Shepherd and David pulled from their boats. The tree dipped and turned, dumping both men off into the swirling water.

Branches whipped around as the tree spun, and Kade dove to avoid being hit. Jake held on to the tree trunk, and a root caught him, pushing him under the water. Shepherd pushed on the tree with his paddle to turn it. The heavy tree dipped again. Jake's weight pulled it lower. They had to get him out.

The tree shifted again, and this time Jake freed himself and came gasping to the surface. One of the rescuers pulled him into a boat, and David looked around for Kade who held on to the house. Another tip of the large tree, and the house loosened and began to move further down the river.

"Kade! Hold on." David pushed the boat back from the tree and cranked the motor. If the house toppled before he got to his friend, it could be bad. It tipped and bobbed along the river with David and Shepherd in close pursuit. When they approached it, they killed the boat motors and used paddles to avoid pushing the house with waves.

"Let's push it over there to the opening," shouted Shepherd. They worked to move the house without tipping it.

Kade swam to the boat, crawled over the side, and helped the others. When the house bumped against the ground, they were able to help the family into the boats and to safety.

They checked up and down the river, making sure there were no others in danger. It would be days before the river people and islanders could return to what — if anything — the flood left of their homes.

On the river

"Man, we need to work together. The prospects are endless if we pool our talents and use our heads." Two men, one young and muscular, the other thin and swarthy, chinked glasses of bubbling beverages and nodded. A waitress set plates of food on the table in front of them, and the swarthy man grimaced as the young one tackled his steak. He lifted his head and swiped his hand across his mouth.

"Yeah, I've been looking for an opportunity to expand my enterprise." A piece of meat stuck out of his mouth. "What do you have to offer?"

"Only the best uncharted area in the country. Untouched by any other syndicate, ripe for the harvest. I have the right connection to make it all ours."

Swarthy handed the young man a napkin, and once again, glasses chinked.

Thirteen

The rain stopped after a week, and the damage done was astronomical. Ms. Emma turned on the television to watch the news reports showing flooded towns, fields, and roads. Oliver came in and joined the rest. They watched pictures of rescuers pulling people from flooded buildings and cars. Heroic rescues and tragic events filled the screen.

"Those poor people," Oliver muttered. Kade raised his eyebrows and David blinked. This came from the same man who wanted the river people to disappear? Of course, this involved more than the river people.

Oliver looked away from the TV. He remained quiet the rest of the day and into the next. Often, he would shake his head and study the ceiling or a wall.

Kade watched his dad through the open door. "What's going on with the old man?"

David shrugged. "I have no idea. He isn't acting like himself." Ms. Emma kept a vigilant eye on him, taking him coffee and offering him honey buns and fried pies. A short time later, he called Kade and David into his office and revealed his concerns.

"I've been wondering what I can do to help these people." He paced the floor. "It won't make a difference this time, but I can do something about preventing another flood from causing this much damage."

"What are you going to do, Dad?" Kade asked.

"I'm going to pool my resources, talk to other businessmen, and build levies. Not levies like we have now that are destroyed by flood waters, but levies which will withstand a raging river. Levies to last for good."

David rose, walked to the window, and looked out at the force which flowed out to the countryside beyond. The city built concrete retaining walls to keep the river back. Those walls did the job at a high cost. He looked around at Oliver. What is he thinking? How would they pay for levies strong enough to resist the force of a flood like this one?

"Kade, you'll do the footwork and find sponsors and supporters who will champion our cause. You'll go to every CEO and tycoon within fifty miles on either side of the river. Make them want to help these people as much as we do." Oliver paced the floor.

"David, you'll help me devise a blueprint for these levies. I hope you'll agree with my idea because I need your help to develop it." He grabbed a pad and pencil from his desk and looked at Kade. "Get going, boy. We don't have a lot of time."

David pulled up a chair beside Oliver and watched in awe as his pencil flew over the pad. He always admired Oliver's skill as an engineer and once again he saw the reality of his talent.

Oliver held a diagram. "What do you think? Will it work?"

David studied the paper, turning it one way then another. He picked up a pencil and made a couple of marks. He turned it so Oliver could see, and they erased lines, added lines, and adjusted numbers until they were both satisfied.

"Want to make the blueprint?" Oliver asked. "I'll let

you. Just show it to me before you print it."

David's whole face brightened. "Me? You want me to do it?"

"Sure, I do. You can, you know."

David picked up the pad and went to his office to work. In a few days he showed it to Oliver and in a short time he had the blueprint complete.

"David, come with me." Kade had knocked on the doors of every CEO and fat cat in the city and prepared to expand his campaign down the river.

"I don't know if I can take off. I have work to do."

"I'll ask Dad. He'll let you." He trotted off to talk to Oliver and David hoped he could make it happen. He did. They would enjoy a road trip like old times, just the two of them joking and laughing at any silly thing they heard or saw. A full-sized fake horse on top of a barn, a real car on top of a building, a naked butt visible under the open door of a van parked beside the road for a potty break.

"Hey, do you remember the time we went to Chicago to pick up your uncle?" David asked. Kade pondered a moment and laughed.

"Oh, yeah, I remember. The pig waddling across the road in a red bikini. Dang, that was hilarious."

David chuckled. "She was the biggest sow I've ever seen. Guess she escaped the petting zoo."

"Reminded me of … Here! Turn here," Kade jabbed his finger and David pulled into the parking lot of a tall building. "I'll get the bag and you grab the poster."

They entered the office and introduced themselves. The secretary showed them the room they would use, and they laughed and talked to several businessmen and women who were receptive to their presentation. More appointments were set up, and more businesses pledged to help with the project.

Quite satisfied with their success, David and Kade turned toward home. The campaign took more than a week, and they were ready to report back to Oliver. A few hours into the trip home, they left the restaurant where they ate lunch and pulled into the lane behind a semi-truck loaded with grain. As they were about to go under an overpass, the truck struck the overpass support pole and toppled over, spilling grain all over the interstate right in front of Kade's black Escalade.

"Look out!" David yelled as Kade struggled to avoid the moving semi and the deluge of grain. When they stopped, they were crossways of the highway with the back of the Escalade filled with beans.

"Man, that was close." David's voice shook. "Are you okay?"

Kade's hands still gripped the steering wheel and his face was a white mask. David crawled out of the vehicle and around to check on Kade.

"Come on, let's see about the driver." He pulled Kade's hands from the steering wheel and straightened his fingers.

Kade shook himself and crawled out. David called 911 as they ran to find the other driver dazed and banged up, but alive.

"Hey, man, what happened?" David dragged him away from the truck and leaned him against a concrete embankment. "Are you all right?"

The man rubbed his face with a shaky hand. "I tried to straighten up. I don't know what happened."

David ran back to the Escalade to get a bottle of water. "Here, take a drink." He poured water in the man's hand. "Put some on your face."

The man did as he was told, and his trembling slowed. He looked up at David and blinked. "Say, ain't you with Crandall Shipping?"

"Yes, I'm David Kingston. I work for Crandall. Are you a client?"

"My boss is moving his business there. I'm taking this load to Pruit Shipping, then the next load will go to Crandall's. He's switching over for some reason. Said something about getting a better deal, but I ain't so sure. I kinda like Pruit myself. Pruit's a nice guy."

"I've heard he is, but I've never met him." David smiled at the man. "Well, I hear sirens. Guess help is on the way."

When they filled out the accident report and the ambulance pulled away with the injured man, Kade and David checked Kade's truck for damage. Other than bean dust in every crevice of the truck, everything looked good. They crawled in and headed toward home.

Kade drove in silence until a huge sigh escaped his lips. Then another. David ignored him, thinking a fit of nerves gripped him.

"That reminds me of something that happened once when I was in college," Kade said. "I had an early class, and when I was driving down the road, I saw a vehicle coming around me on a curve. Scared me silly. I whipped over only to realize it was nothing but my own shadow from the streetlight."

David chuckled and shook his head. "Remember that time I topped a hill and had to take a barbed wire fence to miss Mr. Harris on his John Deere tractor? Sure messed up that little Ranger I drove."

"Didn't you have to fix that fence?"

"Sure did. Took a whole Saturday, and then I spent the rest of the summer fixing my truck." He laughed and slapped his leg. "What about that time you backed into that light pole?"

"Yeah, I looked left and right but forgot to look behind me. Bam! Bent my bumper but good."

"By the way, it's time for lunch. Let's find a place to eat." They were entering a small city and watched for a restaurant.

"Here's one," Kade pulled into a parking area. "It looks busy. That usually means it's good."

"Yeah," David faked a dodge. "Watch out for that light pole."

On the river

"You want me to what?" Willie shook his head in disbelief. The skinny red-headed man rose from the stump where he had perched earlier. Willie shifted his gaze to the big, burly man who stood with his arms folded and his head tilted back.

"Look, kid. If you don't want to nab the child, we'll find someone else."

"Sure," the skinny dude said. "It isn't hard to find someone who'll do such a simple job for this amount of money."

Willie thought a moment. His parents had been struggling since his mom had to quit her job as waitress on the Gold Boat. The baby was due any day, and she would be off for a while. The doctor bills were already coming in. If he could help them pay some bills, they might overlook his failing grades at school. He glanced from one man to the other, then nodded. "I'll do it. Just tell me when and where."

Fourteen

It took David a week to catch up with his work when he returned to the office. That's when he found some of his files changed again, causing the balances to be off on many clients' accounts. Ms. Emma pursed her lips when he talked to her about the problem.

"Like I said before, David, you know what you have to do. Be fair to your clients. They have to be able to trust you."

He changed the ones he could and went in person to talk to clients who had already been cheated. He took the blame on himself, not wanting to implicate Oliver in any way.

"Now, David, I know you." Silas Hebron narrowed his eyes. "I don't believe this is your doings."

David clenched his jaw. "I'll fix this, Mr. Hebron. I'll make it right."

"I know you will. I trust you." He cocked his head. "When you going to start your own company? You have a lot of clients ready to follow you should you ever decide to go out on your own."

David's face turned crimson. "Uh, I don't think I'm ready yet. Thank you for your confidence, though."

"Well, I'm just sayin' when you get ready, you let us know."

One of Oliver's clients arrived in time to hear what David said. "Put me on your list, too." He jammed his hands into his pockets. "I'm tired of coming out on the short end of the deal. Crandall has nothing but excuses when I ask him why my profits aren't up to par. And I'm not the only one."

David rubbed his hands against his pant legs. He sure couldn't afford to make Oliver mad. He needed to keep his job.

A lot of work later, David organized his files and managed to find two new clients. Things were going well until Oliver called him into his office. Kade slouched against the wall on one side of the room, and Oliver stood behind his desk. David looked from one to the other. Kade kept his head lowered, and red ran up Oliver's neck and covered his head.

"Have a seat." A command, not a suggestion. David obeyed. Oliver paced as the red of his face deepened.

"I had a visit from clients who are convinced I'm cheating them. I wonder who gave them that impression."

David frowned and shook his head. Oliver continued. "Well, I have an idea. No, it isn't an idea. I know." He leaned on the desk with his face inches from David's. "In fact, Tom Wade said straight out that he and the others are hoping you'll buy your own shipping company so they can join you."

David stiffened. Why in the world would these clients do this to him? He told them he wasn't ready. They knew he worked for Crandall. Why would they throw him under the bus?

"Tom Wade is an idiot," Kade muttered. He turned to David. "He's the only one who's said anything to Dad. If anyone is being cheated, they haven't mentioned anything about you, David. Dad exaggerates."

Oliver whirled around and walked over to Kade. "Son, I've warned you. Don't cover his butt. He'll have your inheritance one day if you aren't careful." He gestured for David to leave, and as David walked to his office, he could still hear him ranting.

For several days, David avoided seeing Oliver, but one day Oliver called for a meeting of all staff members in the board room. David seated himself on the opposite end of the table away from his boss and tried to keep out of his sight.

"David Kingston." David cringed at hearing Oliver call his name. "Mr. Kingston, are you ready for your report?"

What report? David panicked. His brain spun as he tried to recall anything about a presentation.

"Uh, sir, I don't recall you asking me to do a report." A hot flush creeped up his neck.

Oliver leered, and the staff members stared at David. He couldn't believe it. Why would Oliver do this to him right in front of everyone?

"Kingston, two weeks ago I asked you to prepare a presentation on the condition of the river since the flood. I asked you to show our staff how the levies I developed will prevent future events such as the one we experienced not long ago."

David blanched. Oliver set him up. He planned to denigrate him in front of everyone. He stood and lifted a finger. "Oh, yes, I remember. I do have it ready if you'll give me a moment." He grabbed his briefcase and headed to the door with Kade in close pursuit.

"Did he ask you to present?" Kade asked.

"No, of course not." David clenched his teeth.

"You grab your laptop and I'll get the DVD." Kade snickered. "You'll give him a presentation he won't forget. You've had plenty of practice."

And he did. Within five minutes David had the undivided attention of the staff members while Kade leaned back in his chair with a grin across his face and one thumb lifted.

Things were good for a while. Oliver came to the office two or three days a week, while David earned the trust and admiration of all the clients of Crandall Shipping. Little by little David took over most of the business accounts. Oliver made frequent trips around the country and abroad, leaving David with the receptionist, and the rest of the office team. He enjoyed the company of all the staff members, even more with Oliver out because they were more open and relaxed without the boss.

"David, have you seen this?" Kara, the shipping clerk, handed him a file. He flipped through it and snapped it closed. Then his mouth fell open and he jerked it back opened to the middle. A letter in Oliver's handwriting was paper clipped to the file of Roger Logue, one of David's most valuable clients.

> Mr. Logue:
> I apologize for the discrepancy in your files from January through March. Young Kingston is still in training and didn't notice the mistake. I'm working to help him overcome his weakness with numbers. I will make sure this does not happen again.
> Oliver Crandall

David flipped through the file. Prices were

inflated, and the totals were changed and inaccurate. He knew he did not make these errors. He went to his office and checked the files on his computer. They were the same as in the file. He remembered — he always backed up his files on a flash drive. He riffled through the desk drawer and found it. Sure enough, the backed-up files showed the correct numbers so David could see where the numbers were altered. Besides him, Oliver alone had access to make changes to the files.

He went to Kara's office, and together they scanned all David's files. Several of the others had similar letters. David spent the rest of the day correcting totals and fixing the mess. He determined he would again visit each client in person to make things right. He hoped he could regain their trust.

"I'll go with you and stand behind you." Kade matched strides with David as he went to talk to his clients.

"Thanks, man. It will help to have the boss's son at my back."

When a client hesitated to listen to David, Kade stepped forward to intervene. They went from vessel to vessel, explaining the situation and making things right. Some came around with assurances the files had been corrected with no loss to them, but many refused to listen to David or Kade.

"Kingston, I've already had problems once with you," Paul Sapine said when they visited him on his boat. "Now you're telling me there's been another error in my account? I think Crandall should handle my account himself."

"Mr. Sapine, David has saved you money ever since he took your account. Now you're denying him the chance to make up for his error?"

"Yeah," Sapine replied, "but how many more errors will he make before he learns the business well enough not to make any? And how much will the next error cost me?"

"How much did this error cost you?" David asked.

Sapine's forehead puckered, and he rubbed his neck. "Well, not too much. It could have been more though. And I prefer to make money, not lose it."

"Tell you what," Kade said. "David will return to you what you've lost, and on the next shipment, he will give you a discounted price. Will that take care of things?"

Sapine shook his head. "I'm not sure. I've always liked you, young man. But I can't afford to take unnecessary risks. Think I'll depend on Crandall to handle my business."

A few clients who joined him a short time before scoffed when David tried to convince them. "You're young, Kingston," one said. "Until you learn the business, I want Mr. Crandall to handle my account." When they refused to listen, David assured them their accounts would be entrusted to Mr. Crandall.

"Well, looks like I'll have to start all over," David commented as they drove back to the office. "It's hard to regain people's trust."

"I'm sorry my dad did this to you, David. You don't deserve this kind of treatment."

"Aww, don't worry about it. It'll all come out in the wash."

Kade grinned. "Reminds me of your mom. She always said that. I miss her."

"You need to go visit her and Dad. They'd love seeing you. You know I popped in on your mom a while back. We had a good visit."

"You did? You didn't tell me that."

David shrugged. "I went before Sadie and I split. By the way, how is Sadie?"

"I haven't seen her in a while, but as far as I know, she's fine. Still seeing that guy."

"The wedding is coming up, right?"

"Yeah." Kade raised an eyebrow. "You going?"

David cringed and shook his head. "I don't think so. I know Oliver expects me to come and Sadie wants me to, but it would be awkward. I'd rather not."

"You don't have to. Don't let anyone make you feel like you do." Kade exhaled. "You know as well as I do how persistent my family can be."

"I do. I also know how super they can be. Especially your mom."

"Yeah, she's a great lady." Kade paused a moment. "You know, Dad used to be great, but he's changed. I don't know what happened to him. Seems like over the years he's become...I don't know...different."

They rode in silence for a while. Kade adjusted the radio, and David gazed out the window.

"You remember telling me your dad is like a Venus Fly Trap?"

Kade pulled into the parking area and turned toward David. "Yeah, I remember."

"What did you mean?"

"By now it's clear what I meant. Look at what he's done to you. Don't you see he's like a Venus Fly Trap? He acted nice to you until you got under his influence, then, SNAP! And you're trapped."

David pressed his lips together. "I've always liked your dad. I assumed he liked me."

"It has nothing to do with like. It has everything to do with money and ego. That's all. He hates it when his clients prefer you over him."

"Oh."

"Uh, oh. Looks like Dad is in his office today. Maybe he'll be in a good mood."

"I hope so." They rode the elevator to their floor and waved to Ms. Emma on the way through to their offices.

"David, Mr. Crandall wants you in his office." Ms. Emma turned to her computer, avoiding his eyes.

David headed for Oliver's office with Kade right behind him. Oliver flinched when he saw Kade but gestured for David to sit in the chair facing him.

"Kade, you don't need to be here." He waved his hand in dismissal. "I need to talk to David."

"I'm good." Kade raised his hand. "We need to talk to you anyway."

Oliver adjusted his tie, and his eyes darted from David to Kade. "What do you want to talk to me about?"

On the river

A red speed boat roared down the river, slowing when the Island came in sight. As it drew near the foot of the Island, the driver killed the motor and the boat drifted to shore. A tall, dark-skinned man stepped onto the sand and secured the vessel to a tree. He pulled a bag from the boat and walked up the bank where he stood a moment on the brink of a small hill.

In a few minutes an older-looking man carrying a blanket-wrapped bundle joined him. He handed the package to the swarthy man who gave him the bag. The older man disappeared over the hill, and the man placed the blanket-covered package into a box in the bottom of the boat. As he untied the rope to free the boat, a bird which landed on the box rose, startled by a cry from the blanket.

Fifteen

D avid sat straight up in the chair, waiting to find out what Kade was going to do. Kade leaned forward with his hands on the desk, looked Oliver in the face and straightened. He walked over by the window.

"Dad, it's the river people and the Islanders. You're doing a great thing building those levies. They are happy and grateful."

Oliver studied Kade a moment and his mouth twitched. "That's good." He turned in his chair. "I'm glad they are appreciative. It requires a lot of money and work to do what we're doing to help them."

"They understand." Kade walked back over to the desk. "But there's another thing. The problem with gamblers and racketeers is increasing. The river people and Islanders deserve to be able to raise their children without them being exposed to this kind of corruption." He peered at Oliver's face. "Don't you agree?"

David leaned back in his chair and a corner of his mouth turned up. He watched as Oliver's expression changed from pleased, to upset, then to confused.

"Sure. Children shouldn't have to be around those kinds of things. But what do you expect me to do? I'm not the law. I'm just one man."

Kade scratched his beard. "Yes, you are one man and you are not the law. However," he extended his hand toward Oliver. "You have a lot of clout in this city. You could use your influence to persuade city and county officials and politicians to take action. You did it to improve the levies, and now you can use it to clean up the river."

Oliver rose and walked across the room to gaze out the window. He stood there a while without moving while Kade and David watched. When he turned to face them, they were surprised at the pained expression on his face.

"Over the years I've seen this river change," he said. "The terrain and also the people. It's like a never-ending evolution takes place, and I can't keep up. I can't change with it." He sat at his desk and stared at the wall.

"My ancestors purchased the Island in the twenties, and my family lived there for years. They raised cotton and truck-patched, but mostly they raised cattle. That's where I learned to work hard, and that's where I decided I never wanted to work in another cotton patch.

"Jesse and I owned the island and this part of the river. We knew everyone who lived in a twenty-five-mile radius and were friends with most of them." He walked over to a large painting of a ferry carrying a horse and buggy across the river. He ran his finger over the frame and across the picture before he turned once again to gaze out the window.

"My grandmother gave me this painting." He pointed. "That ferry carried folks across the Chute to and from the Island until it became unsafe."

Kade stood beside his dad with his hand on his

shoulder, and Oliver turned to him. "You know, most islands on the river are covered every time the water rises. But to my knowledge, Crandall Island flooded one time, and that was in the thirties. Not too many islands on this river are even inhabited by people."

"It's a special place, all right." David leaned back in his chair. "I'm glad I grew up there."

"Yes, it is special," Kade agreed. "And that's why we need to take action to keep out the corruption and preserve its integrity."

Oliver agreed. "Yes, I guess we do. You guys get to work and let me think about it. I think I'll try to use my influence to get help for those people."

Kade grinned and high-fived David as they left the office. "Snagged."

David yawned and stretched as he turned off his computer and filed the accounts he completed. It had been a long day, and he needed sleep. He stuck his head out his door when he heard steps in the main office, and saw a beautiful blonde woman standing alone in the middle of the floor. She looked his way, and gray eyes flecked with amber scrutinized him. Dimples appeared along with a wide smile.

"Hello?" David moved toward her. "May I help you?"

The woman stuck out her hand. "Hi. I'm Sophia Odell."

What is that accent? David offered her a chair, but she shook her head and gestured toward Kade's office. "I'm waiting for Kade. He said he would be right back."

"Hey! I see you've met Sophia." Kade lit up as he looked at her. "We're going to Celestial Flame for dinner. Want to join us?"

David laughed. "No. But thanks. I'm sure you don't want a third wheel at the Celestial Flame. Anyway, I'm beat. I'm going home. You have a good time." He smiled at the gorgeous woman. "Nice to meet you, Sophia."

When David saw Kade the next day, he whistled. "Wow! Where'd you meet her?"

"She's from Australia. She moved here last year. I met her on the plane my last trip."

"Maybe I need to fly more often."

"Yeah, you do need to branch out a little. Man, you gotta get over Sadie."

David grimaced and lifted one shoulder. "I guess." He returned to his office and worked until late again. Since his breakup with Sadie, he found himself putting in a lot of hours, and still sleep evaded him most nights.

"You're getting way too thin, David." Ms. Emma brought him homemade cornbread and vegetable soup or another nutritious meal every day.

On his way home, he saw Oliver talking to a man in front of a restaurant. Oliver waved his hands and pointed, and the man shook his head. The man pointed in the other direction, and Oliver shook his head. David slowed to watch. The tall, thin man with a dark complexion looked familiar. It was Jasper, Sadie's fiancée. David saw him once since Sadie's birthday party, and that was when she brought him to the office.

Otherwise, he hadn't seen Sadie since the breakup. So, Oliver and his future son-in-law didn't agree on everything. Maybe he didn't like the guy he chose for his daughter.

Before David passed them, another man joined the conversation. David saw him once on the pier, but he didn't recognize him as a client. Oliver hadn't added any new clients to the business. All the recent clients owed their alliance to David. He had worked hard to rebuild his client base and was making progress.

While he watched, Oliver gave the man an envelope and the man looked from one side to the other and disappeared down the street. Jasper thrust a fist into the air and stomped away. As David passed, Oliver went inside the restaurant.

Kade left on another trip, and David decided to take a short visit to the Island. He could visit his parents and at the same time, check on the river people. He hadn't seen them since the flood.

About nine Saturday morning, he docked his boat on the Island when he ran into Ivy Turner, a neighbor of his parents. After David inquired about the man's family, the talk turned to the troubles on the island.

"Things were pretty rough there for a while," Ivy said, "but we're getting back to normal. Oliver's levy project gave a big boost to our economy since he used Island and river people to build his levies. Man, we're grateful for those levies, too."

"I'm glad Mr. Crandall decided to do the project." David walked up the bank with Ivy. "And I'm glad people are benefiting from it."

"I'll tell you the truth, it surprised me a little when Oliver wanted to help us. Seems like in the past several years, he didn't want anything to do with any of us. We kinda felt like he considered himself above us."

"Why would you think that? He grew up on the Island like a lot of other people around here."

"Yeah, but he didn't stay like the rest of us. Now he drives that big red speed boat up and down the river like a big shot. I even heard he has a new woman to sport around."

David raked his fingers through his hair. "Have you seen him with another woman besides Mrs. Crandall?"

Ivy reddened. "No, I just heard it." He removed his cap and scratched his head. "Tell you what I have seen, though. I saw Oliver coming from one of them gambling boats with the guy that runs it. Heard them talking. Did you know he's planning to build a casino on the Island?"

David's jaw dropped. He jammed his hands into his pockets and stood silent a moment. "You sure you heard right?"

"Yep. I heard it with my own ears. Oliver told the man a lot of money could be made right here on Crandall Island. Said he wanted to make money off this place for a change."

"That doesn't sound right with all the work and money he's investing to help the Island people." Recognition dawned on his face. "Unless..."

Ivy looked across the river and back at David. He

lifted an eyebrow. David chewed on his bottom lip. They stared at each other, and Ivy waved as he boarded his boat. David headed to the Kingston home.

He hadn't walked far when he heard a vehicle. He glanced around but kept walking. It drew nearer and he turned. An ATV was headed right for him. He dove into the bushes beside the narrow road to avoid being hit. He couldn't believe it. It was Jasper.

David stood to watch the retreating vehicle. Maybe it wasn't intentional. *Wait! He's coming back. He's trying to run me over.* David jumped behind a tree and stuck his head out to look. He jerked back when a bullet whizzed by his head. He took a deep breath and ran through the scattered trees. The ATV followed him. As he approached a willow with low-hanging branches, he had an idea. He pulled a branch back as far as he could and waited. The ATV slowed, and Jasper looked left and right. David stepped out far enough that Jasper could see him, and when the grinning man drove the vehicle under the tree, David let go of the limb. Jasper yelled as the branch caught him right in the face. He flew off the seat as the ATV continued forward. David ran through the trees and made his way to his parents' home. Jasper got what he deserved.

On the river

Simon stood at the edge of the clearing, shuffling from one foot to the other. He wanted to go, but he would be embarrassed. What would people think? He'd heard these meetings were good. A friend said the guy who holds the meetings could help people hooked on gambling.

Since the gambling boats took residence near the Island, lots of Island and river dwellers were frequenting the river casinos. As a result, many of his friends had marital and money problems. Now his wife gave him an ultimatum—stop gambling or leave. He wanted to stop and swore to himself he would. But it had a hold on him he couldn't explain. Every time he passed the casino on the way home from work, he stopped.

He straightened his shoulders and joined several others headed for the small building. He loved his family and wanted to save his marriage. He would do whatever he had to do to conquer his addiction.

Sixteen

Jesse appeared disturbed when they talked about the casino Oliver planned to build. He had heard about it but admitted nothing could be done.

"This is Crandall's Island," he said, "so he can do what he pleases with it no matter what we think."

"How are the Island people taking the news?"

Jesse rose and gazed out the door. "Depends on who you ask. Older folks who have lived here all their lives are not happy about it, but most of the younger ones are excited. For one thing, they see it as an employment opportunity." He opened the door and motioned for David to follow. "How 'bout me and you take a little trip on the river?"

As Jesse steered the boat, David was dismayed at the damage done by the flood. Trash littered the banks and splinters of buildings hung entangled in trees and stuck in drifts. Old houses that once stood on the banks were gone, and new structures replaced them. Why would people build back in the same place the flood had washed them out? He asked Jesse about it.

"It's all they know," Jesse said. "Several of these people own property along the river, but many are squatters. They find a place and build, hoping they won't be evicted. The river police ignores them, and they stay put."

They checked on friends and neighbors on the river and walked up narrow paths to deliver sacks of canned goods to those they knew needed help. David checked on Maggie who'd had the baby. He chuckled at the sight of a healthy, smiling little girl. The baby's grandpa beamed with pride at his daughter and grandchild.

David spent the night with his parents and returned to the city the next day after they attended church and ate lunch. On the way home, he speculated about life on the Island. He'd had a good life on the island with his parents. What changes would take place with a casino built there? Yes, it would provide jobs, unless Oliver brought employees over from the mainland. He might do that. Most likely, Island people would become more involved in gambling, which would escalate crime. If that happened, dependence on government assistance would spike as more people became addicted to gambling. Instead of the Island being a quiet haven the paradise he remembered would be filled with traffic and noise.

A week later when David went to work, he found that Oliver had stripped him of his clients. Ms. Emma rubbed her temples and blew out her cheeks when he approached her to find out why he couldn't access his files.

"I'm sorry, David. He made me transfer all your clients to him. He left you Oscar Holmes."

David stormed out of the office and drove to the river. He drove his boat to the Island and instead of his usual place to dock, he drove around to the foot of the Island and docked there. He went straight to his old thinking spot. There he had prayed for solutions to many problems and worked through many choices he faced.

A grove of willows surrounding a fallen log provided a peaceful sanctuary beside the water. The place changed over time as the trees grew and the landscape changed, but he loved to go there when he needed alone time and fortitude. The willow grove was his favorite place to talk to God.

He sat on the log and stretched his long legs toward the river. The musky scent of moss reminded him of earlier days when he and Kade lay on the green carpet, dreaming of adventures and solving life's mysteries. The water lapped against the sand and a school of minnows darted around the rocks on the sandy river floor. A breeze moved the leaves above his head, making a soft swishing sound. A few yards downstream, a doe with a fawn waded into the shallow water to drink.

Now what am I supposed to do? Why doesn't he just fire me? His thoughts slammed against each other like two armies of foot soldiers in arm to arm combat, each yearning to seize control. His brain would be permanently bruised. He leaned forward to watch the minnows swim about without a care. Their only concern was finding dinner and avoiding becoming a meal for bigger fish. Come to think of it, isn't that the greatest concern for anyone? *I work to provide for myself, and I've become a meal for a bigger fish. Haven't I increased Crandall Shipping by bringing in new clients? Yes. I've worked my butt off helping Oliver build his business. I've done everything he's asked me to do. Then why is he treating me this way? Why does he want to destroy me?*

His energy was gone. His eyes grew heavy. He scooted down so his head rested on the log and drifted off to sleep. A brown lizard crawled down his forehead to awaken him. It cocked its head to look him in the eye.

He picked up the little creature and sat it on the log before he stood and stretched. His parents deserved a short visit from him before he headed back to the city. Before heading to his parents' home, he decided to walk down the river. On these walks, he was often rewarded with sights of wildlife that lived there. Water birds with long legs and beaks fished along the edge of the water, and otters swam together close to the bank. A large snapping turtle slid into the water as he approached, and he saw a water moccasin slither through the grass in the edge of the water.

He felt a little better about things, but he still couldn't imagine what the future held for him. He had walked quite a way along the river, and he decided to head across the Island to reach his parents' house.

Just as he turned, he caught a glimpse of movement in a bush. He could see nothing, so he went to investigate. A young boy holding a baby hid behind a large tree. A bay mare was tied to a limb behind the boy.

David pulled back the bushes to expose the blushing boy. "What are you doing here?"

He looked around David as though expecting to see someone else. "Hiding."

"Who are you hiding from?"

"Them." Fright filled his eyes, and he looked

around again. "Them guys who are after this baby." He glanced down at the baby. A wadded-up blanket lay on the grass behind him.

David turned to see if anyone was coming. Nothing. "Who's after your baby?"

"Ain't my baby."

"Geez, kid, whose baby is it? And what are you doing with it?"

"Uh, it's a long story."

David glanced around once more, then guided the boy to a patch of moss under the tree. "Sit here and tell me the long story as short as you can."

The boy sat down and cradled the sleeping child. "You see, it's like this. I was supposed to get this here baby for these guys. And I did. I snuck up on the mama while she was hanging clothes on the line. The baby was sleeping on a blanket behind her, so I grabbed it and ran. She didn't even see me."

"Who are the guys who told you to get the baby? And what are they going to do with it?"

"I don't know. All I know is when I deliver the baby, they give me money. Anyway, now I don't want to give it to them."

"Why?"

"I wasn't far from the house when I heard the baby's mama screaming and crying for her baby." He wiped his eyes. "I just caint take that, man, the crying. Now I don't know what to do. If them guys catch me, they'll hurt me."

"Where does the mama live? How far away?"

He pointed down river. "Not far. She lives right

through those trees over there." His head jerked up. "Listen. I hear them coming. They've got an ATV. I hid my horse here when I came, but they see me riding her, they'll catch me." Again, he wiped his eyes. "I don't know what to do."

David thought a moment. "Tell you what. You hide over there behind those bushes with the baby and wait for me."

"What're you gonna do?"

"I don't know yet. You wait here for me, out of sight. I'll be back. I hope."

"Okay." He cradled the sleeping child and crouched behind the bushes. David walked into the opening until he could see the approaching ATV. It wasn't the same one he'd encountered earlier. He jumped on the horse and guided it to an open field. Soon the driver of the ATV revved its motor and started after him. He urged the horse forward, slumping down so the men would think he was the boy. He reined the horse into a narrow stretch of woods, and the scenery became a blur as the horse and rider dodged trees and vines and leaped over stumps and dead logs. After a while, they were in a meadow moving toward an old abandoned house.

David slid off the horse and ran into the building. He looked around. Except for a broken chair and table, it was empty. Out the window he could see the ATV approaching. He ran from room to room looking for something to arm himself. He jerked off a leg that was hanging from a chair. It would make a weapon of sorts.

He sneezed and gasped for breath when dusty air

filled his nostrils. With little time to wait, he looked for a place to hide. He still wasn't sure what he would do, but he had to do something. He steeled himself when he heard the ATV pull up by the door.

The rickety porch groaned as someone jumped on it, and a deep voice yelled out. "You go look in that shed over there. I'll look inside the house." A barely inaudible voice answered.

David raised the chair leg and waited behind the open door. The screen door squeaked and through the crack he could see a big, burly man. He cringed. *I'll have to make the first hit count, because I won't get a second one.*

He stepped from behind the door and swung the wooden chair leg as hard as he could, knocking the man to the floor. He dragged him to the other room and used his belt to tie him to the table. Then he waited.

The second man stomped up on the porch, and again, David swung the leg. The man saw the movement and ducked. The weapon glanced off his shoulder. He swung a fist, and David fell backward. The man straddled him. David's head jerked to one side, then the other. Blood spewed. Blackness descended. He awoke alone with no idea how long he'd been there.

He felt his arms and ribs and flexed his legs. No broken bones. He touched his swollen eyes and busted lip. He was stiff, but he could walk. It would soon be dark, and he had to get back to the boy. He whistled for the horse, but it didn't come. He rubbed his aching jaw. Blood ran down his chin onto his shirt. At first, he hobbled along, but soon the stiffness left and his steps lengthened.

He found the boy still huddled under the bush. The

baby had awakened, and the boy patted it as it lay on his shoulder. He grinned when he saw David.

"I have a little sister," he explained. His eyes widened when David came close. "What happened?"

David ran his tongue over his busted lip. "They got away, but I got a good look at them. I'll report it and give a description to the police. Of course, they'll want to ask you some questions."

The boy drew back. "Oh, no. They'll put me in jail."

"Look. You did wrong to take the baby, but you didn't give it to them. We'll get the little guy back to his mom and that will look good for you. If you cooperate with the law, they'll go easy on you."

"My dad will kill me. He's already mad at me for skipping so much school." He handed the baby to a surprised David and fled.

"Wait!" David called. "Come back. I need your name and address." But the boy was gone.

It was a long walk back across the Island, but he started off. He would take the baby to its parents and then go to his parents' house to spend the night. They didn't know he was on the Island, so they wouldn't be worried about him. He was thankful for the moonlight. Tiredness pulled at him as he trudged through the tall grass and weeds. The baby wiggled in his arms, and he comforted it.

He cut through the trees in the direction the boy had indicated until he came to a small cabin. He realized the danger of approaching a home at night. Most likely, he would be met with a shotgun. He moved to a clearing so those in the house could see him.

"Hello. Hello in the cabin." His calls aroused a person

inside, and a light appeared.

"Who's there?" a woman called out.

"Ma'am, I need to see you. Is there a man in the house?"

He heard the unmistakable click of a gun and a deep voice. "Yes, there is."

"Sir, I have something for you. I'm David Kingston, Jesse Kingston's son."

A light shone in David's face. "Yes, I see who you are. What are you doing here, David?"

David held up the sleeping baby. "I have your child. May I come in?"

The door opened, revealing a cozy room where a young woman sat weeping in a corner armchair. She looked up when David entered. He moved the blanket from the child's face, and she let out a low cry and ran to him. She reached her hands for the child, and he handed it to her. He and the man watched her inspect the sleeping baby.

"He's all right, ma'am." He handed her the bottle.

"How did you...where did you....?" Her face contorted, and she turned with the child as though to protect him from David. "Did you take my baby?"

His jaw dropped. "Oh, no, ma'am. I didn't take your baby."

She hugged the child until it cried out and looked at David like he was a monster. "Then how did you get him?" The suspicion in her voice made him cringe.

As he explained what happened, her face relaxed and a look of gratitude replaced the suspicion. The family begged him to stay to celebrate the return of their child, but he declined. He did accept a cold wet cloth to put on his face.

He didn't look forward to the long walk across the Island in the middle of the night. But it had to be done. Once again, he was thankful for the full moon. He'd never been afraid and wasn't now. It felt a little eerie walking alone in the dark. He and his dad often hunted at night, but it had been a long time. And then, he wasn't alone.

On the river

Maggie hushed her crying baby and looked down the bank toward the water. She watched her grandpa nestle in a bush and pulled a vine around to cover himself. In the opposite direction she watched Max Shepherd hide in the same fashion. She chewed on a fingernail and swayed back and forth, willing the child to be quiet. It wouldn't be long now.

A boat carrying one passenger drifted toward the bank and the passenger, a heavy bald man, stepped out. He looked around and panted as he ascended the steep embankment to Maggie. Maggie stood as he approached. She clutched the child close to her breast.

The man held out his arms. "Hurry," he said. "Give her to me. Did you bring the items I asked for?" Maggie nodded, and tightened her grip on the baby. The man's cheeks puffed out and he wiggled his fingers toward Maggie. In the other hand he held out an envelope.

Maggie's eyes widened as she watched Shepherd and her grandpa coming behind the man. The man whirled around, but Shepherd managed to grab his arms and restrain him. Grandpa belted the man across the face and Shepherd shook his head. "That's enough, Harvey. He'll get what he deserves."

"I can't even think of punishment enough for a man like him," Grandpa muttered.

Seventeen

The terrain was flat with a tree here and there. Most of the trees grew along the banks of the river. He was stepping along at a brisk pace when he heard a sound behind him. He jumped and whirled around. He thought night shadows were playing a trick on him. But no, shadows didn't make sounds. Whatever it was, it was still coming. He looked around for a tree to hide behind, but there was none. He was wide open for whatever fate awaited him.

The sound came closer. There wasn't even a tall weed or a hole to hide him. He could see a moving figure, a wavering vision in the moonlight. Moving closer. Getting bigger. Suddenly it became clear…it was the bay mare.

David whistled and the mare stopped. She walked up to him and he picked up the reins hanging from her halter. Laughing in relief, David mounted the horse and headed for home.

By now, it was near morning. He stretched out on the porch swing to wait until his parents awoke. He drowsed a little until he heard movement inside the house. His mom was putting on coffee and starting breakfast. He waited until he heard his dad's voice. He could see them as he had so many times before. Dad would put his arms around Mom and kiss her on the back of the neck. She would turn for a good morning kiss and laugh at his flirting. He would comment about the wonderful smell of the cooking food, and she would slap his hand when he reached for a bite. He would fix two cups of coffee, one for himself and one for her, and sit down at the table.

David rose and stretched before he gave a soft knock on the door. Dad stuck his head out. "David! What are you doing here so early in the morning?" Then he gasped. "What happened? Have you been in a fight?"

After her initial shock, his mom Kathleen pulled him to a chair and grabbed the first aid kit. While she doctored his wounds, he explained what happened. He devoured the eggs and waffles she fixed for breakfast while she fussed over him.

"I can't believe that's going on right here on the Island." Jesse pulled on his shoes. "I'm going to call the authorities. This can't continue."

"Yeah, I'll have to fill out a report." David slammed his fist into his palm. "Wish I had found out the name and address of that kid. I have no idea who he is."

"If he lives on the Island, he shouldn't be too hard to find." Jesse said.

Kathleen poured David another cup of coffee. "It's one thing to hear about these things on the news, but when my son gets attacked close to my home by these monsters, something better be done."

Jesse apologized that he had to leave for work. David felt disappointed that he would be gone when his dad returned. But he could trust his mom to offer solid advice.

"Mom, I have a problem. I'm at a crossroad, and

I'm not sure what to do." She watched his face as she listened to his situation. She stiffened when he told her about Oliver taking away all his clients.

"David," she said, "you're qualified to do the job Oliver gave you to do, and if I know you, you're doing a good job. Your dad has talked to several of your clients he met on the river, and it sounds like they like you and trust you."

He put his empty plate in the sink. "I hope so. I've tried to work hard and do a good job for everyone."

"Seems like some major rocks have appeared in your river. Like your dad always says, rocks aren't always obstacles. Sometimes they just cause the river to change direction."

"Yeah, Dad and his river."

Kathleen laughed. "Well, the analogy always works. You'll do the right thing, son."

On his trip back to the city, David recalled one of his favorite scriptures: *When you pass through the waters, I will be with you; and through the rivers, they shall not overwhelm you; when you walk through fire you shall not be burned, and the flame shall not consume you.* Then he knew what to do. He would not be consumed by Oliver's demon. He pushed the throttle and soared along the top of the water.

First, David went to his office to get his portfolio. He checked the information, made a correction, and stuck it in his briefcase. He pulled Oscar Holmes' file, looked it over, and added it. The office had been closed more than an hour, with no one around to question him. It didn't matter. He was doing nothing wrong.

The next morning, he called Holmes and made an

appointment for later in the day. He stared at the tall structure housing Pruit Shipping before he walked up the steps. When he left two hours later, he was an employee of Brody Pruit.

The following day before anyone else came into the office, he formulated a letter of resignation. When Oliver arrived, David handed him the letter. "I'm giving my two weeks' notice."

Oliver did a double take when he saw David's swollen face and black eyes but said nothing. He opened the envelope and skimmed the letter. A flush crept up his face and he lifted his head. "You don't need to do that, David. I've been good to you. I've given you opportunities no one else in this city would. If you want to leave, that's your choice. But you need to leave now."

David winced. He glanced at Ms. Emma. Her eyes were brimming with tears. He returned to his office and within ten minutes he was packed. He hugged her, said goodbye to the other staffers, and left. He would take a couple of days off before he started his new job.

He sat in his car, hands on the steering wheel. He looked in the rearview mirror. He'd wanted to be an important businessman. He'd almost reached that goal. He'd wanted a red Porsche, and he was sitting in it. He'd dreamed of a family. Sadie had crushed that dream. What happened? What did he do wrong?

He turned the key and tires squealed as he left the parking lot. He turned toward the car lot. The Porsche would have to wait until his finances were more stable.

On the river

Cletus nailed the last beam in place and climbed down from the scaffolding. Since he'd agreed to do private work for Mr. Crandall, he felt pretty rich. He asked the construction foreman to let him off at noon. He would take Eva to that nice new restaurant in town and then to the casino boat for a little gambling. Ever since he proposed, she'd bugged him to take her. Now he could afford to.

What did Mr. Crandall want him to do? He didn't say. He said Cletus shouldn't mention it to anyone and it would involve travel up to the Colorado Mountains. That would be great. He would even be paid for the week off for the job. Mr. Crandall said he would take care of everything. Of course, it was his casino the crew was building. He was the boss. What a great guy.

Eighteen

David's phone rang, and when he put it to his ear, he jerked it back.

"Dang, man, what do you think you're doing?" Kade's voice boomed through the speaker. "You left the company without even telling me?"

"I'm sorry, Kade. It all happened so fast and you were gone. I knew you wouldn't be happy about it, but I didn't know what else to do."

"Listen, meet me in twenty minutes at Hoggies." Kade's tense voice made David cringe.

The two young men sat opposite each other at a booth and talked between bites. After David explained his battered face, Kade grilled him.

"Did you call the police?"

"Yes, I filled out a report. I got a distinct feeling they weren't much concerned. They kept asking about the mother of the baby when they should have been asking about the men who did the crime."

Kade frowned. "I don't know what they're doing. They act like the Island and river people are the real criminals."

"I know. It's strange."

Kade changed the subject. "David, I know Dad hasn't been fair to you, but you could have waited till I got back so I could talk to him."

"I guess I should have, but he gave me no choice. I

mean, I had nothing to do. Nothing. I tried to give a two weeks' notice, but he refused and told me to leave. What else could I do?"

Kade massaged the back of his neck. "Are you aware of what's going on now at the office?"

"No, what?"

"Dad's clients are all leaving him. He only has a few left. They told him they won't come back unless you do."

David slapped his forehead. "Oh, crap! I had no idea."

"Yeah. At this rate he won't have a business long." Kade rubbed his forehead. "Will you consider coming back?"

David pressed his lips together. "I don't believe I can. He doesn't want me back."

"He does, even if he won't say it. If you don't come back, he's done."

"Then what will you do?"

"Don't worry about me. Several people offered me jobs." Kade grinned. "I'm popular, you know. Just like you."

David studied a moment. "I won't come back, but I'll tell you what I'll do. I'll go to each of the clients and try to reason with them to give Crandall Shipping another chance. After all, most of them have been with him a long time. They may not listen to me, but I'll try."

"Yeah, you put that Kingston charm into action and work your magic." Kade punched his arm and laughed.

And that's what he did. Most of the older clients agreed to give Oliver another chance, and even a handful of the newer clients gave in to David's pleas. To save face for Oliver, David made them promise not to tell him why they returned and not to mention his name.

David enjoyed his new job and liked his employer. Though not as large as Crandall Shipping, the company showed promise. Before long he gained new clients and became acquainted with older ones. Brody saw the rapport David had with clients and employees alike and before long, promoted him to head the entire shipping department.

David met Kade and Sophia one evening for dinner, and Kade updated him on business at Crandall's. "We're doing okay," he said, "but Dad is still gone a lot. I don't see how he expects to keep clients when he isn't there half the time. When you were there, he relied on you to take care of things."

"Why doesn't he hire another person?"

"He has interviewed a couple of people, but he never follows through, and nothing gets done. I've been helping with his clients' files, doing scheduling and things. Ms. Emma has, too. Without the two of us, the business would fold."

"Why is he gone so much?"

Kade scratched his beard. It was getting a little straggly. "I don't know. When I ask him about it, he gets mad and says it's none of my business."

Sophia, who stayed silent through the conversation, spoke. "David, would you consider going back if Oliver were to ask you?"

Shaking his head, David smiled at her. "No, not now. I have it good where I am. Mr. Pruit respects me and likes my work. He has already promoted me, and I believe I have a secure future there."

Sophia sighed. "That's understandable. I hate this has happened. Kade told me you two have been close since childhood and have always done everything together. What a shame now you won't be working side by side."

"Yeah, it's too bad," Kade turned to David. "Are you about ready for another trip to our old stomping grounds? How about I crank up my new boat, and we head for the Island?"

"New boat? You didn't tell me about that."

"I didn't? Man, you gotta see it. It's a Fountain 35 Lightning, white with a blue stripe. It's fast, roomy and comfortable."

"You sound like a boat commercial."

Kade lifted Sophia's hand and kissed it. "I've an idea, Sophia. You go with us. I'd love to show you the Island."

"Sure," David said. "We'll bring a fishing pole for you,"

Sophia laughed and shook her head. "No, I'd better not."

But she gave in, and early Saturday morning the three headed down the river.

"Want me to bait your hook so you won't get your hands all wormy?" Kade teased Sophia all morning while David laughed at the two. Sophia's blonde hair spilled out from under her ball cap to frame her slender face, and a long braid snaked down the length of her back. David enjoyed her quick humor and gentle demeanor. He could see how Kade would fall for such a beautiful woman.

"No, thanks. I'll do it myself." He handed her the can of worms and she scrunched her nose. She chose a big one but dropped it when it wrapped itself around her finger. "Yuck!" She chose another one and threaded it onto her hook. The look on her face made the boys hoot in laughter, but she persisted with the slimy chore. She threw the line into the water over the edge of the boat. The boat rocked when she peered over the side, and she gasped and pulled back.

"Let me show you how to cast further out." Kade pulled her line back in and showed her the procedure. She proved to be a quick learner, and before long she pulled in a good-sized bass. By mid-morning the stringer was full, so they decided to pay a visit to the Kingston home. Maybe they could talk Kathleen into frying their fish for lunch.

Jesse and Kathleen welcomed the young people into their home, and after they ate, Kathleen lit candles to extinguish the scent of frying fish. She and Sophia became fast friends, and Jesse affirmed his approval to Kade. Cheerful conversation accompanied a delicious lunch followed by a tour of the Island on four-wheelers. Kade and David shared memories about every spot they visited, and Sophia giggled at the stories of their childhood pranks.

David plopped down on a bed of moss and leaned against a large sycamore tree. "Remember the time we were over by the chute with Johnny Flanks and stumbled up on a herd of wild hogs?"

"Yeah." Kade chuckled. "Sure took us by surprise."

"The pigs were surprised, too. Those things are mean." David whistled. "Kade and I got away, but they chased old Johnny up a tree. I thought they were going to climb the tree with him."

Kade threw back his head and howled with laughter. "He did, too."

"How'd you get him down?" Sophia asked.

"David headed home to get his rifle and I hid out to make sure Johnny was okay." Kade slapped David on the shoulder. "This man right here is a pretty good shot, you know. We had enough pork to last all winter."

"Wild pork is a little stringy, but with good cooks like our moms, it makes a fair meal." David rose, and they went back to the Kingston's.

Evening came and while the women chatted in the kitchen, Kade pulled David outside. "I'm going to do it. I'm going to propose."

"I'm sorry, Kade. My answer will have to be no. I'm not ready for marriage yet."

Kade punched David's arm and laughed. "What do you think? You like her, don't you? Your mom and dad seem to."

"Sure," David said. "She's great. How about your parents? Have they met her yet?"

"I took her to meet Mom, but Dad's never around. Mom likes her a lot."

"The most important question is, do you love her?"

Kade gazed skyward and nodded. "I sure do love her. More than anything." He reached into a pocket and pulled out a box. "See? I already have the ring."

"Then go for it. Ask her." David thought of the ring he kept hidden in his desk at home. Maybe one day.

Kade sat on the porch swing and stretched his legs out. "Want to help me?"

David looked puzzled. "Nope. You can do that job all by yourself."

"I need you to help me set up a mood. Do you remember that grove of willows by the river? I want to make a sort of arch there, and tomorrow I'll take her there."

"Sure. I visited there the other day. It's a perfect spot."

The next day they rose early and went to David's favorite thinking spot. They cleaned the area of debris and tied willow branches together to make an arch. Kade picked wildflowers from the field behind Kingston's house, and those were set in wet sand around the area.

After church and lunch, Jesse asked Kathleen and David to go with him to visit a sick neighbor before he and Kade left, and Kade talked Sophia into going for a walk. When they all returned a while later, Sophia glowed as they admired her ring and congratulated the happy couple.

On the river

Bradley whistled his appreciation of the sleek, silver speedboat. He couldn't believe his luck. To get this boat all he had to do was drive fast and scare some dude in a motorboat. Piece of cake. The man said he would give him the keys and the title when he finished the job. He would even let him use the new boat to scare the man. What a great opportunity for a poor river kid. He would be the envy of every guy around.

Nineteen

"David, would you come to my office, please?" David closed his computer and headed down the hall to find out what his boss wanted. He had a good relationship with Brodie. They shared a passion for guitar music and often played together at Brodie's house.

David stood opposite Brodie's desk to wait until he finished writing. He admired this man. He'd built his business from a small warehouse several miles upriver to the present building which housed his company. His clients and customers liked and trusted him as an astute executive who built a network of business associates up and down the river.

When Brodie finished, they walked over to the window and chatted a while about music, about family, and business.

"I have a proposition for you." Brodie watched David's face. "I want to sell you this shipping company."

David stared and gasped. "What? You want me to buy this company?"

Brodie laughed. "Yep. I'm proposing to sell it to you. You have a keen business sense, and you know shipping well even though you haven't been doing it that long. You have people who will back you, and you can make it a success. What do you say?"

David turned and stumbled to a chair. He sat,

speechless. His heart pounded in his temples as he contemplated the idea. *Me? A business owner? But I'm just a kid fresh out of college. What do I know about running a business?*

"Well?" Brodie sat across from David and watched his face.

David's head moved from side to side. "I...I don't know what to say. I don't have enough money to buy a business."

"Oh, that's no problem," Brodie said. "You have no collateral, and no longer than you've worked, I'm guessing not much money in the bank. But I have enough confidence in your ability I'm willing to work past that."

"I don't know what to say."

"I see in you the seed of success. You have intelligence, integrity, and initiative. That's what it takes, and I want to do this for you. I'll back you until you're able to stand on your own two feet. How does that sound?"

David stood, beaming. He stretched out his hand toward Brodie who shook it.

Brodie laughed and slapped David on the back. "Son, don't look so scared. It'll be all right. I'll have my lawyer draw up the contract and you'll be a business owner."

"Before I sign anything, could I have time to pray about it and talk to my dad?"

"Of course. I'd expect that of you. And if you decide you don't want to do it, there'll be no hard feelings. Agreed?" David nodded. "Now you take the rest of the day off to do what you need to do. I'll have the contract ready tomorrow if you decide to go through with it."

David headed to the island. He would visit his Willow Grove, talk to his dad, and sleep on it before he made such a huge decision. His mind blurred as he guided his boat through the water.

Owning his own shipping business would make him a competitor with Oliver. That could be bad. It would load him with heavy responsibility. That could be bad. It would give him an early start as business owner. That could be good. With Brodie backing him, he would have a leg-up in the business world. That would be good. He'd have to do better than two out of four.

At his Willow Grove, David deliberated long and hard. With a stick he made a list of pros and cons in the sand — both lists were short, just like his life. King Solomon told God he was only a child and inadequate to rule Israel. And Solomon was older than he was now. Yet, David hadn't been asked to rule a kingdom. Well, sort of, except on a much smaller scale. Without a doubt, he was inadequate.

What if he failed? What if he couldn't get any new clients to build the business? Didn't he add new clients to Crandall Shipping and to Pruit Shipping? What if they came because of Oliver and Brodie? What if he couldn't handle the business part of running the company? He hadn't done that yet. But Brodie said he would help him. Arrrggg! Why did he doubt himself so much? Maybe Dad could make him feel better.

As always, Jesse referred to a river during their talk. "Son, time is like the water in a river. You can't touch the same water twice, because the flow never stops."

"You think I should buy the business?"

"I didn't say that. Do you know for sure Mr. Pruit is trustworthy?"

"I feel he is. I researched him, and everything I found

about him sounded positive. Several people say he's honest and people who work for him say he's a fair, knowledgeable boss. I know those who work there now like him and seem to trust him."

"What kind of boss will you be?"

David buried his hands in his hair. "I hope a fair one. I have you as a role model, and Mr. Pruit has shown me what it's like to have a good boss. I'll try to emulate his methods."

Kathleen rubbed David's shoulder. "Is this what you want to do with your life, son? Run a shipping business?"

David looked at the faces of the people he regarded as the wisest, most caring people on God's green earth. He knew they would stand behind him whatever he decided. He rose. "I'll sleep on it tonight, and by tomorrow I'll know what to do. Thank you both for being my parents."

The next day he signed the contract and became one of the youngest business owners on the river. He called Kade. Together they would celebrate.

When he'd spent his full month as boss, David took inventory of his business. Brodie checked with him from time to time, and the client list of Kingston Shipping grew steadily. When the clients of Crandall Shipping heard he now had his own business, they asked him to take their accounts. David talked most of them into staying with Crandall, but two or three refused.

"Now Kingston," Ted Stringer said, "you know I never wanted anyone but you to take care of my accounts. I won't take no for an answer, so you may as well accept my business."

Mark Johnson stood beside Stringer, bobbing his head.

"That goes for me, too, David. If you won't handle my shipping, I'll quit the business."

David cringed, but agreed. Of all things, he didn't want to take business from Oliver. Just being his competitor seemed bad enough.

He had no idea how bad it would be until he met Oliver on the street a few days later. When he raised his hand in a greeting, Oliver stiffened and leered. "So, Kingston, you're trying to drive me out of business by taking my clients."

David tensed. "No, Mr. Crandall. I don't want your clients. I have no desire to hurt your business."

"Yeah, like you could." Oliver's hands tightened into fists. "Tread lightly, son, and watch your business." He whirled and stalked away, and David drew a long breath. He walked across the street to his truck when Oliver's silver Jaguar whizzed by, missing him by inches. He crawled under the steering wheel of his truck and sat for a while before he pulled into the street.

When he arrived home, a surprise awaited him. Sadie sat on a bench beside his door.

"What are you doing here?" David put his key into the door.

"I want to talk to you." She stood and wrapped her arms around herself. "May I come in?"

"Sure." David held the door open for her and she brushed against him as she entered his apartment. "Want a glass of tea?" She nodded. "Had supper?" She shook her head. "Want pizza? I'll order one." She nodded again.

As they sat eating pizza in front of the TV, David watched her. *What's she doing here?* "Thought you were getting married."

"That's over. Has been for a while."

"What happened?"

"He turned out to be a jerk." She blinked and leaned back. "I've been staying home a while."

"Aren't you working?"

"Yes. Still writing for the paper."

David gathered the plates and put them in the sink. "How are your parents?"

"Separated. Dad found himself another woman. Didn't you know?"

"No. Kade hasn't said anything."

"Well, he's pretty upset. I am too." She twirled a lock of hair around her finger. "Still doing business as usual for the old man?"

David sat beside her. "Sadie, what are you doing here? What do you want?"

"I want you, David. That's all I've ever wanted." She turned to him, and tears coursed down her face. "I'm so sorry for what I did to you. I've acted like a fool."

David tensed. "Yes, you have. So, what's changed?"

Sadie leaned forward, her lips slightly parted. "I've changed. I've grown up. You'll see, David. I want to come back."

He watched her through narrowed eyes. Had she changed? "Why should I believe you?" He wanted to believe her. Desperately.

She ran a finger over his cheek and tilted her head. "Kiss me. You know you want to."

He did. His breath quickened. The scent of Gucci filled his brain with nostalgic images of dark eyelashes and soft, silky curls tickling his nose. Once again, he buried his face in the curls and the taste of bacon-ranch pizza gave way to a sweetness he'd almost forgotten as he placed his lips on hers, gently at first, then with less abandon.

No. He must take it slow. *Let her prove herself.* He backed away and shook himself. He walked across the floor and looked back at her. She swiped her hand across her mouth and pouted.

"How long since you've talked to your dad or Kade?"

"Quite a while. I haven't seen either of them since I got home."

David scrutinized her a moment. "Then you aren't aware I no longer work for your dad."

Sadie's eyes widened. "What? You aren't at the shipping company anymore?" Her forehead puckered. "Then what are you doing?"

"I bought out Brodie Pruit. Pruit Shipping is now Kingston Shipping."

Sadie straightened in her chair. "You're kidding, right?" David shook his head. "So, you own your own business. Wow! I don't know what to say. Congratulations."

"Thanks." David stood and stretched out his hand. "How about we go to the river?" Sadie smiled and took his hand. Before long they were strolling hand in hand along the bank.

After they walked a while, they sat under the canopy of a cotton wood tree and watched the river. Was this simply a rock in the stream? A distraction? Or maybe a whirlpool? He wasn't sure. His heart beat a melody in his chest as he watched the glisten of her auburn locks. He laughed at her animated conversation, and when those green eyes gazed into his, he lost all ability to think straight. Why couldn't he get over her? He didn't want to.

"David, did you hear what I said?" Sadie tugged at his arm. "Mom called and told me Kade and Sophia are engaged. But I'm sure you already know."

"Yeah, I know. He proposed to her on the Island."

"I've got to find out when they plan to have the wedding. I hope she'll let me be a bridesmaid."

"I'm sure she will." David leaned over and pulled her close to his side. "Sadie, what do you want for yourself? Are you happy with what you're doing?"

She pulled back and gazed at him. "I guess so. I'm busy all the time. I'm hoping to get a promotion before long. I want to have my own beat and get into broadcasting."

"That sounds great. Maybe one day I'll watch you on TV. You could do a story about the shipping business and feature me." They laughed together. It was good.

On the river

"I'm so tired of you being gone all the time." Tammy placed a platter of cornbread beside the bowl of brown beans on the table and sat down beside her husband. "Between the time you spend on the Island and chasing criminals, me and the kids hardly see you."

"I think I've found a solution." Max Shepherd spooned some fried okra onto his plate. "What if we could move on the Island? Then I would be able to help people who need me and be close to the situation I'm investigating."

"What about the kids' schooling? I'd have to boat them to the mainland."

"I know it's a lot for you. Do you think we could teach them at home?"

"I don't know why not. My degree should be good for something." Tammy bit her fingernail. "What about a house? Are there any on the Island that are livable without a lot of work?"

"That's the beauty of it. I've learned that a nice one may be available soon."

"Really? Where? Who's?"

Max kissed her on the nose and grinned. "You'll love it."

Twenty

Kingston Shipping grew, and several of Oliver's employees came to David for jobs. He added several new clients and referred many of them to his old employer. A short time with Crandall Shipping showed that Oliver had manipulated their accounts, and they begged David to take them. He knew if he didn't, they would find another shipping company.

"Kingston!" David would know that voice anywhere. He turned to face Oliver, whose neck and face were beet red. "I've warned you to stay away from my clients. I know you're bribing them to ship with you, and it's not going to work."

"No, I haven't bribed anyone. If you would treat your people right, they would stay with you."

"What?" Oliver shouted. "You don't know what you're talking about. You think you know so much, but you know nothing." Spittle sprayed from his mouth. "I'll tell you one thing, you're dealing with the master of shipping." He whirled around, stopped, and turned back. "And another thing. Leave my employees alone." He lowered his voice and pointed at David. "Stay out of my way, David, or you'll be sorry. You'd better watch your step."

Later, David told Kade what happened. "Aw, don't worry about Dad," Kade said. "He won't do anything to you. He's all bark and no bite."

"But what about Crandall shipping?" David fixed his

eyes on Kade. "Is it holding together okay?"

Kade shrugged. "Not really, but that's not your concern. Like you said, if he would be fair and good to his clients, they would stay with him. I don't know what's happened to the old man. He sure has changed."

"Where do you stand in all this, Kade? It's your business, too."

Kade pressed his lips together. "Yeah, well I'm separating myself from the old man and his mess. I'm with you, David. Never forget that."

David hesitated. "Want to join me at Kingston Shipping? Be a partner? Together we could accomplish great things."

Kade laughed, "Nah, I'll stay with Dad—a while longer at least. I'll not leave. I plan to stay clear of his undertakings, if you know what I mean." One corner of his mouth turned up in a doleful smile. "He's still my dad, no matter." He fixed his eyes on David. "I understand you and my sister are back together."

"Well, you might say that. We're taking it slow. Working things out."

"You may be taking things slow, but I don't know about Sadie. She talks like all is forgotten and she has you hooked and reeled in."

David grinned. "You know my greatest weakness is that woman. She may be the death of me."

"Yeah." Kade smirked. "If Dad doesn't get you first."

David promised a visit to his parents, and he decided to take his motorboat to fish a little. He pulled out from the pier and boated a short way down the river when he heard a ping beside him. He looked at a hole in the side of his boat. A bullet hole. He looked around, and another hole appeared, then another. Someone was shooting at him.

He pushed the throttle forward and sped over the water. The shots appeared to be coming from his left, but he wasn't sure. If he went to the bank, he might run right into the shooter. He had to get to the bank beyond the range of the gun. Even though the holes were only on the sides, water seeped into his boat enough he couldn't make it to the Island.

He spotted a pier ahead. He maneuvered the boat to the dock and inspected the damage. It looked pretty bad. He called Kade to bring a truck and trailer to pick up the boat and him. He didn't tell him what happened, just that he had trouble and needed a ride.

"David, those are bullet holes!" Kade exploded. "Why do you have bullet holes in your boat?"

"Well, obviously, a mad gunman was shooting at me."

"Dang. Who you got mad at you now?"

"I don't know. Probably a misguided hunter." David tried to lighten the situation. "Or an irate turtle. Maybe that one you hooked the last time we were out here."

"Man, this is serious. You could have been killed. Did you call the police?"

When David shook his head, Kade made the call. In a short while, an officer made out a report and promised an investigation. On the way back to the city, Kade remained quiet, and David tried to get his mind off the issue.

"What's going on with Sophia lately? Did she finish the project she's been working on?"

Kade shook his head. "Man. I can't believe someone actually shot at you. You didn't see anyone?"

"No, nothing. Anyone could be hiding in the trees on the bank."

"Did you see a boat close to you?"

"No. I don't remember seeing a boat, but I wasn't paying attention."

"Well, you gotta pay attention to your surroundings. Maybe this was a freak accident, but maybe not."

"Now who would want to shoot me? I'm a good guy." David laughed. Though shaken and scared, he wouldn't allow himself to believe anyone was out to get him. Besides, he had to keep Kade from freaking out.

Kade whipped the truck off the pavement and headed down a gravel road.

"Where are you going?" David hung on as the truck bounced over the rough gravel.

"Is this close to where you were?"

"Yeah, I think so."

Kade parked at a dock and they jumped out. Several guys were milling around, unloading a boat, and checking fishing gear. They looked up when Kade and David approached them.

"You guys know where a fellow can get a boat fixed?"

One guy looked over at David's vessel. "What's wrong with it?"

"It has holes in it." Kade watched the faces of the men. "Bullet holes."

A man spit brown juice and walked over to the boat. "Bullet holes? How'd it get bullet holes?" He inspected the holes and turned to David. "This your boat?" David nodded.

"You got an enemy out on the river?" Another man snickered, but the brown juice man remained somber.

David shrugged. "I don't know of any. At least not one who'd shoot me."

"Well," the man drawled, "you might want to watch your business from now on."

In the middle of the night, David woke from a sound sleep and sat straight up. *Watch your business. Watch your business.* What did he mean? He called Kade.

"Sorry to wake you, but do you remember what the man at the river said? *Watch your business.* Do you think he meant that as a threat, or maybe it was just words?"

A deep sigh came over the phone. "Man, what are you talking about?" A yawn stifled Kade's words.

"He said, watch your business. Could that be a threat?" David hesitated. "I mean, Oliver told me the other day to watch my business. Those exact words."

"Oh, I told you he's all bark. He wouldn't shoot at you."

The image of Jasper on a four-wheeler chasing him flicked across David's mind. "You don't think he would get someone to, you know, try to scare me or something?"

Kade remained silent.

"Are you there?"

"Yeah, I'm here. I don't know, David. He's been acting pretty insane lately."

"What do you mean?"

"He told me the other day as long as you are around, I would never succeed. Said you were taking away everything that should be mine."

"Really?"

"Yeah. I told him he was crazy."

David cradled the phone against his shoulder and pulled on his pants. "Sorry I woke you. Go back to sleep. We'll talk in the morning."

He drank coffee and walked the floor until dawn. When he went to work, an irate client confronted him.

"Kingston, what's this about the cost of shipping going up? We deal with you because you've always been fair. And now this." He shoved a paper at David.

David read the paper and waved it. "Where did you get this? This isn't mine."

"I found it stuck on my boat this morning. They're on all the boats at your pier."

A line of clients came through the door, all with papers. David lifted his hands. "Guys, I didn't put those papers on your boats. Your shipping prices have not changed. It looks like a prank has been played on you."

He assured the men he would find out about the situation. None of the office staff knew the origin of the papers. David went to the pier and asked around, but no one would admit to seeing anything. He was leaving when a mechanic appeared from under the deck of a large boat and waved at him.

"Hey, Henry. How's it going?" David climbed on the boat to talk with him. After responding to David's questions about the welfare of his family, Henry talked about looking forward to retirement. David asked if he'd seen anyone suspicious around.

Henry scratched his head. "Well, early this morning I saw this dude kinda hanging 'round. He did act sorta suspicious, but I didn't think a lot of it until I saw him sticking a paper on the windshield of Lawson's boat. I figured he was leaving a message or maybe an advertisement."

"What did he look like?"

"Well, kinda tall and dark. Taller than you. And kind of thin, you know."

"Okay. Thanks, Henry. Say 'hi' to your wife for me." David jumped from the boat and headed for his truck. He had the answer he needed.

On the river

Troy and Betty watched their small children play in their yard. They used twigs and leaves to create a farm for their play animals.

"Troy, what are we going to do? That flood destroyed everything, and I haven't been able to plant much of anything. My garden spot is covered with litter and is nothing but a mire."

"I know, Betty. Since Crandall started that casino, a lot of the casino boats are laying off people and I haven't been able to get a job on the Gold Boat. I'm just one out of many who lost work. Times are tough for everyone on the Island."

"I'm worried the kids won't have enough to eat. We're down to the last quart of milk, and I'm out of flour. I have a little beans and rice, but that's all."

"I know. I'll talk to Shepherd. Maybe he can help me find some work."

"He seems like a good man. I'm glad he moved on the Island. He's helped a lot of people."

"What are we going to do for a home? We have no place to go and no money for a home on the mainland."

Troy patted Betty's hands. "Don't worry, hon. Maybe Crandall will give us something for this house. Surely he won't make us move without a dime for what we've built here."

Twenty-one

"Mom! Dad! What are you doing here?" David was closing the computer down and straightening his desk, ready to close shop when his parents walked into the office.

"We're here to visit you. Come on. Lock up and take us out to dinner." Kathleen hugged her son and kissed his cheek. She laughed and stroked his beard.

"Have you lost your razor?" she teased.

"Yeah, I know it needs trimmed." David turned to Jesse. "How long will you be in town? I've needed to talk to you."

"A couple of days. We have news, too." Jesse dangled his keys in David's face. "Got a new ride today. Wait till you see it."

David admired the red Buick Regal, and Jesse insisted they drive it to dinner.

"What do you have to talk to us about?" Jesse wanted to know.

"Let's wait until after dinner. Then we'll discuss it." David didn't want to spoil dinner. "Tell me about your news."

David watched their smiling faces as they looked at each other. "You tell him, Mom." Jesse stood grinning at his son.

"We're moving to the city." The twinkle in Kathleen's eyes betrayed her excitement.

"What? You're leaving the Island? How could you do that?"

"Now, Son," Jesse said. "We've debated long and hard about it. Oliver is doing groundwork for his new casino, and you know it won't be the same. Already the noise level has risen, and the traffic is horrendous." He picked up Kathleen's hand. "If we're going to be living right in the middle of a construction site, we may as well move here."

Were they excited about the move? Or had they just accepted the fate of progress? David would never have believed his parents could move away from the home they'd had since they married many years ago.

"Have you found a house?"

Kathleen shook her head. "Not yet. We have an appointment tomorrow with a realtor. She's going to show us a couple."

David scratched his head. "Man. It won't be the same without my home on the Island."

Jesse patted him on the back. "Son, your home is still there, but another family will be living in it after we move." He smiled at Kathleen. "We're renting it to the Shepherds. We met Max Shepherd a while back, and he has a nice wife and kids. They promised to look after it for us."

David recoiled. "Max Shepherd? Do you know anything about him?"

Jesse frowned. "Not much. Like I said, we met him a while back and he seems nice. We did check him out, though. He has a good reputation and he's clean. We know that for sure."

When they finished eating, Jesse turned to David. "Now tell us what's on your mind." David told them what had been going on with Oliver, leaving out the part that had sounded like a threat. He didn't want to worry his parents, and anyway, it was likely nothing.

Jesse sat a while without saying anything. When he spoke, his low voice showed concern. "We've heard things are not going well for the Crandalls. It's too bad."

Kathleen spoke. "Yes, it is. I visited with Melody a couple of weeks ago. We've managed to stay in contact, even though we don't see each other often. I knew she and Oliver were at odds, but now they're separated. Her heart is broken."

"Did she tell you he's seeing another woman?" David asked.

"She's not for sure, but she suspects it." Kathleen nibbled on her lip. "Is he?"

David wadded his napkin and threw it on the table. "Yes. I've seen them together. At first, I didn't want to believe it. But other people have seen them on the river in his red speedboat. Pretty much everyone around here knows."

"How are Kade and Sadie dealing with it?" Kathleen asked.

"They are both angry," David answered, "but there's nothing they can do. They both support their mother, of course. Kade says his dad is insane, and I'm beginning to believe it."

Jesse and Kathleen bought a house with a couple of acres and moved to the outskirts of the city. David enjoyed seeing them more often, and they enjoyed the entertainment features of city life. But he could tell they missed the solitude of the Island. Max Shepherd gave them an open invitation to visit any time, and they accepted the invitation quite often.

"Max Shepherd is an all-right guy," Jesse told David one day. "The more we visit him, the more we realize he's a man of integrity. A good Christian man. In fact, I guess he's a minister because he invited us to a meeting where he speaks on Saturday nights. We're talking about going to visit."

Between classes, Sadie spent time with Kathleen, gardening, crafting, and visiting local museums and art exhibits. Often Melody joined them, and Sophia loved to take time from her law office to go with the ladies on their excursions.

David loved to see his mom and Melody together again. He enjoyed seeing her eyes light up when Sadie and Sophia shared their flea market findings with the two older women. He took pleasure in going fishing with his dad when he had a chance. He was glad to know his parents were happy living in the city.

About daybreak on a Saturday morning, David and Sadie headed toward the Island in David's new blue speed boat. They would spend the day visiting friends and fish a little before they returned to the city. Sadie often fished with David and Kade when they were kids and proved to be good at it.

They docked at the Island after sharing a sack lunch on the deck of the boat. David picked up the stringer of fish, and they headed toward David's old home. The Shepherds might enjoy a fresh catch.

A man with gray fringes around his bald spot opened the door. He welcomed them and introduced them to his wife,

Tammy, and two children, Rodney and Rita. Tammy served sweet tea, and they talked a while about life on the Island. Then Max offered apologies. "Guys, we have to leave for a while. A family down river has a situation and we promised we'd be there this afternoon to help them."

"Is there anything we can do?" David asked.

"No, nothing. We hate to leave right in the middle of your visit, but we'll be back in about an hour or so. We'd love for you to stay here so we can visit when we get back."

David and Sadie sat on the porch swing enjoying the gentle breeze and each other. He wrapped an arm around her as she snuggled against his shoulder. She talked about friends who had come from the Island and he recounted stories of his childhood to the rhythmic squeaking of the swing. He twined his fingers through hers and nuzzled the sweetness of her thick, auburn curls.

"Sadie, let's get married."

She sat up and looked at him with wide eyes. "Married? Is this your idea of a proposal?"

"Yes. Let's get married today. Max is a minister, and he'll marry us. What do you say?"

Sadie put her hand over her mouth and giggled. She nodded, and he pulled her to his chest. With one finger, he lifted her face and looked into her eyes.

"I want to hear you say it."

Her lips quivered. "Yes."

"Do you mean it? No more running off?"

"Yes, I mean it. No more running off. I love you, David, with all my heart."

He leaned down and his lips brushed hers. She pulled his head down and pressed her lips against his. When she pulled back, her lashes were wet. He caught a tear with one finger and pulled her close.

"Shhh, my love. I don't ever want to see you cry. I love you more than life."

They stood silent, reveling in their love for each other. Then Sadie jumped back and put her hands on her hips.

"Let's do it. Come on." She grabbed his hand and pulled him to the back yard where a bed of daisies, zinnias, and sunflowers grew. "We can get married out here. It's the perfect place."

"Yes, perfect." David touched a tall sunflower. "My mom planted these before she and Dad moved. She loved her flowers, especially these."

As they waited on the Shepherds to return, they walked around the yard admiring the flowers and vegetables growing there. They didn't have to wait long.

"We want to get married, here, today." David lifted Sadie's hand to his lips as he broke the news to Max. "Will you help us? Will you perform the ceremony?"

Max glanced at Sadie. "Sure you don't want a church wedding?"

"No." Sadie sniffed a Sweet William she picked from a rock flower bed around a cypress tree. "This is the perfect place for a wedding." Her eyes followed David who walked to the edge of the yard and stood gazing into the distance toward the river. She went to him. "What is it, David?"

He shifted his gaze to her and cupped her face in his hands. He stooped to place a gentle kiss on her lips and enveloped her in his arms. They stood in silence a while, and Sadie pulled back. "You thinking about Kade?"

"Yeah, guess I am. We've always done everything

together. I hate to leave him out of my most important day."

"Then call him. He won't want to miss this big event for his best friend." She thought a moment. "How about our parents? They'll want to be part of our happiness."

"You're right. I'll call mine and you call yours."

A smile spread across David's face as he pulled out his phone. After a short conversation, he nodded. "They're on the way. All of them. Kade said he'd never speak to me again if I got married without him being here."

Sadie pecked him on the cheek. "Mom is coming with them. She's so excited, even though she dreamed of a big wedding for me. But she agrees this will be better."

Off she ran to tell Max there would be a delay.

David and Sadie met Kade and Sophia at the boat dock. Sophia carried a suitcase and Kade handed David a garment bag.

David took the bag and helped Sophia out of the boat. "What's this? Are you going on the honeymoon with us?"

Kade laughed. "We thought you and Sadie might need some things since you are so impulsive. You might want to marry the love of your life with nothing more than a dirty pair of jeans and an old shirt, but Sadie might want a little more sophistication. We stopped by your places and grabbed some stuff."

"Oh." David grasped his hand. "Thanks, Kade. I appreciate you. That was thoughtful."

"Besides," Sophia said. "Sadie asked me to pick up a few things for her."

David strolled beside Kade up to the house as the girls walked ahead. Suddenly he stopped and grabbed Kade's arm, pulling him back. "I have an idea, and it's a good one. Let's have a double wedding. You and Sophia, Sadie and me. What do you think?"

Kade watched the girls a moment, then yelled. The girls stopped and looked around. When Kade motioned, they waited for the guys to catch up to them.

Kade pulled Sophia to one side, and they talked a moment.

"What's going on?" Sadie wanted to know.

"How do you feel about making this a double wedding?"

Sadie gasped. "Oh, yes, yes, yes! I'd love that."

David gestured for her to be quiet. They didn't have to wait long for the other couple to return, smiling.

"Let's do it!" Sophia and Sadie hugged each other, and the guys shook hands. They hurried to the Shepherd house. There was much to do before evening. They had a wedding — or weddings — to plan.

As they waited for their brides to prepare for the occasion and their parents to arrive, the men talked on the front porch. Both David and Kade had unanswered questions about Max Shepherd.

"How long have you been in this area?" Kade asked him.

"I was raised on down the river a piece, on the other side. My family moved there when I was a baby."

"I thought I knew about everyone, but I don't remember any Shepherds."

Max laughed. "Probably because we lived further down. And both my parents worked in the city. Dad was in law enforcement and Mom in social work. They weren't around much. Most of the time, I stayed with a neighbor, Granny Livvey. She about raised me."

"What do you do? I mean besides helping people around here," David said.

"Actually, I work for a Federal agency. I patrol this area for things like bootleggers and such." He seemed uncomfortable with the subject and changed it. "You guys grew up on the Island, right?"

David nodded. "I did. Kade lived in the city, but he spent most of his free time here with me. We had a lot of fun exploring and playing on the river."

Max looked thoughtful a moment. "Say, did you guys ever build a raft for the river?"

Kade looked at David and laughed. "Sure did. That project about did us in, too."

"What happened?"

"Well, once we built a raft out of logs and boards tied together with vines and ropes and took it out on the river."

David interjected, "We wanted to be like Tom Sawyer and Huckleberry Finn."

Kade continued. "Trouble was, we weren't paying attention to the time or the weather. It was later than we realized, and a storm came up."

"Yeah, a bad storm," David said. "The wind blew hard, causing waves that made it near impossible for us to control the raft. Then it got dark, and we couldn't see anything."

Kade stared off into the distance. "The lightning strikes helped us see the bank enough to grab low hanging branches. I fell into the river, but David grabbed my pants and pulled me up. Then..."

Max jumped up from his chair. "Then someone pulled

you both to the bank."

David and Kade stared at him. "You? It was you?" David said.

Max nodded. "I'd been staking out a bootlegger a while, and that night I came up on him at his still. He ran, and I almost caught him. That's when a bolt of lightning and a yell for help drew my attention to the river. I saw the two of you in trouble, so I saved you and lost the bootlegger." He laughed. "I guess it was worth it. Anyway, I caught him later."

David grabbed Max's hand and pumped it up and down. "We've always wondered who saved us that night."

Kade pounded him on the back. "Yeah, and we've always wanted to thank him for saving us. Thank you, Max Shepherd. Thank you for saving us."

Max bowed. "My pleasure, men, my pleasure. I sure am glad I happened to be there and happened to hear you."

"I don't think it was by chance," David said. "I think Almighty God was looking out for us." Max and Kade both nodded their agreement.

By early evening their parents arrived, and David and Kade stood in front of Max Shepherd waiting for their brides. The guys had concocted an arch of ivy, wisteria, and honeysuckle vines while the ladies fashioned bouquets of daisies and sunflowers. Tammy wove yellow star-like coreopsis flowers into Sadie's auburn hair and purple asters into Sophia's thick blonde locks.

Rita sprinkled zinnia petals on the ground, creating a path for the brides. Rodney carried a small basket with temporary wedding rings he had shaped from hammered wire. The laughing girls held hands and danced toward the waiting men who looked quite charming in their light summer shirts and blue jeans. Tammy recorded the event for the parents, and the happy couples vowed to love each other through thick and thin from beginning to the end. Max pronounced them married, and they raced off in their boats to begin their married lives.

On the river

Late in the afternoon, a riverboat cruised through the water close to the Island. Only three people could be seen on the lower deck, but an observant viewer would notice two men lounging on the top deck. Otherwise, the boat appeared empty.

A red speedboat pulled up beside it, and a dark-skinned man shouted to those in the speedboat. A passenger leaped from the speedboat to the riverboat before the speedboat pulled away. In a little while, a man pointed toward the bank where a pier extended out into the river. A group of boys waited with a stack of boxes and jugs, and the riverboat stopped beside them. When the riverboat moved again, the pier was empty, and the boys disappeared in the trees.

Twenty-two

A week after Sadie moved her things into David's apartment, David received a call from Oliver.

"You think you're so clever, Kingston, but I'm way ahead of you. You may have weaseled your way into my life by marrying my daughter, but you won't get away with it. I won't allow you to ruin my family or my business."

David gasped. "I married your daughter for no reason other than I love her."

"Yeah, right. You may fool my little girl, but I'm wise to your conniving tricks." The sound of the slamming phone made David jump.

Sadie came into the room with a towel around her wet hair. "Who was that?"

"Ah, just a telemarketer." David picked up his briefcase. "I'm going to the office. Have a good day at work." He took her face in his hands and kissed her. He vowed to himself nothing — no one — would take her from him, not even Oliver. Especially Oliver.

He hopped in his truck and drove down the street when from nowhere an old black Jeep Wrangler slammed him in the rear and sped around him. He didn't see the driver, and when he pulled over, he saw the Jeep coming toward him, fast. He pulled his truck into an alley on the right and jumped out. The Jeep turned and headed for him. He ducked into a doorway and looked out. An older man with white hair sat under the steering wheel. The Jeep backed out of the alley and sped away.

"What happened to your truck?" Kade and David met at the diner for lunch as they did every Tuesday, and Kade inspected the bumper.

"Had a little fender-bender this morning. I'll take it to Jim's Auto to get it fixed."

Kade stared at David. "I'd say that's a little more than a fender-bender. It isn't even a fender. Your whole back bumper is destroyed. Did you get rear-ended?"

"Yeah. I stopped too fast and a guy slammed into me."

"Did you file a police report? He had to be following too close. It would be his fault."

"Nah, I just let it go. It was a white-headed old man driving an old Jeep. I didn't want to cause him any trouble." He didn't *really* lie.

Kade laughed. "Always the softy, feeling sorry for a poor slob." He punched David's arm. "One more thing I love about you, David."

"Oh, hush. You'd do the same thing."

One day as he walked across the street headed for work, David was forced to dive between two parked cars to escape the same Jeep. Someone was out to get him for sure. He must be more observant of his surroundings.

He glanced up when he heard the door open. "Ms. Emma! What are you doing here?"

Ms. Emma tightened her lips and narrowed her eyes. "I've had it, David. I'm done. May I come work for you?"

David put his arm around her shoulders and pulled her toward a desk. "You sit here, my love, and we'll get you started right away."

"First, I need to talk to you in private."

David led her to his office and sat facing her. "What's going on, Ms. Emma?"

"I kept quiet as long as I worked for Mr. Crandall, but this morning I reached the limit. I will no longer work for a man who is a criminal, and that's what he is. A low-down criminal."

"Why do you say he's a criminal? What has he done?"

She lowered her eyes and rocked back and forth, clutching her purse.

David moved around his desk and put his hand on her shoulder. "You don't have to say anything if it makes you uncomfortable."

She looked up. "No, I just want to say it in the right way. Guess I'll have to say it straight out. Oliver is determined to destroy you."

David drew back. "Destroy me? Why?"

"Why, because you are a better businessman than he is. Because your business is growing while he struggles to keep his afloat."

"How does he intend to destroy me?"

Ms. Emma's nostrils flared. "He has contacted every business around, telling them you are not trustworthy, and they should stay away from Kingston Shipping. He devised a letter with false information about your business. He threatened me when I refused to type the letters and again when I refused to mail them. So, I left." She leaned forward. "He mailed them yesterday. By now most everyone will have them."

David went to the window. He'd tried to keep things

fair with Oliver. In fact, he'd tried to help him. He referred clients to him—although most either refused or came back in a few weeks—and he tried to persuade Oliver's clients to stay with him. Could he help it if clients disliked being cheated?

"Kingston, what's this?" A scowling client shook a paper at him. David looked at the paper and groaned. It was the letter from Oliver.

"Look, Hebron, you know me. Have I ever done you wrong? I've worked hard to earn the trust of my clients."

Hebron wadded up the letter. "I should have known Crandall would pull something like this." He shook David's hand and left. For the next week, David fielded calls from disturbed clients, assuring them he hadn't changed from when they first signed up with the company. He encouraged them to call Brodie Pruit if they were in doubt of the competence of Kingston Shipping. He shook the hands of those who decided to move to Crandall Shipping, and wished them well. Ms. Emma proved to be a lifesaver. She bustled around organizing interviews, serving coffee, and interceding between clients and David until he could debunk the false information they had been given.

David stalked into the apartment and slammed the door. "Sadie!" He threw his briefcase on a table, opened the refrigerator, and pulled out a bottle of green tea. "Sadie! Where are you?"

"I'm in here." Sadie came running from a back room. "What's wrong? Are you all right? What's going on?"

"Nothing that a little vacay on the river won't fix. Pack up and be quick. We're leaving now." They packed a bag, threw food into a cooler, and were off.

David and Sadie cruised along with their bare feet sticking over the sides and the radio blaring. They snacked on peanuts and Pepsis and ate dinner on the deck. They waved at passing boats and laughed at fishermen pulling in their catch. They motored up a tributary a little way and anchored in a safe place under some low hanging branches to spend the night. The songs of frogs, loons, and night creatures lulled them to sleep as they cuddled below deck.

About midnight, the sound of a motor startled them. Rubbing the sleep from his eyes, David climbed the steps to the deck and looked out. At first, he couldn't see anything. He started to go below when a light flashing on the bank caught his attention. Voices, at first low then louder, pulled his attention to a small boat he hadn't noticed before. As he watched, he saw people getting into the boat. It appeared to be small children. They were being herded into the boat by two or three larger people. A child cried out for Mama, and another wailed. Then another. A deep voice shushed them with threatening tones. It looked like several kids of various sizes, but David couldn't tell how many. The men rowed the boat out into the stream, cranked the motor, and opened the throttle.

When they were gone, David went below and called Kade. A sleepy voice answered, and David pulled back the phone when loud coughing and hacking filled his ear.

"Kade? Are you awake?"

"You moron. Why do you always ask that when you call in the middle of the night?"

"Sorry to wake you. Listen, something's up on the river." David explained what he witnessed while answering Kade's questions for clarification. "I'd call the river police, but

I don't have a number."

"Hold on a minute." Kade gave him the number.

An operator directed David's call to an agent who refused to believe David's complaint. "Kid, go peddle your crap elsewhere," he snapped. "We have enough to do around here without answering prank calls." The phone clicked.

Early the next morning, David and Sadie docked at the Island in time to have breakfast with Max and Tammy Shepherd. When David filled him in, Max called the river police, and before long an agent appeared at the door to fill out a report.

"I'll check this out." The agent closed his report book. "I'm sorry for the way you were treated last night. We get a ton of prank calls and we get a little cranky on the night shift."

Max exploded. "Look, this stuff has been going on a while now. We've made report after report, but nothing ever gets done. People's kids are disappearing left and right, but you people turn deaf ears to the cries of the river people. What's the problem?"

The agent's face reddened, and he stuttered. "I...I don't know anything about that, sir. We try to investigate all the reports given us. I'll check on it." He bolted.

Back at the office, David talked to several of his clients, asking if they heard of anything unusual going on down the river. They hadn't noticed anything. He visited the pier to talk to the boat crews, and they had plenty to tell.

"Yeah," a deckhand remarked. "I keep seeing a big ole beat-up lookin' river boat trollin' up and down the river. Didn't think much of it at first, but after a while, you wonder what it's doin'. Don't appear to be much of anybody on it.

That's what's strange."

Another hand from a towboat spoke. "What's botherin' me is a certain red speedboat keepin' the water churnin'. There are boats galore on the river and I see speedboats all time, but it zips around like there's no tomorrow. I caint put my finger on it, but something ain't right."

"Yeah, I seen that." A guy with greasy coveralls joined the conversation. "The other day I saw a barge loaded with grain chugging along when a fancy red speedboat pulled alongside and a guy yelled to the driver. Next thing I knew, another guy leaped onto the barge from the speedboat. In a little while he jumped back, and the red boat zoomed on up the river." He scratched his head. "Kinda dangerous if you ask me."

"You wanna talk about dangerous, did you see a kid on the Henderson barge the other day?" A fuzzy-headed man smacked his forehead. "Who ever heard of having a kid on a barge? He ran around like he belonged there."

Others commented on things they saw and heard, everything from strange actions of boats to children crying in strange places. David left, determined to find the underlying cause of the issue.

He and Kade took the girls to a favorite restaurant and soon the conversation turned to the strange events of their evening on the river.

"What can we do?" Kade drank the last of his Pepsi and put a tip on the table. "If the river police or the Port Authority won't do anything, where does that leave us?"

David added to the tip. "I'm not sure. Guess we'll have to notify a person higher up the ladder. This'll only get worse if we don't take action."

. "We'll have to have proof."

"Yeah, they won't listen to words. We need solid information to give them."

Sophia held up a finger. "I have an idea." She nudged Kade. "Remember that camera I bought the other day?" She turned to David and Sadie. "I needed a powerful camera for a new venture I'm working on. This camera will zoom in on a butterfly a half-mile away. Well, maybe not that far, but it's powerful. And, it'll take videos as well as still life."

"That's a great idea." Sadie scooted to the edge of her chair. "But what are we going to do with a camera?"

Kade laughed and popped her on the top of her head. "We're going to do a stake out. We're going to get proof bad people are doing bad things."

"Yeah," David said. "We're going to catch them. Then the river police will have to listen to us, or we'll get the FBI."

On the river

Leo watched until the cabin lights on the boat went out. He waited a while longer to make sure no one was around and slipped onto the deck. He rummaged around, looking for valuables he might take. He picked up an item, grinned with delight, and shoved it into his pocket. He leaned over to look through a pile of hoses and pushed them off the deck into the water.

He looked around as if he heard a noise and waved his hand in dismissal of whatever made the sound. Reaching into a small bucket, he took out a rag dripping dark liquid. He put an arm over his nose and crept toward the engine room. A short time later, he slunk back to the pier and disappeared into the darkness. There was no sign of the bucket.

Twenty-three

David and Kade borrowed a small fishing boat from a friend who lived on the river. The boat was large enough for a third person to hide and manage the camera while two fished on the deck. Sophia taught the other three to work her camera.

"Remember, this thing costs a lot of money," she reminded them. They promised to take good care of it.

At first, they all went together, and the girls took turns manning the camera. Then the couples took turns to divide their time better between work and stakeout. They wore old clothes, hats and sunglasses to disguise themselves and trolled both sides of the river, always watching. They purchased binoculars from a Bass Pro to use as well.

David and Sadie were on stakeout when Sadie called David's attention to a red speedboat soaring toward a barge. Sure enough, the boat pulled up beside the barge and an exchange took place between the man on the speedboat and one on the barge. Sadie gasped as she zoomed the camera in on the face of both men.

"It's Dad," she whispered. "In the red boat."

"What's he giving the man?" David grabbed the binoculars and focused them. He could see a manila envelope handed from the speedboat to the man on the barge. "Crap! It is him. What's that all about?"

Sadie lowered the camera as the boat sped away. "I

don't know, but if it's sneaky, you can bet it's illegal. I can't believe Dad is involved in devious activities and probably dangerous!" She remained quiet the rest of the day, and David tried to excuse Oliver.

"He may be giving a paycheck to an employee," he suggested. "Or maybe it's a bonus for a worker who did an extra good job. It's probably nothing, Sadie."

When they told Kade what they had seen, he shook his head.

"No, it had to be something else. Dad couldn't be involved in the trouble on the river. Look at all the good things he's done to help those people. Like you said, he was most likely paying the guy for work he'd hired done." A muscle in his jaw twitched. "Often things are not what they seem." David and Sadie agreed with his theory—it could be easily explained. They had no proof of any wrongdoing.

Things were smooth for the next couple of weeks, with nothing else said about Oliver's involvement. Until a bomb dropped. Right on David's head. A bomb that unsettled his world.

Arty Holt, a security guard at the dock, came running into David's office. "Mr. Kingston, you gotta come quick."

David ran after the man to the dock. Out on the water one of his boats was on fire. It had already pulled away from the dock, so the boats at the dock were safe, but a few boats were too close to escape. Fire shot out of the craft in all directions and men leaped into the water. Those gathered on the dock stood in shock while nearby water vessels moved in to rescue crew members. The fire took boats and cargo, but no one was hurt.

David turned from watching the event to find Oliver

behind him. "Well, boy, looks like you got trouble." Oliver stood with his arms folded across his chest.

"Looks like it."

"Hope you renewed your insurance. If you didn't, this could ruin you."

David stiffened. "I'm sure my insurance is good. I'm sure my secretary took care of that."

"I wouldn't count on it." Oliver smirked and stalked away.

The fire occupied David's mind, so he didn't give much regard to Oliver's remark until later. He had Ms. Emma turn in the insurance claim the day of the accident, and the insurance rejected it. David called the agent who said the policy was canceled two weeks before the accident.

"I know I renewed the policy." Tears glistened in Ms. Emma's eyes. "I always do that at the beginning of the year. Look. Here's where I sent the check."

David could see the company had endorsed the check. Then what was the problem? He knew he didn't cancel it. Or did he? He raked his fingers through his hair. Since he took over the company, he found the exorbitant amount of paperwork to be almost paralyzing at times. The secretary he'd had before Ms. Emma did a good job, but she often missed work to care for her children. Could he have missed something?

He rose and paced the room. He walked over to the large office window. He could see the tree line bordering the river which wound around the edge of the city into the surrounding countryside until it disappeared into the distant south. He leaned forward and clutched the facing. He loved that river. That mighty river where he made so many memories. That mighty river where he made his living. That same mighty river could end up causing his ruin.

He and Ms. Emma combed through files and papers trying to find the error. Everything they found indicated the insurance policy was current. David called the agent again, and he insisted David canceled the policy. He brought the papers showing the cancellation, and when David saw it, he knew what happened. The signature was David's name, but not his handwriting. The handwriting belonged to Oliver.

David slammed the papers on the desk in front of the agent. "You let Mr. Crandall sign these papers?"

The agent frowned. "Sir, that's your signature."

"It may be my name, but I did not sign that paper. Did you see me sign the paper?"

The agent tugged at his shirt collar. "Well, no, but it's your name."

David glared at the agent. "Look, Mr. Foley, I acknowledge the name on that paper is mine. There's no debate. But I did not sign my name to that paper. The signature is not mine." He grabbed a file from the desk and pointed to the bottom of the page. "*That's* the way my signature looks. See the difference?"

Foley nodded. "Yes, there is a significant difference. But the policy is still canceled. I don't know what to do about it."

"My lawyer will be explaining what you will do about it." David shoved the papers into Foley's chest. "He will be calling your boss."

Foley reddened as David ushered him out the door.

For the next weeks, chaos ruled the office. Clients

demanded payment for their cargo while David assured them they would lose nothing. And how would he manage that? He couldn't cover the cost of their losses. Neither could he lose his best clients. David paced the floor at home and at the office, sleeping little and eating less. Sadie made all his favorite foods which he shoved aside. She begged him to take a sleeping pill, but he refused.

"What in the world is going on?" Kade asked. He had been out of town and only heard bits and pieces about the accident. David tried to explain about the insurance issue without implicating Oliver. But it was impossible.

"How could you allow your insurance policy to expire?" Kade wanted to know.

David shook his head. "I didn't. It was canceled."

"You canceled it? Why?"

Sadie listened until she'd had enough. "Kade, David didn't cancel the policy. Someone else did."

"Who? Ms. Emma wouldn't do that. Was it one of the other staffers? Did you fire her?"

"No." David slumped in his chair. "No one at the office. The insurance agent, Fowley, did it. Or at least helped do it."

"It's the insurance company's fault. That should be an easy fix. They are responsible."

"My dear brother, listen to me." Sadie sat on the arm of the chair by Kade. "Your loving father, Oliver Crandall, canceled David's policy."

Kade jumped to his feet. "No way. Dad wouldn't be involved in such a mean-spirited thing. Besides, how could he cancel a policy that isn't in his name?"

"He forged David's name."

"That doesn't make any sense. You can't just cancel a person's insurance. Not unless the agent . . ." His head jerked toward David who turned away. "What's the insurance company saying about it? You've talked to them, right?"

David scowled. "Of course, I have. They're looking into it. My lawyer has contacted their lawyer and for the time being, that's all we can do." He rose and began pacing. "In the meantime, my clients are threatening to sue for the loss of their cargo."

Kade took David by the arm and pushed him into a chair. He sat straddling a chair facing him. "My friend, here's what we're going to do. We're going to sue the insurance company for their part in this. We're going to file a charge against Oliver Crandall for fraud. We'll pay those who've lost their cargo. It may take us a while, but we'll get this mess straightened out."

"But I don't want to ruin your dad." David looked at Sadie.

"David, you have a responsibility to your company and your employees. You shouldn't worry about a man who is trying to destroy you."

Kade looked around at Sadie and Sophia. "Are you in agreement with this, ladies?" Solemn faces stared at him and heads nodded. They were family.

David paid the ones he knew could not survive without payment, and his clients were understanding and worked with him to settle their accounts. Kade made good on his promise, and a lawyer from the insurance company came pleading with David to drop the lawsuit. The company would reinstate the insurance and honor the claim. He could pay everything in full and drop all the lawsuits. He had one more thing to do.

He and Kade walked up the steps to Crandall Shipping, briefcases in hand. They ignored the receptionist and walked into Oliver's office. David adjusted his tie and laid his briefcase on Oliver's desk. Kade sat in a chair facing the desk.

"What do you want?" Oliver growled.

"Mr. Crandall, I know you forged my name to cancel the insurance policy. The company has reinstated my policy and the costs of the accident are all covered."

Oliver's face turned crimson, and he shoved his chair back from the desk. He looked from David to Kade and back to David.

David continued. "I have all the evidence I need to prove you forged my name. At my demand, the insurance company has agreed to keep silent unless I want to press charges for fraud."

Oliver rose and paced around the room. "What do you want, David?"

"I want your promise to leave me and my business alone. That's all."

Oliver blanched. "That's all?"

"Yes, that's all." David held his hand out toward Oliver. Oliver stared at it as though it were a weapon. David leveled his gaze and continued to hold it out.

Oliver took his hand and shook it. "Okay, Kingston, I'll leave you and your business alone. You have my word."

On the river

"Man, I can't believe my luck. A hundred dollars, just like that. And all I have to do is pretend my boat is stalled." Lucas strutted around bragging about getting hired on one of the Kingston Shipping boats and already earning extra money.

Valance shook his head. "You should'na done that, Lucas. Your boss is a good man, and you won't last long working for him. You pretend to be in trouble when you ain't, he'll fire you for sure. Then no one'll hire you."

"Ah, I ain't worried. I can earn more money working for this other guy and I don't have to do much a' nothing." His laugh echoed off the metal walls of the tugboat that bore the name Kingston Shipping on the side.

Twenty-four

Kingston Shipping flourished as did the love of David and Sadie. They enjoyed periodic fishing trips and visits to the Island, often accompanied by Kade and Sophia. Jesse and Kathleen often went to visit the Shepherd family, and Melody liked to join them for a wiener roast around a bonfire on the Island. Everyone came except Oliver, and even though no one mentioned him, they were aware of the pain caused by his absence.

After months of peace, David learned Oliver was stirring things up again. A Crandall employee posted fliers along the Kingston Shipping dock offering special shipping rates and a signing bonus to anyone who would change an account to Crandall Shipping. Most of David's clients knew the score with Oliver and scoffed at the offers, but a few new ones showed interest, and a couple moved their accounts to Crandall.

David dismissed the issue, but Sadie insisted Kade speak to Oliver despite David's objections. Kade returned red-faced and angry. He refused to tell David what transpired, but Sadie filled him in. She had accompanied Kade to Oliver's office and heard Oliver explode on Kade.

"You're weak like your mother," he said to Kade. "When I'm gone, this business is yours. But as long as Kingston is around, it'll never amount to anything. You'll never amount to anything."

Sadie cried. She couldn't believe her dad would talk to Kade that way.

"I wish I'd never made Kade talk to him," she moaned.

"Don't blame yourself, sweetheart." David comforted her the best he could. "You were just defending me." His kisses moved from her hand to her forehead and to her lips. "I love you so much."

"You have the best heart, David, and I don't want you to be hurt. Especially by my dad."

"Don't you worry, my dear. I can defend myself. Even from your dad's angry assaults."

"Kade reminded him of his promise, but he brushed it aside. Said it didn't matter." She pulled back and looked in David's face. "Will you consider pressing charges for what he did?"

David pushed her head back to his shoulder. "No, I won't. Whatever he does is between him and God. I won't be a part of his mental labyrinth."

Days later, David received a call from one of his boats. The boat captain needed help with a boat that had stalled. The boat was anchored about a mile upriver, and the captain insisted David go himself instead of sending a dock hand. David called for a boat mechanic to accompany him and headed out to check out the trouble in a small motorboat. About the time he saw the boat, he noticed another boat approaching from the left. A silver speedboat barreled toward him at full speed, but before it hit, it careened and went the other direction. The motorboat lurched, and David fell over the side of the boat. He floundered about, and the speedboat came at him again, barely missing him. The maintenance man pulled him into the boat.

"Who in the world was driving that thing?" The maintenance man checked David over to make sure he wasn't hurt. "He sure needs lessons in common courtesy." David removed his soaked shirt and wiped water from his face. He looked for the boat which reported trouble, but it was gone.

"I guess he didn't need much help after all." The mechanic headed the boat back to the dock.

Later when David drove across town to visit his parents, a silver Jeep ran him off the road into a shallow ditch. Then it almost hit him when he got out of his truck at a grocery store.

"David, this is no coincidence." Kade flipped when David filled him in on the near accidents. "Dang, man, your life is in danger. You're getting out of here, now."

"No, I'm all right." If he was all right, why was he having bad dreams and night sweats? Why did he look over his shoulder every time he left the house? Why did he jump at every noise he heard and movement he saw?

He agreed when Kade insisted he and Sadie take a short trip. They would fly to a ski lodge in Colorado on a little vacation.

The next day, Kade pulled in by David as he parked to go to work. "Hey, man. I got a little something special for you." He reached into the back of his truck and pulled out a black bag. He handed it to David. "Open this."

"What is it?" David peered into the bag and gasped. "A gun? You got me a gun?" He pulled out a rifle. "Thanks. It's nice. But what for?"

"You're going to carry this on your boat at all times. And here's another item for you to carry." He held out a

Glock. "Be careful, it's loaded. You're to keep it loaded and carry it with you. You'll need to get a license to carry as soon as possible."

David grimaced. "I don't know, Kade. I don't like the idea of carrying a gun."

"Look, friend, you grew up shooting guns. It's not like you haven't shot one before."

"Sure, I did. I shot at wild game. Not at humans."

"Dang, David, you've got to protect yourself. Come on, man, face the facts. Someone wants you dead."

"I don't think so. It's scare-tactics."

"No matter. You need to scare whoever is scaring you. No arguments, man. Put this rifle on your boat and keep it loaded."

"Okay. I'll get a carry license, but I won't carry this on me. It will only be in my truck or boat."

"Okay, just so you have it with you. Now go get ends tied up so you and Sadie can leave."

They decided not to tell Sadie the reason for the trip, and she jumped at the chance to spend time alone with her husband. They were at the airport early the next morning and arrived at the lodge by evening.

"The first thing we have to do is go shopping." Sadie rubbed her hands together to heat them. "I don't know why you wouldn't take me shopping at home. I'm freezing."

David laughed and pulled her close to keep her warm. They caught a cab to the nearest mall and stocked up on warm clothes including boots, gloves, and scarves.

"Have you ever been skiing?" Sadie clapped her hands with excitement.

"No, this will be a first for me."

"Me too. Can we go tomorrow?"

"Yes, but tonight we'll enjoy each other and hot cocoa with marshmallows." A fireplace burned in their room and David called room service to bring hot chocolate and peanut butter cookies. They snuggled on the thick rug in front of the warm fire, enjoying their sweet treats. Enveloped in their love for each other, they paid little attention to the soft music playing in the background.

The next day they were out on the slopes with a ski instructor. Sadie squealed as she stumbled and landed in a deep snowdrift. Before long, the instructor said they were ready and led them to a gentle slope. Things were going well until David swerved and tumbled. Sadie, who was close behind, piled on top of him. They worked to untangle their skis, giggling and wallowing in the snow until they looked more like snowmen than skiers.

"Wow, skiing is hard work." Sadie puffed out her cheeks. "I'm about ready for a nice cup of hot chocolate."

"That sounds like a good idea." David pulled her up and they headed back to the lifts. The evening activities included hot cocoa and marshmallows roasted in a rock fire pit in the middle of a large room, and friendly conversation with other lodgers. David almost forgot the dangers he'd encountered at home.

The next day they went to the slopes a while before they decided to explore the local shops. A small plaza and a couple of eateries were within walking distance, and they laughed as they puttered through an antique shop they found.

Sadie clipped a huge pair of earrings onto her ears. "Look, David. These would be perfect with my new black dress."

He laughed at the gaudy jewelry and held up an old, ragged book entitled, *New Brides: How to Care for Your Husband.* "Look, I'm getting this for you." They giggled as they read passages such as "Always make his favorite food for dinner and have it ready at exactly six p.m.," and "Shine his shoes and set them out each morning when he prepares for work." They enjoyed eating lunch at an open-air restaurant and were returning to their room when a man and woman came stumbling down the sidewalk toward them. The man bumped David hard, sending him sprawling into a pile of dirty snow shoveled from the sidewalk. Sadie rushed to help David to his feet and the couple stumbled on, laughing.

In the evening, the resort hosted a dance. David and Sadie floated around the dance floor, rejecting offers to dance with other people. One man kept trying to cut in and dance with Sadie, but David held her firmly. After the third try, the man grabbed Sadie's arm and jerked her away from David. Sadie gasped and tried to pull away, but he held on and pulled her to the other side of the room. David followed them, but Sadie shook her head and gestured for him to back off. David knew she could handle herself. To prevent an ugly fight, he went to the punch bowl but did not let his wife out of his sight.

Sadie allowed herself to be led around the dance floor for a dance. When she excused herself, the man held on to her arm. She smiled as she put her arm around his waist and danced him close to the door. She stepped on his foot and brought up a knee, and the man grunted and doubled over. She rushed to David and they left the room.

"Didn't you recognize that man?" Sadie asked.

"No. You know him?" David avoided a cleaning cart sitting in the hall.

"Only as the guy who knocked you into a snow drift."

David squinted his eyes. "Are you sure? What's he up to?"

"I'm not sure, but he told me you were cheating on me. Said he saw you with another woman."

"What? He said that to you?"

"Yes. I told him he didn't know what he was talking about. That's when I gave him a knee."

David scrutinized Sadie's face as he unlocked the door. Sadie flopped on the bed and David dropped beside her. "Sadie, never doubt that I love you."

"I don't." She cradled his face in her hands and kissed him. "Your love for me is the same as mine for you. I know that." She kissed him again. "But, David, do *you* know that?"

"What do you mean? Of course, I do."

"Why aren't you honest with me?"

He pulled back to look into her eyes. "I am honest with you. Why would you say that?"

Sadie sat up and pulled her knees to her chest. "Because I know things have been going on that you haven't told me. That's dishonest." She twisted a curl around her finger. "And I'm not talking about another woman. I'm talking about what's been happening to you the past weeks. You've been hiding things from me."

David dropped his head. "Oh." He moved over to touch her hair and pull her close again. "I want to protect you. And I don't want you to worry about me. That's all."

"But there's one thing you don't seem to understand.

You are part of me. I'm part of you. We're one. Anything that happens to you, happens to me. Right?"

Silence.

"Right?"

"I know that's right, but it's hard when it's your dad after me. I wouldn't do anything to hurt you, Sadie, and I know you love your dad."

"I do love my dad. But you are my husband. Remember? Leave your father and mother and cleave to your spouse? Would you want me keeping things from you?"

"No, of course not. You're right. I should never keep anything from you. I want you to trust me like I need to trust you, completely."

"Yes, you do," she murmured as he buried his hands in her hair. She took a deep breath and turned off the light.

On the river

"Hey, you. Wanna make some extra cash?"

A man in a red speedboat pulled up beside the long johnboat where Ben sat, baiting a string of hooks on a trot-line. He had pulled in several catfish from lines he set out last night and would have more tomorrow. Maybe he would catch enough to pay for his kids' school clothes. Kitty was in a tizzy because the girls had to wear hand-me-downs from their cousins, and he was tired of her fussing. It would feel good to hand her some cash so she could go clothes shopping.

Ben looked over at the older man. "What do you mean? What do I got to do?"

"Just a little target practice." The man's grin made Ben suspicious, but he sure could use an extra dollar. And he did like to shoot.

"You wanna explain?"

"Do you have a gun?"

"Sure do."

"Are you a good shot?"

"I can hit a flying mallard at two-hundred yards."

"Say, that's pretty good. You'll be perfect for this job, then."

"Tell me about the job."

"Well, tomorrow when you come on the river, watch for a young man in an old red motorboat. He usually comes by around mid-morning. Blond with a clean-cut beard."

"Yeah, I've seen him about."

"All you need to do is scare him a little. Just shoot a few holes in his boat. That's all."

"How much?"

Ben gasped at the amount quoted and nodded. Baby's gonna get some new shoes.

Twenty-five

The trip back home proved to be uneventful. Sadie napped on the plane while David watched a movie and stared out the window. He'd taken a trip to escape the wrath of Oliver, but would anything be different when he returned? Had his desire to hurt David lessened? Time would tell.

And it hadn't. In fact, it had increased. David knew Oliver had set out to get him and nothing or no one would stop him. When he went out on the river alone, he returned with his boat shot full of holes. Therefore, he seldom went. When he drove to the store or gas station, a car ran him off the road, and several times while he walked across the street, a vehicle tried to run over him. He limited his drives to work and back. He determined he would not tell Sadie and Kade, and he would not involve the law. He would try to be more careful and trust God to take care of him.

One day he had to go upriver to handle a business matter. As his boat skimmed the water, he heard the familiar sound of bullets riddling the sides of his vessel. The attack became so violent he fled to the Island to find sanctuary. He pulled his boat onto the bank midway on the Island and hid it in a patch of tall grass and weeds where he lay behind a sand dune until the shooting ceased.

"Whatcha doing?" David looked up into the face of a tousled headed teenage boy standing on top of the dune.

"Oh, I'm just resting." David stood and stretched as

though he'd been asleep.

"Ah, come on. You caint fool me. I saw what happened." The boy stepped closer. "Who ya got mad at ya?"

David gave a lop-sided grin. "It's nothing. Don't worry about it. What's your name?"

"I'm Shelton. Shelton Lynch. I ain't gonna worry 'bout it, but I think maybe you should."

"I'll be all right." David waved his hand to dismiss the idea just as the sand around his feet sprinkled his shoes. He and Shelton dove into the tall grass behind the dune.

Shelton gasped and peeped over the grass. "Tell ya what. I'm gettin' outta here and I advise you to do the same. My place ain't too far and you're welcome to run there with me."

He took off running with David close behind. They didn't stop until they arrived at a cabin almost hidden behind low hanging cedar branches. A large man carrying a baby goat turned when they stumbled through the branches into the yard.

"What in the Sam Hill is going on?" He looked from Shelton to David. "Who're you?"

Shelton hooked a thumb toward David. "This here's David, and he's in trouble. He's got an enemy who's aiming to get him for sure."

The man put the goat on the ground and stuck out his hand. "Good to meetcha. I'm Shelton's dad, Travis. Come on in and tell me what's going on."

Travis offered David a chair and served him a cold glass of tea. Shelton told his dad what he witnessed and the two seemed genuine and concerned. That's when recognition dawned on the face of Travis. "Say, I know who you are.

You're Jesse Kingston's kid."

"Yes, I am."

"Ole Jesse's a good guy. A fine neighbor. Guess we moved here after you'd left the Island." He sighed. "We sure hated for him to move. But it's understandable now a casino is being built here."

"Yeah, I hate that, too." David glanced around the cabin. It was roomy and neat with stairs leading to a loft. Colorful quilts hung on the banisters and baskets of yarn and knitting needles hinted at the presence of a woman.

"Now if you would, David, enlighten me. What's going on? Who's after you?"

David shuddered. He no longer cared who knew his problems. He may as well start from the beginning. Well, at least close. David told his story from the day he went to work for Oliver. Travis and Shelton listened to his story with periodic nods or an hmmm now and then. They only interrupted if they needed clarification. When he finished, they stared at him in disbelief.

Discouraged and deflated, David slumped in his seat with his head lowered. Travis and Shelton looked at each other and Travis slapped David's knee. "Listen, young man, your story sounds far-fetched, but you must be telling the truth. They always say truth is stranger than fiction. Your story is strange, all righty, so it must be true." He cocked his head. "This guy got other reasons to be mad at you besides you marrying his daughter?"

David looked down. "Well, he may be mad because I'm a business competitor now."

Shelton whistled. "Man-o-man! That Oliver dude must really hate you. He wants to kill you, all right. Seems to me like you ain't gonna last long with a man like that after you. He musta hired some bad dudes to hunt you down."

David splayed out his hands in frustration and looked at his watch. His gun was in his boat, but he couldn't bring himself to use it. "I gotta get home. It's getting late."

"Tell you what," Travis said. "We'll go to the river with you to make sure the shooter ain't still there. If no one shoots at you, you're okay. If the shootin' starts back up, then you have a problem."

Travis and Shelton accompanied him to the river, and when he boarded his boat, the shooting began. All three dove into the sand, waited a moment and ran back to the cabin.

"Well, looks like that guy ain't givin' up." Shelton sat cross legged in the floor while David slumped by the window.

"Wait a minute." Travis climbed the stairs, taking two steps at a time. In a couple of minutes, he came back carrying a bundle of clothes. He handed them to David. "Here, put these on."

David pulled on a plaid shirt and a pair of ragged overalls. Travis stuck an old hat on his head. Shelton grinned and nodded his approval. He pulled a skein of yarn from the basket and tape from a desk drawer and made David a long, black beard. It looked a little rough, but Shelton declared it would look real from a distance.

"Now, walk like this." Travis demonstrated a humped over, stumbling kind of walk to David. "We'll watch from behind those trees to make sure you'll be okay. You take our old boat from that patch of bushes over there. We'll take your boat down river next time we go, and that won't be too long."

David hunched over and hobbled along the riverbank

when he moved from the shelter of the trees. He pulled the old boat out of the bushes and hunkered inside. He waited. Nothing happened. He paddled out into the river and started the motor. Still nothing happened. He headed toward home, watching every water vessel he met. He didn't want to give a passerby any chance to figure out his disguise.

He rubbed his stomach and grimaced. What in the world had he done to deserve this? Was God angry with him? Maybe he'd sinned without realizing it. He couldn't think of anything. He watched a hawk soaring over the water and remembered the comforting words of his mom when he was scared as a child: God's eye is on the sparrow, and because you are made in the image of God, you are more valuable than a bird.

Trying to keep a low profile, David chose different routes to and from the office and when not at work, he stayed inside the house. He jumped at any little noise or sudden movement. Even though Sadie knew nothing of the dangers threatening him, she worried about the difference she saw.

"David, you need to get out of the house a while," she would say when she arrived home from class and found him sitting in front of the television or pacing the floor. "You're acting like an old man. Go fishing!"

He would make an excuse or look for something to do. He kept the laundry done, and the floors were spotless. She began to fuss at him to take her places.

"We never go out anymore." She pleaded with him to take her out until he agreed to go out to eat or to a movie. Once she caught him looking over his shoulder. "What are you doing? You act like someone is after you."

He had to do something before his wife thought he was a coward. Before *he* thought he was a coward. He conceded to talk to the man who'd guided him all his life — he paid a visit to his dad.

"Son, you're looking a little sickly. Have you lost weight?" His observant Dad missed nothing. They walked around the huge yard while Jesse showed David the work he had done, planting trees and setting out bulbs for spring blossoms. He admired a row of blackberries and a couple of blueberry bushes which would bear fruit the following summer. As they walked, David vented to his dad.

"I don't understand why God is letting all this happen. Has He left me? I can't think of anything I have done to put a wedge between us."

"God hasn't left you. Every person has a will, a choice. And right now, Oliver is choosing to hurt you when you haven't done anything to him. God won't force him to do the right thing."

"I wish he would leave me alone. I'm getting tired. Sometimes I want to kill him before he kills me."

"I don't blame you, but then you'd end up in prison." Jesse sat on a lawn chair.

"Yeah, I guess. I know that wouldn't be right anyway. I'm always aware that he is Sadie's and Kade's dad. What should I do, Dad?"

"I understand you don't want to get law enforcement involved, but this is an extreme situation. You could get killed. Oliver has lost his mind if this is his doing."

David rubbed the back of his neck. Maybe Oliver had lost his mind. After all, he'd left a wonderful woman. He seemed unconcerned about his children. He seemed oblivious to his own role in sinking his own business. What other explanation could there be?

Jesse slapped his knees. "Tell you what. Let's take a trip. Just you and me. If she doesn't want to stay alone, Sadie can stay with Kathleen or her mom, and we'll get away for a while. Do you have an employee who can handle your business a week?"

"Sure. Jacobs is trustworthy, and it would be good for him. Give him a little experience. I want to send him to hunt for a good place to open another Kingston Shipping anyway." David heaved a sigh. "Where're we going?"

"I think a hunting trip in the mountains would be good, don't you?"

"That sounds wonderful. When are we leaving?"

In two days, Jesse and David were on a snow-capped mountain hunting wild game. Sophia had loaned them her powerful camera with a stern admonishment they take care of it. They rented a cabin on the side of the mountain and stocked it with enough food for ten people. Sadie and Kathleen both insisted they make it two-weeks and Jesse said they were right.

Stomping around in the snow and climbing rough terrain gave David plenty to keep his mind off things at home, and he fell straight to sleep when he went to bed at night. He and Jesse had long talks as they watched for game and while they made potatoes and deer steak to eat.

Jesse loaded David's plate with greasy fried potatoes and corn bread. "We need to add meat to those bones."

The fresh air and time with his dad were like medicine, and David ate the delicious victuals with zeal.

One day a blizzard kept them indoors and David

paced back and forth from the door to the window, gazing at the snow. Jesse watched him a while then suggested they use a checkerboard he found in a closet.

"Son, you may not have a choice of things that happen, but you do have a choice of how you handle them. As long as you keep a good attitude, you'll be fine."

Jesse jumped David's black checker with his red one. "Dangers in rivers include whirlpools which can drown an unsuspecting victim. You have to be constantly aware of what's inside you, or you could be drowned by your own whirlpool."

David found the expedition exhilarating and couldn't wait to show Sadie pictures of the beautiful scenery and various animals they saw on their daily excursions. He would text them to her when they found a place with phone service.

They set out early one day, determined to find game. When they lived on the island, they hunted and often enjoyed fresh game, but they took this trip to enjoy the region and witness as much new scenery as possible. They walked at least a mile through the woods when Jesse motioned to David and pointed. A huge elk stood straight ahead, part of its antlers hidden by a tree. It stared straight at them.

David pulled his backpack around and pulled out Sophia's camera. He walked around a grove of trees for a better view and snapped pictures of the magnificent animal. He looked around for Jesse but didn't see him. Maybe he had walked further under the trees. He couldn't locate him anywhere.

"Dad!" David's whisper resounded through the snowy timber like a shout. "Dad! Where are you?"

Nothing.

David shoved the camera back inside the backpack and walked the direction they came. Their tracks were still there, and he followed the trail until he came to a clearing. He pulled out his binoculars and viewed the area, but still no Jesse. He heard a crash to his right and looked there. A limb which broke under the weight of the snow lay on the ground. How in the world could Jesse have disappeared without a trace? He wasn't too far from David when they saw the stag. He wouldn't have left him.

On the river

Cletus had never been to the mountains before. The cold wasn't the same as the cold back home, and the beauty of the snow-covered mountains warmed his heart. One day he and Eva would come here for a vacation. Right now, he had a job to do. Why did that old guy want to scare these men? Oh, well, not his business. He would do the job and head back home. He had seen the guys he was to attack. In fact, his cabin was down a short way from theirs. Seemed like two nice dudes. Looked like a father and son. He wasn't hurting them, at least not bad. Such a small deed for a nice sum of money. They'd probably do the same thing for the same pay.

Twenty-six

David decided to return to the spot Jesse disappeared. He didn't know what else to do. Earlier he saw what appeared to be ATV tracks leading in the direction they came. He could follow them back to the cabin. It had started snowing and the tracks were getting dim, but he could still make them out. How would he find his way back once the tracks were covered? The compass he had would have to do.

He studied the area they traversed and could see nothing amiss. He looked up into the trees. Could he be hiding to play a trick? No, he would never do that. He had to be close. David stomped around beneath the trees, moving bushes and vines, checking every log and stump he saw. Because his dad refused to use a cell phone, there was no way to contact him, wherever he was. Besides, there was little or no service out here. All he knew to do was search.

The snow thickened, covering the tracks he'd made. David moved in circles, trying to stay within a radius of the point Jesse disappeared. He used his compass and landmarks to check himself. He couldn't afford to get lost. A broken limb, a tall stump, a bent tree, a large nest high in the branches — all these helped him stay focused and on track. As his trek widened, he decided to move in one direction at a time to save distance.

He worked his way around the area until it was late. He had to get out before nightfall. Using his compass, he went north back to the cabin. In his search, he moved further west, and to get back on track he started east. He remembered a large boulder which stuck out of the side of the mountain near where they saw the elk. He needed to find that boulder. He also remembered a highway ran north and south near the cabin. If he could get to the highway, he could find his way.

Trudging through the deepening snow, he faltered several times. Tiredness consumed him, and fear and loneliness threatened to dominate every thought. He couldn't allow that, and he couldn't stop. He had to find his way out. He had to find his dad. He might not be able to find the boulder. Darkness approached, and he couldn't wait. He traveled north.

Lights flashed, and he knew he must be approaching the highway. He climbed the incline to the blacktop and headed north. The first cabin appeared, and he could make out the forms of others scattered along the road. The one he and Dad rented stood on the south end of the resort. As David neared the door, he glimpsed a dark figure through the window. Was it Dad? He fumbled for his key and unlocked the door. A small lamp lit the room. Had they left it on this morning? As he entered, he heard a noise coming from down the hall. He watched a moment and went to investigate. When he reached for the bathroom door, it opened, and there stood Jesse.

"Dad! Where have you been?" Blood ran down Jesse's swollen face. "Oh crap! What happened to you?" David led Jesse into the living room to inspect the damage.

"It isn't that bad." Jesse touched his bleeding forehead and winced. "I don't know what happened. I was watching the elk when something from behind knocked me down. I think I hit my head on a rock. I don't remember anything else. I don't know how I got here."

"I'm taking you to Urgent Care. You could have a concussion." David dabbed Jesse's head and face with a wet towel.

"I do have a splitting headache." Jesse sat in a chair while David fussed over him. David helped him into the truck and drove to the Urgent Care where a physician ex-rayed his head and gave him something for pain. He cautioned him to rest a few hours. Back at the cabin, David made burgers and read while Jesse rested until bedtime. David hung the wet coats close to the fireplace to dry when a card fell from Jesse's coat.

"What's this?" David read the crude message printed on the card. WATCH YOUR BUSINESS. "Who in the world wrote this?"

Jesse scratched his head. "I guess the same one who hit me on the head. That sounds like a warning. Who is warning us and about what?"

David cringed. "I don't know. With everything that's been happening, I'd hoped this trip would get me away from whoever is after me. Guess not."

"Want to leave a little early and go home tomorrow?"

"Yeah, might as well. All the fun has gone out of being here."

"We'll have to be more cautious from now on." Jesse yawned and stretched. "I'm ready to hit the sack. Good night, son."

David tossed and turned, wishing his phone worked. He needed to call Sadie. With his troubles and her classes, they hadn't spent much time together in the past several months. He would plan to take her away so they could have time to themselves. He knew class work and her internship stressed her, and it seemed like the closer graduation got, the harder her classes were.

He drifted off when a loud noise outside his window awakened him. He pulled back the curtain and found himself looking eye to eye with a huge, black bear. He jumped back, and the bear rose to his feet. Could he see inside the room? Did bears have night vision? The light of a small clock behind David illuminated the room, and he might see inside. It would be nothing for him to break the glass, while he wouldn't be able to get his body through the small window, he might be able to reach through if he saw David.

The bear turned away for an instant and David eased back and out the door. He woke Jesse and motioned him to follow. They slipped into David's room. The bear peered through the window and growled. David unplugged the clock to make the room black, and in a couple of minutes the bear headed back into the woods.

"Well, I'm glad we didn't encounter that guy while we were in the woods. He'd be worse than the one we did encounter." Jesse went to the coffee pot, but it was empty. "Think I'll sleep a little more before dawn."

"How is your head? Still hurting?"

Jesse touched his bandaged head. "It's a little sore, but the headache is gone."

They stopped to sleep at night and to eat, and they were home in two days. David tried to call Sadie when they were out of the mountains, but she didn't answer her phone. When he called Kathleen, she told him Sadie left with her mom for a couple of days, and she hadn't heard from her.

"Why won't she answer my calls?" David fretted, and Jesse tried to think of reasons to pacify him.

"She could be busy. You know how women are when they get together."

"I guess. But even if she's busy, she would still call me back."

"Maybe her phone's dead and she forgot her charger."

"Not for this length of time." He tried to call Melody, but she didn't answer. A call to Kade didn't get much better results.

"I haven't heard from Mom or Sadie, but I've been gone. Sophia hasn't said anything about them. I'm sure they're okay. If she's with Mom, they'll be attending a conference or shopping."

They were close to home and stopped for lunch when David's phone dinged. Charlie, one of the deckhands on a client's boat, sent him a private message.

Jesse stopped with his fork halfway to his mouth. "What's wrong, son? You look like you've seen a ghost."

David clenched his jaw and stared at his phone. "Charlie messaged me saying Sadie is gone. Says she left with a guy." He typed on his phone.

What do you mean, gone?

David continued to stare at his phone. "Charlie says she has left me for another man. Says Oliver's gloating about it." His heart rate quickened. He must get home. Now.

"Son, you know you can't believe everything people say. Who is this Charlie anyway?"

"He's a deckhand on Roger's boat. I believe him to be an honest man." His brows drew together. "No, this can't be right. Sadie wouldn't do that."

"No, she wouldn't." Jesse gestured to the waiter for the check. "Come on, let's get home to find out what's going on."

David drove in silence most of the way home, and Jesse reminded him to stay within the speed limit. They unloaded Jesse's things, he hugged his mom, and he drove home to open the door to an empty house. He ran into the bedroom and jerked open the closet door. The scent of her Gucci filled his nostrils. He turned, expecting her to be behind him. No such luck. Her clothes hung in the closet, but several empty hangers hung between brightly colored blouses and dark pants. In the kitchen, the refrigerator shelves were almost bare, and nothing except a bottle of Worcestershire sauce and a box of pasta filled the pantry. Where could she be?

He drove to his office and tried to finish a client's file, but he couldn't focus. They seldom disagreed, much less fought. She knew he loved her and assured him of her love before he left. No, he couldn't allow himself to think she would leave him. It would never happen. His shipping manager came in to ask about an account, and the office manager filled him in on new orders. He stayed late and stopped on the way home to buy groceries. When he returned to the apartment, the lights were on.

The door flew open and Sadie threw her arms around him. "David! You're home. I didn't expect you until Friday." David's heart sang as he kissed her long and hard. She chatted as they put the groceries away and made spaghetti and salad for dinner.

"I'm glad you bought groceries," she said. "I intended to when Mom and I got back, but I had to meet a deadline and didn't have time."

A sigh escaped David's lips and he smiled. "Yeah, if I hadn't, we'd have nothing to eat."

She chattered on. "I donated a few items of clothes to Goodwill the other day. I have way too many and decided to clean out my closet. You need to go through yours, too."

"That's a good idea. I'll do it."

"Don't get tomato sauce on your shirt. Here, let me wash that pot. You dry." She yelped and popped him back when he popped her with the dishtowel. He put away the last pan, tossed her over his shoulder, and carried her into the living room. The recliner held them both, and he stroked her hair while she continued to talk.

"You want kids, right?"

"Yes." He snickered. "What do you have on your mind?"

"I want us to have a child of our own someday, but I've been thinking about adoption. What do you think about that?"

"I haven't thought about it."

"I've been reading about the lack of foster parents in our area." She kissed him on the cheek. "Maybe we could have one of our own then be foster parents."

"I think I'd like to start now." He nuzzled her neck and bit her earlobe.

Sadie smacked him on the side of the head. "David, this is serious. I've been looking into foster care. It's a dire need around here."

He pulled her close and kissed her, smothering her words. She gave in and again, David's heart soared as he loved his beautiful wife.

On the river

"Dad, I want this job. I can make good money working at the casino."

Larson looked at the ground and back up at his son. He'd always dreamed that his children would finish school and go to college. Working hard labor and still struggling week to week to pay bills was not what he wanted for them. They were smart, and he wanted them to have better lives than he'd had.

"Lee, construction work is hard. You only have a few months to graduate, then you can go to college. You're getting scholarships. You're smart. Get an education so you can make a good living without working your butt off."

"But Dad, it's my life, and that's what I want. Mr. Crandall is paying a lot, and I can get that Jeep I've been looking at."

Larson shook his head. He'd always regretted not attending college, and Lee would, too. But he refused to listen, just like his dad. He couldn't see the future when the present seemed so bright.

Twenty-seven

David and Sadie were ready for another river trip. Since he returned from the mountains, he longed to visit the Island and fish a little. They sped down the river to their favorite fishing spot, Sadie standing behind the windshield enjoying the fine spray of cool water blowing on her hair and face. David loved seeing her happy. She had been promoted and began taking classes for broadcasting. Life was good.

"Let's drop in to visit the Shepherds before we head home." David finished a chicken leg and gulped a bottle of green tea. They caught a good mess of fish and had to get back in time to clean them.

When they approached the Island, they saw the road equipment moving dirt and laying concrete. Crandall Casino neared completion, and the construction crew worked building the port and driveway visitors would use. They built a special ferry boat to carry people to and from the Island. Lounge chairs faced wide windows on one deck, and a bottom deck would be used for transporting vehicles. A fully stocked bar accentuated one end and a grand piano faced a stage on the other end. According to crew members, Oliver hired a band to entertain casino members as they traveled to and from the casino. Vehicles would be left in a parking area on the mainland and visitors would be shuttled from the port to the casino and back.

David pulled the boat around to the dock and he and

Sadie walked to the Shepherd's home for a short visit. He enjoyed reminiscing as he walked around the place talking to Max while the ladies chatted. Max expressed concern for the river and Island people who frequented the casino boats.

"I have so many coming for help," he said. "Marriages are dissolving left and right because of addictions. Men and women alike are neglecting their families, and children are suffering. Even teenagers are being lured into illegal activities. The other day a single mom committed suicide because authorities caught her son selling drugs and sent him to prison."

David's jaw tightened. There had to be a way to solve this problem. "What can we do about it?"

"I've increased my meetings to two days a week and one weekend night to offer help to those who will come. I've reported the problem to authorities, but they do nothing." He scratched his head. "David, I'm sure a crime gang is heading this. We've got to find out who the leader is. I've got an idea, but until I'm sure, I can't say anything."

David glanced at Sadie who laughed at something Tammy said. How did I end up with such a beautiful, wonderful woman? And how is she the daughter of such a vicious, devious man? Did Max suspect her father was behind these crimes? It sure seemed possible. He grimaced and turned back to hear Max.

"How would you feel about staying here on the Island a while to help me do a little investigation? Think Sadie would be willing to be without you a few days?"

He glanced again at Sadie. "I'll talk to her about it. She's concerned about things around here, too. She's busy with classes and work. She may be glad for me to be gone a while."

Sadie agreed, and Max arranged for David to stay with a family at the head of the Island. He would be in disguise for the duration of his stay for his undercover work. Max laughed at the old man who stumbled along beside him on the narrow path. One of the locals had given Max a walking cane he designed from a vine and branch which had grown entwined together. David used the cane along with a disguise he had found in a costume store.

Under the alias Jack, David traversed the small island from head to foot, talking to Island dwellers and fishermen who frequented the area. Mentions of red and silver speedboats, an old beat-up looking river boat, and missing children sprinkled the conversations. Several doors slammed in his face when the gambling boats were mentioned. The subject was a sore spot for many because of addictions, and others for whom those boats provided an income.

He sat on the steps of a cabin, talking with the man and woman who lived there. "You folks sure have a nice place here. Looks like you take a lot of pride in your work, Frank."

"Yeah, me and Shirley want it to look nice. We built this here cabin ourselves, you know." His shining eyes took in the rich loam of a large fenced-in garden, a small orchard, and the picket fence around the yard of the neat log cabin which housed a family of five. Behind the cabin stood a barn surrounded by a board fence. Several cows and a mule milled about, and hogs grunted in a nearby pen. A flock of chickens pecked and scratched in the dirt beside their coup. By Island standards, they were well off.

"Mind if I ask where you work?"

"Nah, I don't mind tellin' ya. I work on one of the

gamblin' boats that travels the river." He hesitated. "The way I see it, it's an honest living for me. I got three kids, an' I want them to go off to college. I want them to have it better'n me and Shirley." Shirley stood behind him and put a hand on his shoulder. He continued. "I don't gamble, if'n that's what you're thinkin'. I know a lot who do, though."

"I admire a man who works hard." David tried to remember to use his old man voice. "It's them who take advantage of others I have trouble with. You know the kind."

"Sad to say, I'm afeared I do. There's quite a few around here, I tell ya. In fact, seems to be more all the time."

Careful not to arouse suspicion, David waited for him to say more. He didn't have to wait long.

"On the boat where I work, I see cheatin' goin' on all the time. The tables are rigged so the customers win once in a while. That way they keep comin' for more. The dealers make sure they keep most of the money on the boat."

"Hmmm. That's bad. And no one does anything about it?"

"Nah. They caint. Those who tried disappeared. I value my life. I keep my mouth shut."

"Can't blame a man for that." David swigged a glass of tea Shirley handed him and wiped his mouth on his shirt sleeve. "Ma'am, you sure make good tea. Thanks. Say, Frank, I've an idea. Think you could get me a job on a boat?"

Frank looked startled. "You want to work on the boat? Well, I don't know. You're a little...uh...."

"I know. I'm a little old. But I could do janitor work or maybe assist the clerks."

"I don't know, Jack. I guess I can try. You got a way to get there? You'll need a boat."

"Oh, sure. I have a motorboat. So, you'll try?"

"Yeah, why not. I'll talk to Jim tonight. Where can I find you to let you know?"

"I'll come by tomorrow around one. Sound okay?"

Frank went with David to the boat the next day and showed him around. It was crowded, and the air was filled with smoke and the smell of liquor. As the boat floated along, gamblers, bar keepers and dealers jostled against each other, often cursing in angry tones. David couldn't imagine anyone choosing to be here.

Gamblers and dealers alike ignored him as he wiped down slot machines and cleaned spills from the floor. He watched as a dealer manipulated cards to cheat gamblers. He saw a dealer with his foot on a pedal, stopping the spinning wheel at a spot of his choosing. He watched as money exchanged hands under the table. People's livelihoods were taken by dealers who in turn gave them to the owners of the gambling boat. Young and old alike entered the boat, laughing and dreaming of a win that would change their lives. Most left with a loss that could cost them everything when they didn't have enough money to pay their bills. His heart ached for these people who were blinded by the notion of becoming rich by gambling.

He returned to the Shepherd house about midnight to tell Max what he saw. The two men drank coffee and discussed the matter.

"I think we'll have to stay back until we can catch the real criminals, the ones running this ungodly organization," Max said. "We may be able to help, but it will take someone higher than us to find and stop the main character in this drama."

"That's about right." David licked the icing from a cinnamon roll and then ate it. Max wrinkled up his nose as he watched him. "It makes me sick to see this happening to the peaceful haven we once had here."

"Once had is right. It is becoming less a haven every day."

"That's why it needs to be investigated. It may take time to learn who heads the organized crime. Meanwhile, people are being ruined with addictions. They're losing their homes and their families. I try to help those who come, but I can't reach everyone."

David rose. "True. And many don't want help."

They finished their midnight snack, and David slept on the porch swing when Max went to bed. The next morning, David would go home to sleep the rest of the day in his own bed.

On his way to the pier, David heard someone call his name. A tall, scruffy-looking guy walked toward him. "Kingston! You don't remember me, do you?"

David squinted his eyes and stared until recognition dawned on his face. "Cosmo! Cosmo Rouge. When did you get back here?"

"I've been back a while now. Hey, I've been hearing good things about you. You married Sadie Crandall? And you own your own shipping company? Wow!"

David grinned. "Yeah, well, you know. So, what have you been up to since you left the island? You still into sports? I heard you played for the Charlotte Hornets."

"I did for a while. But I left them. I kinda figured I have

one body, and I need to take care of it. My knees were giving out. Anyway, I made enough money to do me for a while."

"I guess. Say, I had to check on a barge down river, but I'm headed back to the office. Why don't you drop by the house later and we'll rehash old times? Kade is keeping things going until I get back. I'll invite him over. It'll be fun."

"Sounds great, but I'll have to take a rain-check. I'm going to the boat for a little while. Want to join me?"

"No, I've got to get home. Sadie wants me to take her out tonight, and I don't want to disappoint her."

The two men waved as they parted, and a surge of happiness made him smile as his boat parted the water toward home and his Sadie.

On the river

"I don't care what he said, you're not going." Arthur slammed the door and shoved his wife down on the couch. "We don't need that preacher telling us how to live. We're doin' fine the way we are."

She whimpered and drew back. His temper had always been explosive, but since he had started visiting the casino, his drinking had increased and likewise, the abuse. Every day she feared for her life. When she mentioned the counseling services offered by Max Shepherd, he flipped.

It had to be more than just drinking too much and gambling. Whispers of illegal activities circulated among the other wives and paralyzing fear for their husbands and children overwhelmed them. They felt hopeless and alone.

Twenty-eight

"Sadie, you've lost weight. What have you been doing?" David embraced his wife. Her slim body seemed even more fragile through the thin dress she wore. Her wan face turned to him for a kiss and she held onto him for support. She turned and collapsed on the couch.

"Oh, David, I've been sick. Every day. I can't hold anything down but a little sweet tea."

"Have you talked to your mom?"

"I told her I didn't feel well, but since then, I'm feeling even worse. She's been out of town anyway. I think she came home today. I'm glad you're back. I've missed you."

David dialed his phone. "I'm making you an appointment to see Dr. Lucas. You should have let me know before now. I would have come home."

When they left the doctor's office, they each called their parents. "Meet us at Georgio's at six. We want to have dinner with you." Jesse, Kathleen and Melody agreed. They called Kade and Sophia and made reservations. The news for their family was so important, they had to share it in person.

They ate and visited, filling everyone in on recent events—David shared the news he'd heard on the Island, reserving the part about the Gold Boat for later when he and Jesse were alone. Sadie shared school events and chatted about her classes.

"Okay," Kade burst out. "There's something else going

on. It's written all over your faces." The others nodded in agreement. "We want to know now."

They pushed back their plates and looked at those facing them. David put his arm around Sadie, pulling her close. He nudged her and smiled into her face. "You tell them."

Sadie pulled out items from her bag, handed one to each person, and watched as her family members unfolded them. Melody opened hers first and read her tee-shirt. She squealed and ran around the table to hug Sadie.

"A grandma! I'm going to be a grandma?" By then Kathleen and Sophia were squealing with delight and smothering Sadie and David with hugs.

"Congratulations, son." Jesse shook his hand and Kade slapped his back. For the rest of the visit, baby talk and pregnancy stories dominated the conversation.

When they were alone, David served Sadie a cup of ginger tea. "Are you going to tell your dad?"

The idea of becoming a father consumed David's thoughts. Dr. Lucas gave Sadie medicine for her morning sickness, and she was better. David refused to allow her to lift a finger around the house. He always did his share of the housework, but now he did it all despite her protests. He insisted she focus on finishing her school assignments and studying for finals. Her graduation was close, and he didn't want her to be stressed.

"I'll tell him." Sadie stuck a pencil behind her ear and opened her laptop. "I don't know when, but I'll tell him."

"Don't wait too long. He needs to know."

"Why? He doesn't care about us. He won't care about our baby."

"Yes, he will. He cares about you and Kade, Sadie. He may be too irrational to know it right now, but he does love you. Let him know."

"I will. Not right now, but I will. Please go get me a sandwich while I finish this paper."

David fixed her a chicken sandwich and a glass of sweet tea. "Is there anything I can do to help you?"

"I need peace and quiet. This is my last paper and I need it to be good." She made a face at him. "You need to go visit Kade."

"There's something I need to do at the office anyway." He placed a light kiss on her forehead and a lingering kiss on the lips. She laughed and pushed him away. "I'll be back later. You rest."

Kade's Escalade pulled up beside him when he arrived at the office. "What are you doing here?"

"How's Sadie? Is she feeling better?"

"Yes, she is. The medicine is working. Now she wants to eat all the time."

Kade sidled around and leaned against the bed of the truck. "Dad is talking about moving to Colorado. Did he say anything to you?"

"No. I haven't seen him for a while. I don't think Sadie has talked to him either. I told her to tell him about the baby."

"Did she?"

"She said she would later." David shrugged. "What about Crandall Shipping?"

"He wants me to run it for him. What do you think?"

"Do you want to?"

Kade thumped at a grasshopper that landed on the fender of his truck. "I don't know. I guess I could do it."

David chuckled. "Of course, you can do it. You know the business as well as he does, maybe better. I wouldn't tell him that, though."

Kade leaned his head back and hooted. "No way! I'd tell him that if I wanted to die quick."

"Did he say when he plans to leave?"

"No, it isn't definite. He's just thinking about it. I can see him doing it, though. He's alone now. I heard his woman dumped him. Guess she found herself another sugar-daddy."

"That's so sad and unnecessary. Such a waste." David blew out his cheeks and sighed. "He had everything. A wonderful family, a great business — everything. Why would a man throw all that away?"

Kade ruminated a moment. "Your Dad told me something once I can't get out of my head. He said a river without borders becomes a slough. The way I see it, borders represent self-discipline. For whatever reason, Dad has no self-discipline and his life has become like a back-water swamp."

"Yeah. It makes me sad for such a great man as your dad to lose all control. He's always so angry."

"He wasn't always like that. I remember when I was a kid, we had so much fun fishing and camping. He took me to ball games. Well, you know. You were with us most of the time."

"I remember. We sure had a lot of fun times. In fact, we still do."

Kade opened his truck door and climbed in. "True. I think we're due for another river trip." David raised his thumb as Kade drove away.

He ran up the steps and opened his office door in time

to hear the phone. An older client wanted to meet with him.

"If you want, come on up now. I'm in my office for the afternoon."

In a little while, he and Abe Sanders were laughing over coffee and donuts. "David, I have an opportunity you won't believe. It's a business deal of a lifetime."

David looked over the paperwork and stared at Abe. It would be a great opportunity, but it could ruin Oliver. Abe wanted David to partner with him.

"Kingston, you don't want to pass up this deal. Think of how it will benefit you. I heard you're going to be a parent. Have you considered the cost of raising a child? It's astronomical. College alone costs thousands of dollars."

"Yeah, I know." David looked again at the proposition, hoping for a way to accept the offer without damaging Crandall Shipping. But he saw none.

"Let me have a little time to consider it."

"Sure. Take a couple of days. This window of opportunity won't be open long."

David stayed in his office the rest of the day, pacing the floor. He gazed out the window, watching the river. He talked to his board members who encouraged him to accept the offer.

"David, you can't turn down this offer. You're not doing it to hurt Crandall, but to help yourself. You'll be set for life. Crandall has done nothing but try to sink you ever since you started working for him. Think of yourself for once." The next day, they begged and pleaded. His office staff tried to convince him, and even his older clients expressed their opinions in favor of the deal. David paced the floor. He didn't tell Sadie or Kade about the offer. He slept little.

He decided to end his dilemma and called Sanders. He would not take the deal. He would not be the downfall of his nemesis.

"I understand," said Sanders. "Kingston, you are a man among men. I'm glad to be your friend. I'll find another businessman further down the river to share this opportunity."

A week later, David came out of a gas station to find Oliver leaning against his truck. "I've been waiting on you, Kingston." Oliver scanned David's face and seemed content with what he saw.

"How are you?" David reached for the door handle, but Oliver put his hand on his arm.

"I'm doing okay, David. I heard you and Sadie are going to be parents. Congratulations."

"Thank you."

"I have a question for you, if you don't mind."

"Sure. What is it?"

Oliver kicked a tire and scratched his nose. "Why didn't you do it?"

"Do what?" David watched his face.

"You know. Accept the deal Sanders offered you."

"I thought about it but decided against it."

"But why? I would have jumped at the chance for a deal like that."

"I'm not you."

"No, you're not. You're not like me." Oliver grimaced. "You could have ruined me, you know."

"I know."

He turned to leave but whirled around and stuck out

his hand. "Thank you, son. You're a better man than I am." He turned to leave again, glanced back, hesitated, and walked back to David. "Come back to Crandall Shipping and help me, Kingston? With your help I could restore the company and save my clients. We could even merge our companies and have one successful business. What do you say?"

David stared at him. *Go back to Crandall? Merge? What's he thinking? He's kidding, right?* "You want me to give you my business?"

Oliver blinked. "No, that's not what I said. We could join forces and together build an unbeatable shipping company. Together. The two of us."

"Except for you, I would never have left. You forced me out."

"Ah, let's not talk about old conflicts. It's water under the bridge. We can give it another try and make it work. What do you say?"

"I'll have to think about it and pray about it," David said.

"Well, okay. I know that's important to you. Go say your prayers and let me know when you decide."

David watched him leave, not believing what took place. No way would he ever merge with Crandall. That would be suicide for Kingston Shipping and for him personally.

On the river

A soundless motorboat with a lone passenger moved around the perimeter of the Island. Jesse cast his line close to a dead log in hopes of catching a catfish. He missed his home on the island and came here often to fish a little and spend quiet time in prayer and meditation.

A red speedboat pulled up beside him. Jesse raised his hand in salute when he saw who drove the boat. They hadn't spoken for a long time, but they were friends from childhood. This man had endangered the life of his son numerous times. What could possibly want now?

"Kingston! Pull up." The speedboat docked, and Jesse pulled next to it and stepped onto the bank. "Have you heard the news?"

Jesse secured his boat. "What news?"

"I'm moving to Colorado and taking the kids with me. We'll be leaving in a month."

"Have they agreed with your plan?"

"Of course, they have. I talked to them about it last week. They are happy about the move."

Jesse shrugged. "They haven't said anything to me. I'm sure David would have told me of such a move."

"Well, Sadie wants to go, and she'll convince David. It's the best thing for them."

"And David's business? What about that?"

Oliver's laugh was bitter. "What about it? He's losing it anyway. I've made sure of that."

Jesse reddened. "What do you mean, you've made sure of that? What have you done?"

Oliver snickered. "Oh, you'll find out." He jumped back into his boat and sped away.

Twenty-nine

"David, help." Sadie's cries woke him from a sound sleep. She doubled over the commode with blood running down her legs.

"Oh sweetheart. What's wrong?" David lifted her and carried her to the bed. He grabbed his phone and dialed 911. His heart pounded in his chest, and he held her hand on the way to the hospital. The crowded waiting room had no seats, so he waited in the hall next to the door where he last saw her white face as the nurses wheeled her away.

Nurses and doctors scurried in and out of doors and hurried from one place to another. Pungent odors of medicine mixed with disinfectants filled his nostrils, and stark white walls and floors made him feel alone. He retched when a hacking cough came from the waiting room. An intern raced down the hall guiding a stretcher holding a small boy. Parents followed, sobbing and holding one another. Pleading supplication rose from white lips as David gripped his stomach and watched the stainless-steel doors.

After what seemed like hours, the door opened. In his blurred vision someone in a white coat walked toward him, and a hand took his arm to guide him to the chapel. *The chapel?* The blood drained from his face and his heart lurched. The door of the chapel opened. One foot in front of the other. He stumbled toward a bench. The nurse was speaking. *What was she saying?*

"Mr. Kingston, we've called Dr. Lucas and he's on the way. Please have a seat."

He looked at the pews.

All in nice rows.

All covered with nice, blue cushions.

She had been so white, but her lips were blue.

The blood…why was she bleeding?

How could he ever live without…? No, he wouldn't think of it.

When would the doctor get here?

He glanced at his wrist, but it was bare. He hadn't thought to grab his watch.

The door squeaked when it opened. The doctor came in and sat beside him.

"Sadie. Where is she? Is she all right?" His chest felt tight.

What if she wasn't okay? What if…no, that wasn't possible.

"She's resting now. She'll be okay. We'll watch her for the next day or two. I'm sorry, but she lost the baby."

David blew his breath out in relief. His Sadie would be all right. *But wait, she lost the baby?* He leaned over and put his face in his hands. He pulled them back, wet. The doctor patted him. "I'm so sorry, Mr. Kingston."

"When can I see her?"

"She will be in recovery an hour. You may see her then. A nurse will come for you." He started to leave but turned back. "When she wakes, she won't know about the baby."

She was sleeping when he entered her room. He sat beside her and held her hand until she woke. "Hi, Sleeping Beauty." He kissed her and stroked her hair. She licked her dry lips and looked around, confused.

"What happened?" She rolled her head, and foggy eyes gazed out the window. "Oh, I remember."

"The doctor says you'll be okay. You have to rest."

"The baby? Is she okay?"

David stroked her arm and kissed her hand.

"David! Is the baby okay?" He shook his head and tears gushed when she squeezed her eyes shut. Together they cried.

Sadie's mother came every day for the next couple of weeks to help care for her. She and David fixed all her favorite foods, but she refused to eat. When she soaked her pillows with tears, David brought her dry ones. Why couldn't he could take her pain away? Her white face against the pillows was a constant reminder of her anguish. Dr. Lucas gave her anti-depressants and said she needed to get out, go shopping, or go on a trip to help her get better. She refused to get out of the house for anything.

"Sadie, let's go down the river. A fishing trip would do you good." She glared at him and refused. Her mom begged her to go to New York shopping. She gave an emphatic 'No!".

David slammed his clenched fist into his other hand. How could he pull his beloved Sadie from the dark pit? She kept sinking deeper and deeper.

At last, she completed her classes, and he managed to talk her into going to the grocery store once a week. Still, her sadness dampened the hearts of everyone who entered the room she inhabited. David took her to a therapist until she refused to go. Her smiles were strained, she never laughed, and the light in her eyes no longer existed. She became a walking, talking mannequin. One day David came home from work to find her gone. She had packed her bags and left, with a short note explaining. But it didn't explain anything.

David, I've gone with Dad to Colorado. I won't be back.
I'll send papers for you to sign for a divorce. Sadie

His Sadie left. His phone calls went straight to voice mail at first, then 'the number you dialed is no longer in service' was all he got. She cut off all means of communication.

Dear God, what have I done to deserve this? His prayers bounced off cold, steel heavens. God had forsaken him. His heart had shredded into tiny pieces. *If only I had been shot. If only that Jeep or that boat had hit its target. I wouldn't be here. This pain is too great to bear.* Even encouragement from his parents and Kade failed to lift his spirits.

Once again, he sought the solace of his Willow Grove. He spent one day on the sandy beach, praying and thinking. He tossed a small stone into the river and shuddered as he watched the ripples move across the water. *What was the article he read the other day about the Ripple Effect? Every person is six steps from being connected to every other person on the planet. So that means everything he says and does could – or would – have an effect, not only on those around him, but those around the globe.*

If the ripples from a little stone had so much impact, what would happen if he tossed a big rock? He found a large one and threw it as far as he could into the river. He cringed as waves from the rock extended far into the water. He wasn't responsible for what Sadie did, but he had to make right decisions for his own life. His employees and their families depended on him for their livelihoods, and he couldn't disappoint them. He wouldn't let them down.

While boating back to the city, he saw a woman running along the bank. He slowed his boat and watched her a moment. She appeared to be in desperation. He pulled close to the bank ahead of her and went ashore to wait. She spotted him and stopped. Her red, swollen face showed signs of bruises, and blood smeared across her face from a gash above her eye.

"Do you need help, ma'am?" She leaned against a tree, holding on to a limb jutting out beside her. Her body went limp, and she slid onto the ground. David ran to assist her. It appeared she'd been beaten, and in addition to new bruises there were signs of old bruises on her neck and face. Her arms were purple and scarred, and new cuts bled on her hands and wrists.

"What kind of brute did this to you?" David muttered as he applied a wet rag to her forehead, careful not to touch her wound. Her eyes opened in narrow slits and she groaned. He dabbed at her face with the rag until her eyes flew open. She tried to rise but collapsed back onto the ground.

"No, I have to go." She took David's arm, and he helped her to a sitting position. Her eyes darted to the path behind her and back to David's face. "Who are you?"

"I'm David. Ma'am, you're going to be fine. We have to get you to a doctor."

"No! I have to go home. Please help me." She struggled to rise, then gasped and winced with pain. David saw the blood covering her legs. Red gashes along her legs and knees were raw and swollen.

"Who did this to you? What happened?"

Her eyes darted beyond David toward the river. "No. I fell. I'm always falling."

"Can you tell me your name?" David lifted her to her feet, holding on to her arm to keep her from falling.

She lowered her head. "Tashina."

"Tashina, I have to get you to a hospital. You need medical attention."

"No, I have to go home." She let go of his arm and tried to walk, but her legs gave way. David guided her to sit on a log.

"Is someone after you?"

"No." She looked around. "He can't see me here with you."

"Who? Your husband?" She hung her head.

"Did he do this to you?" She blushed and kept her eyes lowered.

"Look, you don't have to be ashamed. You're not responsible for what another person did to you."

Pleading eyes met his. "It's my fault. He gets so mad at me. But he's always sorry after he hits me. This time was worse, though. I feared he would kill me."

"He could have, and next time he probably will. It's not your fault." David helped her up again, this time with a firm grip on her arms. "I'm taking you to the hospital and I'm calling a friend who can help you. I can't make you leave this man, but I will promise to find you help if you'll accept it." He lifted her small, frail body and carried her to his boat.

Tashina seemed relieved, though still afraid, as a nurse checked her over. The doctor admitted her, and David called Sophia. She talked to Tashina who admitted she wanted to leave her abusive husband. Together they found a social worker who would help.

"There are so many of these women needing a place to stay." The social worker, Carmen, showed sympathy for Tashina and others like her. "Because they are beaten down and feel they have no value, they need special counselling. If they don't get it, they tend to return to the men who beat them. You'd be surprised how many spend their lives in terror and how many actually die from abuse."

A few days later David went back on the river to check on a transport boat. He tied his boat and stood talking to the captain about the situation when an old john boat pulled up beside them.

A rugged looking man with a cigarette dangling from his lips yelled over to David. "You own this boat?"

"Yes. May I help you?" David walked closer to hear the man.

"You're gonna need help if you don't keep out of my business." The man's face flushed. He removed the cigarette to avoid losing it while he ranted.

David leaned toward the man. "What are you talking about? I don't even know you."

"I don't know you either, but it was your boat that took my wife. Go ahead and deny it."

Realizing it must be Tashina's husband, David stiffened. "Your wife named Tashina?"

"Yeah, that's her. She's my wife and you got no business bothering another man's wife."

"You the guy who beat her? You scumbag. A big ole guy like you beating up a little woman like her. You're the scum of the earth to do such a thing. You're no man."

The man shook his fist in the air and roared. "Why, I'll kill you. You got no call to talk to me that way."

David gestured. "Come on up, mister. I'm not a helpless woman. I'll show you how it feels to hit a man. Come on."

The man swore and turned his boat back down the river. The captain of the transport boat laughed when David exhaled and wiped his brow.

On the river

Ally wiped her tears as she watched her one-year-old playing on the floor. She didn't know what to do. She had no one to rely on. Her mom was sent to prison and she didn't even know who her dad was. Her baby's daddy left when she told him she was pregnant. She tried to take care of the little girl, but she was too young to get a job that paid anything. She got some government assistance, but it wasn't enough. Her rent was overdue, and the landlord had given her a week to move.

If only she knew someone who would take the baby just long enough for her to get a good paying job. Then she could provide for her baby. Then she could feel good about herself. There was nothing for her on the island. She had a friend who left the island to find a job. Maybe she could help her. She didn't want to abandon her baby, but she had nothing to offer a child. She just needed a hand up.

Thirty

Days were filled with work, and nights were lonely without his Sadie. Melody tried to contact her, but to no avail. Sadie seemed to have dropped off the face of the earth. One morning a man in a suit handed David a manila envelope, turned, and fled. Divorce papers. David looked them over and laid them on the table. He would not sign them. If she wanted to get a divorce, she would have to do it all by herself.

Sitting in his office having a pity-party threatened to get the best of him, so David decided to take a walk in the River Park. He watched the ducks and a pair of swans out on the water when someone spoke his name.

"Mr. Kingston? Nice to see you again. Do you remember me?"

"Sure. Tashina, isn't it? How are you?" She looked great. When he took her to the hospital, she appeared frail and distressed. Now her face shone, and she'd put on enough weight to look good.

"Thanks to you, I'm all right. I'm looking for a job. I want to make enough money to take classes. I'm thinking about getting into nursing."

"That sounds great. Say, why don't you come to my office and put in an application. I could use extra help right now."

A smile spread across her face. "Oh, thank you. I'll do it."

The next week she was working at Kingston Shipping. Ms. Emma trained her as an office clerk, and David encouraged her to take a night class in computers to expand her training. He also advanced her pay to buy necessary apparel for work, since she left all her possessions when she left her husband. She would stay at the women's center until she earned enough to rent an apartment and was certain her husband would leave her alone.

"That girl was so shy when she first came," Ms. Emma said to David. "But she isn't shy anymore. I think she has her cap set for you."

David laughed. "Nah, she's just getting her wings. For the first time in a long time, she's seeing herself in a good light."

"You know, it's amazing how a mean husband can make a woman feel worthless. When a good one comes along and treats her nice, she starts feeling like a desirable woman." She thumped him on the head. "Be careful, David. Don't make her fall for you."

He was busy at his desk when he looked up to see Tashina at his door. She smiled and leaned against the door frame.

"Working on something important?" Her voice had a soft, musical quality. David smiled and motioned for her to come in. The fragrance of her perfume filled the room, reminding him of the honeysuckles growing on the Island. Everything about her reminded him of the Island. He stood.

"Want to go grab lunch?"

Her face lit up. "Sure. I'm hungry."

They laughed together as they ate, learning about each other's lives.

"You mean you and Kade were raised on the Island?" Her brown eyes twinkled as he shared memories of the two playing along the river.

"I moved there when I married Arthur. At first, it was great. Then things turned sour for us." Her face contorted, and she changed the subject. "How did you get into the shipping business?"

She watched his face as he told her about his journey, and her countenance mirrored her emotions as he talked. The warmth of her hand when it covered his caused him to glance down, but she didn't seem to be cognizant of her action. She laughed at his humor and made interjections as he talked.

"You are a very good listener." David's words brought a wide smile to her face. "Good listeners are hard to find."

"I've had plenty of practice listening." She opened her wallet, but David raised his hand and paid the waitress. "Sometimes a person doesn't have a choice but to listen."

"I'm sorry you've had such a hard time. No one deserves that kind of treatment." David put his hand on her back as they exited the restaurant. He led her to his truck and opened the door for her. As she slid into the seat, she took his hand and held it a moment. He raised her hand to his lips but dropped it like it was hot. His face turned pink and he hurried around the truck.

At work, Tashina found reasons to visit David's office. Questions about a document or an article to show him. They laughed over YouTube videos and shared funny jokes and stories. David complimented her on the work she did and bragged about her to Ms. Emma within her hearing. He noticed Ms. Emma frowning as she worked and often shaking her head as she watched them together.

Tashina stuck her head around the door facing. "Let's go to lunch."

David jumped up and as they left, Tashina reached for his hand. David glanced at Ms. Emma whose eyes were wide. As he helped Tashina into his truck, she kissed him on the cheek. He dismissed the kiss as nothing but a friendly gesture.

They talked and laughed as they ate. "Can we go for a little walk before we go back to work?" Tashina pulled him toward the park, and he yielded.

She laughed at the waddling ducks and squealed when a goose chased her. He encouraged her to pull off her shoes and wade in the shallow water. She splashed him when he stooped down to watch a crawdad.

"David, hold me up." He held her arm while she used a tissue to dry her feet. She leaned into him, and his arm went around her shoulders. He pulled her close and looked into her eyes. She turned to him and lifted her face.

Instead of green eyes, he saw brown. Instead of soft, auburn curls, he saw straight black hair. In place of Gucci was a floral scent. Nice, but not his Sadie.

He smiled at her and took her hand. He entwined his fingers in hers. She touched his wedding ring.

"Still wearing that thing?"

"Habit, I guess." He twisted it off and stuck in in his pocket. He didn't leave Sadie. She left him. What was he supposed to do? Suspend his life in midair until she decided to snap it back at her pleasure? Hadn't his heart bled enough over her?

Days in the office were filled with laughter and teasing as David and Tashina fused work and pleasure despite Ms. Emma's disapproving glances. Frequent evening walks in the park ended with long talks under the stars. Images of auburn hair and green eyes dimmed as the tangible slim body with black hair and brown eyes snuggled against him as they talked.

"Won't you please come in?" Tashina opened her apartment door and stepped inside after a passionate kiss on the welcome matt. David hesitated but then entered. After a cup of coffee, she pulled him to the couch and turned on soft music.

"Thanks, Tashina. Thanks for your companionship. Thanks for making me laugh." He kissed her lightly on the lips and rose.

"No. Please stay." Tashina laced her fingers through his and lifted her face. He touched her cheek and leaned down as he embraced her. The kiss was hard, and she gasped but returned the kiss with fervor.

David pulled back and stared into her face.

"What?" She put her hand to her mouth. "What are you thinking?"

He pushed her shoulders away from him and reached into his pocket for his truck keys. When he pulled them out, something fell on the floor between them. It was his wedding ring. He stared at it, then at her. He reached to pick it up and rotated it between his fingers.

"You still love her."

"I don't know. I'm not sure how I feel." He grabbed her and pulled her against his chest, but she pulled away.

"Did you sign those divorce papers?"

David shrugged. "No. They're still lying on the table where I threw them."

She frowned and stepped back. "Then you're still married." She turned her back to him.

"Tashina, I..."

"No." She walked to the door and opened it. "I thought you were a good man, David. I won't be involved with a married man. I could fall in love with you, but it's obvious you love Sadie. I don't understand why you haven't gone after her before now."

"She left me."

"Do you even know why?"

"No. I haven't been able to contact her to ask." An unexpected shudder rose in his chest.

"You need to find her and ask her. She's gone through a lot and she needs you. Now go."

"Thank you, Tashina. You are a rare friend." His lips brushed her cheek, and he headed for his truck. His heart felt lighter than it had in a long time.

The next day he packed a bag and went to the office. "Ms. Emma," he called, "would you please come in here?" She raised her eyebrows when she closed the door.

"Don't say a word," he said. "I need you to tell Jacob to take care of things around here. I'm leaving, but I'll be back."

Ms. Emma put her hands on her hips. "Humphf! It's about time you do something constructive. Go get that child. I'll handle things around here."

David laughed and squeezed her shoulders. "I know

you're well able."

He jumped in his truck and drove to Crandall Shipping where he found Kade with his feet on his desk, eating celery and peanut butter.

"Come on, we're taking a trip."

Kade jumped to his feet. "We going to Colorado to find a lost sheep?"

"Yes. That's exactly where we're going." Within an hour Kade's bags were packed, and they were on the road. He would find his Sadie and bring her home.

On the river

Lila slipped on her red high heels and grabbed her purse. Dan was taking her to the casino. She had been wanting to go but living on a little social security plus a small pension from Dan's job was hard. When she saved money from selling eggs to neighbors, Dan agreed to take her.

Her eyes sparkled as she waited on Dan to open her door. He was such a gentleman. Since he was conscious of spending too much, she would be thrifty and spend only what she had saved. The time spent out with her husband would be worth all the weeks she had worked to sell the eggs. She silently sent up a thank you to God for her laying hens.

Thirty-one

They took turns driving because David wanted to get there as soon as possible. They would look at the resort where David and Sadie stayed on their previous visit. Every time they stopped to eat, David rushed Kade.

"Come on, man. You don't need to eat so much."

"Yes, I do. I'm still a growing boy. You need to eat. You're nothing but bones. My sister has sure done a number on you."

They arrived at their destination late and would search for her the next morning.

"Come on, David, let's find food. There's a restaurant over there."

His heart lifted. At least he was doing something. He would find his Sadie and take her home. He ordered the house special—cut-with-a-fork pork steak, buttered potatoes, corn-on-the-cob, and hot rolls—and dug in.

Kade laughed at him. "Son! You must be starving. You'd better slow down."

"I haven't had more than a bag of potato chips and a Pepsi in three days. In fact, since Sadie left, I haven't eaten a solid meal." David drank a glass of sweet tea and asked the waiter to refill it. "That's over. I'm going to find my lady and take her home."

They chose pecan pie for dessert and were paying the bill when David saw him. The man who knocked him into the snow the night he and Sadie were at the resort. He sat at a table with a woman, laughing and talking.

David walked over to him. "Excuse me. Haven't we met before?"

The man stared and shook his head. "I don't think so. I don't remember you."

"May I sit a moment?"

The man nodded his head. "Sure. Have a seat. I'm sorry I don't recognize you. What'd you say your name is?"

"David. David Kingston."

The man's eyes widened. "Kingston. Oh, wait, I do remember. You were at the resort with that...oh!" He shoved back his chair. "I'm sorry about my behavior, Kingston. I...I...I didn't know she was your wife. I didn't know what I was doing. I was drinking."

"Yeah, I'm sure you were. I have one question. Were you acting on your own, or did you have another reason to single us out for that little escapade on the sidewalk and at the resort?"

The man held up both hands. "I told you I was drinking."

"I just wondered. No hard feelings." David rose to leave.

The man extended his hand toward David and chuckled. "That little wife of yours — now she can take care of herself, that one can." David ignored the man's hand and started to walk away when the man called him back. "Look, buddy, I'm sorry for my behavior that night. But you're right. I acted on orders from my boss. He's a manager at the resort. He gave me a bonus for harassing you. I don't know why. But you know, a buck is a buck. Sorry."

David scowled. "Humph. Some people have no regard for others. I guess you don't care who you have to hurt to make a dollar."

"I didn't hurt anyone." The man sneered. "I guess you don't know how it feels to have to work for what you get, rich boy."

Kade stood close by, listening. He walked to David's side. "Well," he drawled, "at least you got one thing right." He put his hand on David's shoulder. "This boy is rich. He's rich in ways you'll never know. He's rich with integrity. He's rich with values that would never allow him to harm or harass anyone for any amount of money. He's rich with family and friends. And you need to thank God I'm with him, and he's my role model. That's all that is keeping me from hurting you." He turned to David. "Come on, family and friend. Let's get out of here."

On a hunch Sadie might be at the resort where she and David stayed before, the next morning David and Kade headed there. People were milling about the large lobby and the busy restaurant, but they saw no sign of Sadie or Oliver.

David went to the desk, and the clerk shook his head when David asked about them. He and Kade found a table in the restaurant and ordered. At least they could have a bite to eat. They were digging into the food when they heard a commotion behind them.

"I won't do it! Why do you always do this to me?" David's head jerked up when he heard the voice followed by angry sobbing.

Kade put his hand on David's arm and shook his head. "Wait," he whispered. "Listen and learn. Let them alone for now."

David's face grew crimson as the conversation escalated. "Sadie. Be reasonable. He doesn't want you if you can't give him a child."

"Yes, he does. I love him. I don't love Jasper." The sobbing grew louder. David sat erect in his chair, but Kade gripped his arm.

"Then why did you leave him? Answer that!"

The sound of a chair hitting the floor and the answer brought David to his feet. "Because you told me to. I never would have left him if you hadn't convinced me I should. You're the one who's always wanted me to marry Jasper. Do you even know how evil he is? Why would you do that to your own daughter?"

Sadie whirled around in time to collide with David as he rushed to her. She gasped as he pulled her into a hard embrace, then realizing who held her, she sobbed into his chest.

David glared at Oliver whose face turned from red to white. His fists clenched and unclenched as he struggled with the prospect of flattening the older man. Before he made up his mind, Kade stepped between them.

"Come on, Dad. You've made enough trouble." With a firm hand, he guided Oliver toward the door, paying the waitress on the way out. Oliver yielded, and Kade shoved him into the elevator. "Sadie will be up to get her things. You'd best stay in your room until she leaves."

While Sadie went to get her bags, David and Kade waited in the lounge. David stood, staring out the window while Kade paced the floor.

"Tell you what, I'll stay here with Dad, so you and

Sadie can have time alone," Kade said.

"Actually, Sadie and I may stay awhile to get things sorted out. I'll have to find out what she wants to do." David twisted the wedding ring on his finger.

Sadie had other ideas. "David, I don't want to go home yet."

"But Sadie, I thought…"

"Oh, don't worry." Sadie stroked his bearded face. "I need a little time to get my feelings sorted out. My aunt lives a little way from here, and I'd like to go see her."

"Okay, we'll go see her."

"No. I mean I want to go alone."

David pulled back. "Alone? You aren't coming home?"

She turned her back to David. "I…I left you, David. I let my Dad influence me to leave my husband. I need to figure out why I listened. I have some major soul searching to do to get my life straightened out. You understand, don't you?"

"No, I don't. You can search your soul at home. I'll help you figure it out. You need to go see a therapist or doctor."

She shook her head. "Please let me do this. You deserve better, and I don't know if I can be that for you. I promise I won't take long to figure it out."

David ran his hands over his eyes. He couldn't believe it. He came to get her. He heard her say she still loved him. She acted like she did, so then, what was the problem?

She touched his cheek and pecked him on the lips. Then she left. David watched her walk to the elevator. He watched her move from one foot to the other as she waited. He watched her walk through the doors and disappear when they closed. His whole life vanished through those doors. He gritted his teeth and swallowed hard several times.

The pressure of a hand on his arm made him turn.

"Come on, David." Kade led him out the door and to the truck.

On the river

"How did it go today, sweetheart?" Lucy lugged her swollen body up from the armchair and waddled to the kitchen. She pulled a container from the oven and put it on the table with a glass of sweet tea.

Ronnie removed his dirty boots and threw his greasy shirt into the washing machine.

"It's hard, Lucy. But I'm glad to have this job. Maybe we can save enough to get our own place, then we can get married." He looked around. "Where's Mom and Dad?"

"They went into town. Your dad asked me today when we're moving out. I don't think he likes me."

"Ah, you know Dad. He's mad because you're pregnant and we're not married. He says we're living in sin under his roof."

"I know. My parents are the same way. I wish they'd let us live with them until we can get our own place. They don't even want to admit I'm pregnant."

Ronnie put his arm around her and patted her belly. "It's their loss. One day both our parents will regret the way they feel. If they don't, they'll never see this child."

Lucy patted his bearded face. "Ronnie, I know this job is hard and dangerous. Please be careful climbing that scaffolding. After the baby is born, I'll go back to work at the diner. I promise."

Ronnie planted a kiss on her forehead. "It'll be okay, Lucy. I'll be careful. You just take care of yourself and little Ronnie Junior."

Thirty-two

Back at home, David walked around like a robot. He ate only when his family and friends insisted and slept little. He did his work without thinking. Ms. Emma fussed over him. She corrected mistakes he made and covered for his lack of attention to his clients. She insisted he eat the food she brought for him. In the weeks of Sadie's absence, he became pale and gaunt. One day he came home from work to find his wife in the kitchen, making dinner.

When he came in, she turned and waved a spatula. "Hungry?"

He held her gaze until she turned back to the stove. "What're you making? Smells good."

A slow smile spread across her face. "Your favorite. Shrimp scampi with angel hair pasta."

He watched her as he set at the table and poured glasses of sweet tea. She would have to come to him. He watched as she chopped vegetables for a salad and set Italian dressing on the table beside it. She sat across from him and reached out her hand. He took it, bowed his head and blessed the food. For a while, they ate in silence.

"How's the company doing?" Sadie asked.

"Fine."

"How are your parents?"

"Good."

"Are you going to talk to me?"

David raised his head and gazed at her long and hard. "I don't know what to say, Sadie. My family is good, my company is good. Is that what you want to talk about?"

"No. I want to talk about us."

He shoved back his chair. "What about us?"

She sat in his lap and ran her fingers through his hair. "Are we going to still be us?"

"I guess that's up to you. You're the one who left and refused to come home when I went for you. I've done all I know to do."

"I know. Things have changed."

"What, Sadie? What has changed? I'm still the same."

She moved to sit beside him. "I have. When I went to Aunt Lottie's we had a long talk, and she prayed with me. I hadn't done that in a long, long time. It's what I needed more than anything. She helped me see things the way I never saw them before."

"That's good. So how do you see things now?"

"I see I'm too gullible. I should have never listened to Dad. I should have stayed with you." She bit her lip. "Dad has been hounding me a long time to leave you."

David jumped to his feet. "WHAT? How dare he? Why, I'll…"

Sadie pulled him back into the chair. "Don't, David. I couldn't tell you. I didn't know what you would do."

"When did he do that?"

She stood and walked to the window. "You remember when you refused that deal with Abe Sanders? You know, he wanted you to merge Kingston Shipping with Crandall Shipping? That's when it started."

"Oh, Sadie! You've been through so much pressure. I

can't believe he did that to you. His own daughter! It's all my fault."

"No, it isn't." She put her hand to his cheek. "You haven't done anything wrong. Dad put pressure on me, and I gave in." Once again, she stood. "I'm weak. I've put you through a lot, David."

He pulled her back onto his lap. "Sweetheart, I'm so sorry you've been put through this. I know losing the baby hurt you. I understand you went through a dark time. I wish you'd let me share the good and the bad. You don't have to go through hard times by yourself. I hurt too, and I'm here."

"I realize that now. I'm sorry I lost our baby." Sobs racked her body, and he tried to soothe her.

"I just wish you had told me what he was doing. I wouldn't do anything rash, Sadie. I could have done something."

"I was afraid. I don't want your life ruined because of him." She closed her eyes and leaned her head against his shoulder.

"You can't carry such a heavy burden alone, and I don't want you to. You have to tell me what you're going through and what you're feeling. I can't even put into words how much I care for you."

"I don't know why I didn't realize it before. I know now you would've known what to do."

He stroked her hair. The scent of Gucci drifted into his nostrils, bringing back memories of their first date. He nuzzled her soft curls and ran his fingers along the curves of her neck and down her shoulders. For a long moment they were lost in the circle of their embrace, seeing, hearing, and feeling their love for each other. David pulled back first.

"You said you've changed. What has changed, Sadie?"

"When I stayed with Aunt Lottie, I saw things I've never realized. A passion awakened in me, David. I want to do something different with my life."

"Like what? You don't want to be a television broadcaster?"

"I don't think so. I went to college to be a journalist because it's what I always dreamed about. But a lot of things have changed. The field of journalism has changed, until it doesn't feel real anymore." Her head leaned back, and her gaze shifted upward. "I'm looking at taking classes in social work."

"Really? Why?"

"I saw Aunt Lottie work with children, and I admired her involvement. She's a therapist in a school and she helps those children who have such serious problems. I think I'll be good at working with kids."

"You do like little kids, don't you?"

"I do. Do you know there are hundreds of children left alone every day, hungry, abused, and neglected? Hundreds, David. There aren't enough foster homes to house all those kids." Her face glowed and her eyes sparkled as she talked. David was entranced.

"A lot of times the Department of Human Services has to leave children in abusive situations because there's no place for them. DHS can't remove children from a home until they find a place for them. It's sad. I guess people don't care."

"Maybe people do care, but they don't know what to do."

"I guess. Seems to me the people who care most are the poor people."

"That may be true, but I'm sure it isn't always. Maybe if you tell people about the problem, they would care more and want to help." He kissed her fingers. "Sounds like you have a lot of work ahead of you."

"Yes, and I'm going tomorrow to get registered." She jumped up and pulled David to his feet. "Come on. I have a lot to do."

David whistled a tune as he threw his briefcase on the desk, opened it, and riffled through the contents. Ms. Emma laughed as she watched him. "I sure am glad you're happy again, David. You're looking better, too. Putting a little weight back on. Looking buff."

David patted his stomach. "Yeah, Sadie's a better cook than me. I hope I don't get fat."

"A little fat never hurt anyone." Ms. Emma patted her own plump form and giggled. "How is she doing in her new classes?"

"She's working hard, but she loves being back in school. It's all she talks about anymore."

"I'm proud of her for what she's doing. She'll be able to help a lot of kids, and I know there are a lot who need an advocate to help them."

"Without a doubt she has changed since she's come home. She's like a different person." The change in his wife amazed David. A passion grew in her like he'd never seen. Every night she researched children's advocates and organizations focused on helping children. As she studied, she shared with David things she learned and things her professors discussed during class.

"Hi, Sadie. Come give me a hug." Ms. Emma's greeting made David look up from where he stood in Tashina's office. He was helping her with a computer program glitch when he heard Ms. Emma's greeting. He leaned over Tashina's shoulder to move the cursor, showing her how to fix the problem when Sadie came through the door. She stopped short when she saw Tashina.

David moved to her, leaned to give her a kiss, and saw the fire in her eyes as she stared at the pretty, black-headed woman at the desk. "Oh, Sadie, I guess you haven't met Tashina. She started working here while you were gone."

"Hello, Tashina." Icicles almost formed on her words.

"Tashina, this is my wife, Sadie."

Tashina stood and extended her hand. Sadie gave it a limp shake and held on to David's arm. Tashina looked at David and back at Sadie's blazing eyes. "Your husband has saved my life, Sadie, and I'm grateful. He offered me a job until I get on my feet. You're a lucky woman to have such a man. All women aren't so blessed."

"Yes, I am." Sadie kissed David's cheek and smiled at Tashina. "Nice to meet you, Tashina. I hope you get on your feet before long." Tashina chuckled and sat to continue her work.

Max Shepherd called one evening, wanting David to come to his house on the Island. He had a problem and needed David's help. David kissed Sadie and promised to be back in time for dinner. When he docked at the Island, he cringed at the flashing lights of the huge casino. Oliver built an adjoining hotel and a small plaza behind the colorful building. People were milling about everywhere. The gambling establishment threatened to consume the entire Island.

He made his way around the buildings to a narrow road which would take him to the Shepherd home. There he found Max alone. Tammy and the kids were on a trip to the city, and Max stayed to counsel those river people who needed help.

"Glad you came, David." Max invited him in and handed him a glass of tea. They chatted a while before the subject moved to Oliver and the casino.

"I've been talking to a couple of Fed guys. I think they're ready to look into things around here." Max swigged a glass of tea and wiped his mouth.

"Really! It's about time." David looked out the window, then back at Max. "You think you know who the top guy in this mess is?"

"I've got an idea." Max pulled a dill pickle from the jar and ate it. "I hope I'm wrong to think Oliver has something to do with it. I don't think he's the boss, but he sure seems guilty."

"Who do you think it is? And why not Oliver?"

"The casino has to be a lucrative business for him." Max ate another pickle. "He'd be a fool to risk losing it. Besides, I think he's too obsessed with his own problems to deal with the hazards of organized crime."

"Or his obsession of ruining me." David tapped his fingers on the table. "Say, I know you didn't call me to come here to discuss Oliver's obsessions."

"He's asked us to leave the island. Says he needs the room to develop his business here. Do you know he's closing Crandall Shipping?"

David blinked and shook his head. "No, I didn't. When did this all come about?"

"Last week when I ran into him in the city, he hinted around about it. Last night he came to the house. Said it's time he retires. Said this casino will bring in enough money to support his lifestyle."

"You think Kade knows? He's been out of town the last couple of weeks." David ran his finger around the rim of his glass. "Sadie hasn't said anything. But she probably hasn't talked to him in a while. I try to get her to call him, but she always says she'll do it later."

"I hate to hear that." Max led the way out to the porch. He stood looking across the tree-lined yard. Crepe Myrtle, Rose of Sharon and Lilac bushes bloomed in the spring and summer months along with daffodils, lilies, tulips and various other plants. A garden behind the house provided fresh vegetables for the family, and fruit trees, grape vines, and blueberry bushes gave them fruit to have juice and jellies all year long.

"I sure hate to leave this place. Since we've move here, it's been a haven for us. It's also near the people who need me. I'm not sure what we'll do now. Of course, it isn't just us. Everyone on the Island has been asked to leave."

"Wow! What will they do? Most of the people have lived here for years. This is unexpected for them, I'm sure." David sighed. "And what about those who have rebuilt after the flood? Guess they'll lose everything. Wish there was something I could do."

Max swung around and stared at him. "Oliver is your father-in-law, right?"

"You know he is. What are you thinking?"

"You need to get on his good side and talk him into at least giving the Island dwellers more time to find homes off the Island."

David scratched his beard. "I don't know. I've tried to do right by him, but I think he hates me. I'm none too happy with him, either."

"See if Kade will help you. Or have Sadie call him. Invite him for dinner." Max grinned and slapped David on the back. "You can do it for your friends, right?"

David shrugged. "I'll try. We'll see if we can get him to change his mind." He gazed toward the new construction visible over the tops of the trees. "Think he'd be willing to hire the Island people to work his business? Or they'd be willing to work for him?"

"Well, most already have jobs, but I guess there would be some who would." Max sat on the porch swing. "Tell you what. You see what you can do with Oliver and let me know. If it sounds promising, I'll hold a meeting and see what can be done on this end. Maybe together we'll get these people help."

"What about you and Tammy? What will you do?"

"I'm not sure yet, but don't worry about us. We'll be all right."

"I'm going to have to think and pray on this."

Max offered David a pickle. "There's another thing I need to ask of you."

David waited while Max filled a glass with ice. He poured sweet tea from a pitcher and pointed at a chair. David sat. This must be serious.

"David, you've helped me before, and I hate to involve you again, but I need a person I trust to look around for me.

An agent friend needs to know who is hanging around at the casino."

David laughed. "Sure. I'll fix up a disguise. I don't mind cleaning up spills if I can glean information in the process."

On the river

"No!" Lucy screamed and the man helped her to a chair to keep her from collapsing.

"I'm so sorry, Lucy. He was a good worker."

"What happened to my son?" Ronnie's dad, Harold, loomed in the doorway.

"Sir, he fell from the top of the scaffolding. Another worker spilled oil and Ronnie didn't see it. He slipped."

Harold rubbed his face and his shoulders slumped.

The man patted Lucy's back. "The boy did have an insurance policy. You'll get the money in no time at all."

Harold lifted his head. "You think Lucy will get the insurance money?"

"Yes, of course. Lucy, we'll get it to you when the forms are completed."

"Humpf. She won't be getting it. Ronnie's my son."

"But isn't Lucy...?"

Harold tittered. "No, she isn't his wife. I'll come by for the check."

"But the baby...?"

"That's her problem. My son is gone, and she will be gone after today. Goodbye, sir."

Thirty-three

David hobbled along with his cleaning cart, mumbling to himself. He was getting good at this old man guise. "Oh, excuse me." He pulled back his cart and chose another direction to avoid blocking the aisle. He hated the bright lights and loud noise of the crowded casino. He swept a pile of trash next to a door when he heard angry voices.

"You have a job to do, and I expect you to do it." It was Oliver. "Now get out there and do what you're paid to do."

"But sir, the gentleman says we're cheating him. And we are."

"You heard me," Oliver bellowed. "You can do it, or I'll find someone else."

A man wearing a black shirt with a Crandall Casino logo emblazoned on the back ran out, holding a bag. A quick glimpse into the office revealed a smirking Jasper standing behind Oliver. David watched as the casino worker whispered to another associate, and they hurried to one of the game tables. A well-dressed elderly man stood glaring at the red-faced dealer. A frowning woman wearing furs and bright dangly earrings stood beside him.

"We demand to see the manager of this joint," the man shouted. "We want our money back."

The dealer glanced toward the back where Oliver's office was. "Sir, please lower your voice. We'll take care of this situation. Just be patient."

"I won't lower my voice. Everyone in here should know how this place cheats its customers." He yelled even louder. "You hear that people? You're all being cheated."

A large, burly man approached from behind the couple and grabbed the man's arm. "Come with me, sir. You too, ma'am." The elderly man winced and tried to pull away, but he was no match for the strong man. Jasper came up and grabbed the lady's arm. As they guided them out the door, Jasper whispered to a security guard who took over from there.

David watched the incident as he moved his broom over the floor. Where were they taking the protesting couple? Could they be in danger? He moved his janitor cart toward the door. The security guard was leading the couple out a side door toward a shuttle used for carrying guests from the shuttle boat to the casino. He would send them back to the city and likely tell them not to return.

On his way home, David went out the same side door the elderly couple exited. He walked down the same route the security guard took them. A bright item close to the sidewalk caught his eye. It was a red high-heeled shoe. The same kind of shoe the woman was wearing. David remembered because earlier she'd almost stepped on his foot and he noticed the bright shoe.

He looked around but saw nothing unusual. He walked toward the casino shuttle boat, watching along the ground. When he neared the boat, a sparkle in the sun a little way from the concrete dock caught his eye. It was a bright dangly earring laying on a path that led to an old motorboat.

David filled Max in on what he witnessed and what

Frank told him.

"It's bad enough to know he is involved in unethical and illegal practices, but I sure hope he isn't involved in murder." David couldn't get the image of the elderly couple out of his mind. "I guess he runs the casino with the same ideology as he runs his shipping business. If he does, the casino will suffer the same fate."

"I guess," Max agreed. "He has to make enough money to pay for it. It had to cost a bundle for him to build."

"Not only children are disappearing, but now people are being knocked off to keep them quiet. We've got to get something done." Max scratched his head and picked up the phone. "I'm going to call my agent friend."

David emptied his glass of water and picked up his disguise. "I'm headed home. Gotta catch up on gossip from my wife and get some work done at the office." He waved and left. As he pulled his boat from the dock, he looked around in regret at the changes he saw. He had to help Max and the Island people.

The doorbell rang just as David and Sadie sat down to dinner. David grinned when he saw Cosmo Rouge standing there. "Hey, man. Come on in. You're in time for dinner."

Sadie called Kade and Sophia, and the two couples and Cosmo enjoyed a dinner of goulash and shared memories.

"Remember the time ol' rubber legs Roddy stole the ball, made a long shot and won the game at Cedar Fork? Dang, that was awesome." Kade slapped his leg and hooted.

"Yeah, that guy could run down the court so fast no one could catch him. That's why they called him rubber legs." Cosmo explained to the girls. "What ever happened to him?"

David chuckled. "He works for the IRS catching people who owe the government money."

Cosmo almost choked on his drink. "Oh, that's rich! How fitting for a man with rubber legs."

"Cosmo, David says you quit basketball for health reasons. Are you okay now?" Sadie asked.

"Sure, only the ole knees give me fits. I have to take care of them. I'm too young for a knee replacement."

"So, what are you doing now? I know you too well to think you'd sit around doing nothing."

"Ah, Sadie, you do know me well." Cosmo winked at her. "I keep busy. Actually, I've been helping at the casino."

"You mean gambling?" Kade raised eyebrows.

"No, not really, although I do like to throw the dice once in a while. I'm helping Oliver keep order. He doesn't want any trouble, know what I mean?"

David tittered. "Yeah, you're a bouncer."

"Nothing wrong with honest work."

"Not a thing." Kade rose. "Come along, Sophia girl. It's late. We need to head home."

David and Sadie saw their guests out and straightened the room.

"Did you sense a little tension when I asked him what he's doing?" Sadie put dirty glasses into the dishwasher.

"I did. Something's not quite right." David agreed. "I don't know what it is."

"Maybe it's because he's been gone for a while. Things always change when you've been away. He may still feel a little awkward."

"I guess. We need to have him over again later. Give him time to loosen up around us."

One day David arrived home to find Sadie looking through brochures. "What are you looking at, sweetheart?"

"Remember when we talked about foster care? Before...you know."

His eyes widened. "Are you pregnant?" He couldn't go through another pregnancy if it put his Sadie in danger.

"No, I'm not. But look at this." She handed him a brochure.

He glanced through the brochure and she handed him another one. He gathered piles of brochures laying on the couch next to her and sat in a nearby chair. "Are you serious about this?"

"Yes, I am. You know Dr. Lucas says I can't have kids. So I think I'd like to adopt."

He flipped through the pages, looking at the smiling faces of children and families. They all looked so happy. Beautiful babies and older children. He had been terrified at the thought of losing Sadie when she miscarried. When he knew she was safe, the hurt of losing their child hit him like a blind force he couldn't control. However, in the face of her pain, he couldn't allow his to surface.

"I'll get my degree in Social Work, and I've checked out the job market. It looks pretty good." Sadie rose and went to the kitchen to start dinner. "I think I'm ready to be a mom. Are you ready to be a dad?"

David turned on the oven and pulled a meatloaf he'd made earlier from the refrigerator. "You know, I believe I am. I can see myself playing ball with a little boy or reading a book to a little girl."

"Or playing ball with a girl and reading to a boy."

Sadie giggled. "Wow! I'm going to talk to Professor Harris tomorrow. She has ties with people who might help us. I know there's a lot to it, so the quicker we get started, the quicker we'll become parents."

David rolled his eyes toward the ceiling and laughed. "Time to look for a minivan."

On the river

All the river men taught their sons and daughters gun safety from the time they were big enough to hold one. Hunting was a means of obtaining meat for the family, and guns were considered necessary tools for the home. Josiah called a meeting with the other river men to discuss the situation. This time, their guns would be needed to protect their own. It was time.

Thirty-four

Sadie came home from class one day excited about what she'd learned. "Professor Harris is hosting an event for potential foster parents and she wants us to attend," she told David. "It will be at the River Park next Saturday. People with answers to all our questions will be there. They'll have tons of information about fostering and adoption."

They attended the event where they acquired useful information about foster care and adoption and formed a network of enlightened individuals in the field of social work and child advocates. A case worker named Shelby would work with them through the process.

After the event, they talked and prayed about what they should do. They wouldn't make this decision in haste. David's parents and Melody were on board with the young couple, and Kade and Sophia were constant encouragers. Sadie would take a heavy load and go every semester so she could graduate with a master's degree in social work and find a job working as a therapist in an area school.

David's phone rang in the middle of a meeting with his board members. When he saw Sadie's number, he knew it was important. She wouldn't call him at work if it were not. He excused himself and went into his office.

"Yes, sweetheart, what is it?"

"David, we have a baby. A baby!"

"What? A baby? Already?"

"Yes. We need to go to the hospital immediately. Shelby called and said a young woman at Central is giving birth and her family talked her into allowing the baby to be adopted. She said the baby's father was dead." Her voice trembled. "Can you come now?"

"Yes. I'm in a meeting, but I'll end it now and be right there."

"Come get me and we'll call everyone on the way." Sadie notified everyone to meet them at the hospital.

While family members gathered in the waiting room, a nurse led David and Sadie into a room next to the nursery. She fitted them with gowns and left them to wait. In about an hour a doctor walked in with a blue bundle and a smile. "Congratulations. It's a boy."

Sadie jumped to her feet and opened her arms to receive the blue bundle. With tears streaming, she held it close. David put his arm around her and together, they inspected the tiny red infant from head to foot. A perfect little baby. Sadie handed him to David who wiped his eyes before he took him.

He pulled the small, warm bundle to his chest and kissed the tiny face. The baby opened dark blue eyes and looked at David. "Can he see me?"

Sadie smiled at her husband. "Yes, he can see you. He knows you're his daddy." She touched the dark hair and lifted a tiny hand. The baby grabbed her finger and held on. With his arms surrounding his wife and baby, David swayed in rhythm as Sadie hummed a lullaby she learned from her mom.

David handed the baby back to Sadie and looked toward the door. "Guess we'd better share our joy with our family." He went to the door of the waiting room and motioned for them.

"What are you going to name him?" Kathleen joined Melody who now held the baby. They passed him from one to the other as they admired his soft round face and oval eyes. She nudged Melody. "Grandma, we've got to go shopping! This baby has no clothes."

"Or anything else," Kade said. "We have work to do. Come on, Sophia, we've got to find a car seat."

David laughed. "The doctor says we have to wait twenty-four hours to take him home, so you have time to get what we need."

Jesse extended his hand. "Come with us, Melody, and we'll go find baby things. This little one has to have bottles and blankets and diapers and...oh, my! We have a lot of shopping to do."

They agreed to meet back at the hospital later and scattered. David and Sadie would do the paperwork required to check the baby out. They called their lawyer to prepare legal documents needed for the adoption and would visit his office the next day to complete the paperwork.

A nurse came to check on them and to take the baby for blood work and other necessary tests.

"How is the mom?" Sadie asked.

The nurse shook her head. "There were too many complications. She didn't make it."

"Oh." Sadie winced. "I'm so sorry."

"Can you tell us her first name?" David asked.

"Sure." The nurse checked her chart. "Her name was Lucy. She was a sweet young woman. Concerned that her baby has a good home and a family to love him."

"We'll tell him about her when he's old enough to understand," David said.

When the nurse returned the baby, David watched as Sadie ran her finger along his soft cheeks.

"We have to have a name, David." She felt the tiny fingers and toes. She kissed the sleeping eyes and touched the pink, heart-shaped lips. She caressed the baby, bringing it to her face to feel its breath on her cheek.

"This is sudden. I haven't even thought about a name." His wife looked so natural holding the tiny addition to their family. *How could this be happening?*

Will I be a good father?

Is it enough that my parents did such a great job raising me?

Have I learned enough to raise a child?

What if I blow it?

He could ruin a child's life if he didn't do it right.

What if I don't do it right?

"David, did you hear me? Didn't the nurse say her name was Lucy?"

"Yes. It's Lucy. She didn't say the last name."

Sadie shook her head. "I guess that doesn't matter."

"Should we incorporate her name?"

Sadie smiled. "What a wonderful idea." They started brainstorming names.

"My son." David swelled with pride. He admired his own father and wanted to be as good a father to his own son. With God's help, he would be. He would make sure of it.

"How about Benjamin? In the Hebrew it means son of the right hand. We could use that, and a name related to Lucy."

"I like it." Sadie rocked back and forth, cuddling the

small bundle. "Lucy, Lucas, Luke, Lukah. How about Lukah? Do a search to find out what it means."

David swiped his phone. "It means gift of God."

Sadie's eyes widened. "Gift of God? David, it's perfect. Benjamin Lukah. I love it." She repeated the name several times. David held out his hands to take the child.

"Hello, Benjamin Lukah. Son of my right hand and gift of God." He looked at Sadie who smiled through her tears. "Our son, Sadie. He's our son."

By the time they signed the documents, Kade and Sophia were back with a car seat, blankets, bottles, formula, and a bag of other necessities for the baby. A little later, the grandparents came in with shopping bags full of clothes.

"All these will have to be washed before you use them but look what I found." Kathleen held up a baby blue sleeper set complete with a soft knit hat and a fuzzy yellow blanket. "These were David's when he was a baby."

"Oh! They're beautiful." Sadie held the items to her breast. "He can wear this home."

"Jesse said they were getting a cradle until you guys find a crib. We have a little time to get everything you need." Kade slapped David on the back. "Congratulations, man. You're a dad."

When the twenty-four hours were up, they buckled Benjamin into the car seat and headed home. Immense joy added to their lives in a few hours would change their home forever.

On the river

A buck and doe lifted heads and listened. A blue jay sounded a warning cry from a tall oak tree. A squirrel jerked its tail as it carried a hickory nut to hide in a large hole in the trunk of a sweet gum tree. A blue lizard skittered up a stump and stopped. The forest paid attention to the cries of a child. His mother did not. She was passed out on a broken couch in a filthy living room. She had drunk herself into a stupor the day before and failed to awaken when her hungry son tried to rouse her.

He hadn't eaten in two days and could barely walk because of the soiled diaper that covered a red, blistered bottom. He didn't understand why his mama wouldn't wake up to take care of him. No one lived close enough to hear him. Only nature heard. Only the animals cared.

But wait—someone else cared. Boards creaked as feet climbed the steps. The door squeaked as it opened. Gentle hands lifted the little boy and comforted his cries. Food and a bucket of clean water appeared, and soon, a clean, fed child was asleep on the shoulder of someone who carried him to safety.

Thirty-five

David took time off work to get acquainted with his new son. Would he ever stop smiling? With the help of their support system, he and Sadie found a house and moved closer to Jesse and Kathleen who would keep Benjamin when they both worked. Melody also found a house close by so she could help with the baby.

"This baby will be spoiled." Melody placed the sleeping child in the crib. They decorated the nursery in soft cream colors accented with sea-foam green and yellow. Melody gave them the antique rocking chair she had used to rock Kade and Sadie, and Jesse built wooden toys including a rocking horse in his workshop.

"He's such a good baby," said Kathleen. The two women doted on the child while David and Sadie reveled in the joys of parenthood. "I'm going to teach him to call me Nana. What do you want to be called?"

"That's a hard decision." Melody tapped her fingernail on her chin. "I think I'll be grand-mama with an accent on the last syllable. Grand-Mamá."

Sadie hugged the two ladies. "I love it. You two are the best."

David hadn't forgotten the plight of the Shepherd family and the Island people. He and Sadie agreed they should tell Oliver about the baby. Perhaps he would soften enough to change his mind about making the people move from the Island. She called, but he didn't answer the phone. She went by his office, but the secretary said he left town for a few weeks, maybe months. None of them had seen or heard from him since Sadie returned to David.

He had to return to work, even though he wanted to stay home with his wife and new son. Business would wait no longer. Clients demanded attention from the boss, and although his office staff proved to be capable, some things required his personal attention.

He left the office to head home one evening and was surprised to find Oliver leaning on his Ford. To avoid confrontation, David pushed past him to open his door, but Oliver stood against it.

"Excuse me." David reached again for the door handle, but Oliver stood firm. "I have to leave."

"I need to talk to you." Oliver put his hand on David's arm. David pulled back and lifted his hands.

"David, I mean you no harm. I'll say my piece and leave you be." When David consented, he continued. "I don't know why I've treated you like I have. I know I've been wrong. I'm asking your forgiveness."

David stood, unmoving. Oliver shoved his hands into his pockets and rocked back and forth. "I know I don't deserve anything from you, least of all forgiveness. I've tried every way to destroy you, but nothing has worked. Instead of failing, you keep succeeding. I've tried to turn my family against you, but they love you more." He threw his hands into the air. "What is it? How is it possible the more I try to harm you, the more you prosper?"

"Mr. Crandall, why do you want to destroy me? What have I done to you?"

Oliver put his head back and laughed a bitter laugh. "My business is barely alive. I've lost my wife, and now my daughter. And you ask what you've done?"

"And how am I responsible for your losses?" *This is incredulous. How can he think all this is my fault?*

Oliver snorted. "I was a successful businessman, husband and father until you joined my company. Who else could be responsible?"

"You. You are responsible."

A fist slammed against the truck and Oliver shoved David aside. "Will you explain that to me? Only a stupid imbecile would think that."

David whirled and shoved Oliver against the truck. "I will explain it, and you will listen." His soft, calm voice prevailed over Oliver's angry demeanor. "I joined your company hoping to learn from you, and I did. You trained me well. And when I brought in clients to grow *your* business, you pushed me out."

His voice deepened. "When I had an opportunity to buy my own business, I convinced several of my clients to move to Crandall Shipping, but they came running back when they found out how you treat your people."

Oliver gasped, but David raised his hand to silence him. "You lost your wife because you were unfaithful to her and pushed her away. Your daughter loves you but seems like you're trying your hardest to kill that love. How dare you manipulate her during her weakest time into a relationship *you* think would benefit your business?" Breathing hard, he leaned toward the truck with both hands against the fender.

Oliver slumped, mouth agape, his face tortured. When he spoke at last, it was with chagrin and recognition. "Have I done that, David? Is that what I have become?"

He opened the door of his Jaguar and sat in the passenger side. He leaned over with his elbows on his knees and his hands over his face. David's gut wrenched as he watched the older man. How could anyone come to this place and not even know what brought him here? How can a person become unrecognizable even to himself?

How many chances should a man get? Two? Three? Fifty? What good would it do to hold a grudge? David knelt in front of the tormented man. "Oliver...please."

Oliver raised his head, running his hands over his wet face. "Uh, I...I'm sorry. I don't know what else to say." He bowed his head and shuddered.

David waited a while. "Did you know Sadie and I have a baby?"

Oliver mumbled. "Yeah, Melody sent word to me."

"He's beautiful. So small and helpless."

When he raised his head, his face softened. "I bet he is."

"We named him Benjamin. Benjamin Lukah."

"It's a good name. I like it."

"Why don't you come over to the house for a visit? You'd love holding him."

Oliver sat up straight, and his eyes shone. "Would you let me do that?"

"Of course. We'd be glad for you to come. Sadie will be thrilled to have you."

A smile spread across his face, and he stood. "I'll be there. You live on West Court, right?" David nodded. "I'll call and drop by one day. Thank you, David."

Sadie gasped, and then did a little happy dance when David told her the news. She hummed when she did the dishes and sang when she vacuumed. David rocked Benjamin, put him to bed, and then helped Sadie with the laundry. They checked on Benjamin before they sat in the swing on the porch, listening to the night sounds and talking about the future.

"Where do you see us ten years from now?" Sadie snuggled against David.

"Uh, Benjamin will be ten, and I hope we'll have one or two more by then. Don't you?"

"Yes, I do. Maybe three."

"If we have that many, you'll have to be a stay-at-home mom."

"Sounds wonderful, but who would help those poor children who have no parents or bad parents? They need someone who cares about them."

"That's true, but our children will need you."

"Our children will always have many people to care about them. These kids don't. I want to help those who can't help themselves. Does that make sense?"

David kissed her. "Yes. I see your point. Those children do need you. With the help of our parents, our children will be the most loved and cared for children in the world."

Oliver made good on his word and came to see Benjamin. He beamed with pride as he held his grandson and stayed for dinner. It was a good visit on all accounts. They laughed and reminisced about Kade and Sadie's childhood, and Oliver's eyes misted as he watched Sadie hover over her child.

"I'll come by to see you again," he crooned as he said goodbye to Benjamin. "We'll have a lot of fun together, you and me. I'll find a train set when you get a little bigger. And we'll play ball. You'll be my quarterback." Benjamin latched onto his little finger. "Look. He doesn't want me to leave." He smiled at Sadie and David. "He's a great little guy, and you'll be great parents." He waved as he drove off, still looking back.

On the river

A group of angry men gathered under a tree in the Petersons' yard. Anger boiled over onto the women who served meatloaf and scalloped potatoes. It boiled over onto those who arrived late and stood around the edges, watching. It boiled over onto rowdy children who played chase around trees, over stumps, and through and around the legs of the adults.

"Wade, you said yourself we caint keep doin' nothin'. Nobody else'll help us. It's up to us to fix things around here."

"You got that right, Josiah. I'm sick of the law ignoring us. They don't care when it comes to river people."

Other piqued voices joined in and everyone talked at once. A man near the center of the crowd raised his hand and shushes spread through the group until all became quiet.

"Pa Eli is speaking," a woman said. All eyes turned toward the small, grizzled man.

"Folks, anger and bitterness will get us nowhere," he drawled. Heads bobbed and he continued. "We gotta consider the truth, and we gotta have a plan." He perched on a tall stump and contemplated his audience. "The truth is people who got no rights are interrupting our lives and taking what's ours. We've asked for help and got nothing. We gotta take matters into our own hands."

Fists pumped the air and heads nodded. Once more, all grew quiet when Pa Eli opened his mouth. "One thing we gotta remember—people, good and bad, have value. We have to be careful to protect the innocent." A long hesitation punctuated the importance of his statement.

"Our creator gave us soul to balance us. We have emotions

to stir us, a will to move us, and a mind to guide us. We don't need to get all riled up and act stupid. We have to use our brains to get us going in the right direction so's there's no unnecessary hurt to anyone or anything."

Thirty-six

David arrived early and was working on a new client's file when the office door slammed open and Kade barged in. "Come on, David, there's trouble on the Island."

They headed to David's boat which was closer, and water slapped the sides of the blue speedboat as it skimmed over the river.

They circled the foot of the Island where several other boats of various descriptions bobbed on the water. Something was going down for sure.

"I'm going back to the pier," Kade said. "Dad is here, but I have no idea where."

They docked the boat and rushed to the front door. The casino hadn't opened, and the doors were locked. Kade started back toward the pier but turned around.

He dug in his wallet. "I just remembered — the last time Dad came to the house he gave me a key." The door swung open and they were inside. They headed down the hall to Oliver's office in hopes he would be there. Kade reached for the door but pulled back when loud voices came from within. One of them was Oliver.

"You can't do that," Oliver shouted.

"Oh, but I can, and I will." At first, David didn't recognize the voice. It was calm but strong. "Crandall, you have to realize who's in charge now. It isn't you."

"This is my casino, you fool. I am in charge."

"You gave up your rights when you signed my contract this morning."

"No. I signed a partnership agreement, that's all."

A cruel laugh preceded the harsh voice. "Look closely, my man. My part in this deal gives me rights to use this casino any way I want, and this is what I want." That's when David recognized the owner of the voice. Cosmo Rouge.

The door slammed open and Oliver erupted through, almost hitting David. Unintelligible words spattered out from between purple lips as he rushed toward the offices in the back of the building.

Through the open door, they saw Cosmo. A wisp of smoke drifted up from a cigar he held between his teeth. His feet were propped up on a huge walnut desk. Just before the door closed, they heard him laugh. "He's such an idiot. Is it my fault he needs help to keep his business from going under?"

A short, bald man sitting in an armchair snickered. "Yeah, his real problems started when that blonde broad latched onto him. He can't spend enough to keep her happy. Poor guy."

"Poor guy? Humpf! He gets no sympathy from me. He's an idiot." The door slammed, muffling the sound of laughter.

Kade and David looked at each other and started off to find Oliver. They found him standing in the middle of an office by the casino bank. He looked lost. He turned toward them.

"What are you guys doing here?"

Kade walked over to him and peered into his face. "Dad? You okay? What's going on? Why is Cosmo Rouge in your office?"

Oliver collapsed into a chair and covered his face with his hands. "Son, I'm in a mess. I don't know what to do."

David and Kade pulled up chairs facing him. "Why don't you tell us why you're in trouble?" Kade's soft voice encouraged the troubled man to lift his head. The younger men watched as he gripped the arms of the chair. His eyes darted back and forth as if searching for the answer to his dilemma.

"Well, I, uh…"

"Okay, Dad, I don't know what's going on. Right now, tell me how Cosmo got hold of the casino."

Oliver lifted his eyes toward the ceiling. "Confound it, it's all my fault. I've made bad decisions." He ducked his head. "Son, your dad is no good. He's a real…"

Kade interrupted him. "I'm glad you're finally owning your failures. But right now, we need to focus on this Cosmo thing. How did he get the casino? If we know that, maybe we can figure out what to do about it."

Oliver stood and began pacing the floor. "I had money problems, and he offered to help me out. I didn't realize the price I would have to pay."

"Why didn't you come to me? I could have helped you."

"I didn't want you to know what I'd done." He spread out his hands, palms up. "I'm ashamed. Can't you see that?"

Kade folded his arms across his chest. "What have you done, Dad?"

"Son, I've lost everything. My bank account is empty. My clients have all left me. The only way I could save the company is to borrow money. That's when Cosmo offered me a loan."

"How did he know you needed money?"

Oliver looked surprised. "I never thought about it. He just seemed to know."

"Have you talked to him before this? Have you had dealings with him?"

"Not really. I know he's friends with Jasper Harris."

"Yeah. Jasper of Harris Shipping. The guy you wanted for Sadie."

Oliver looked toward David and lowered his head. "That was rotten of me."

A muscle in David's jaw twitched.

"I guess Jasper told him I needed help. Jasper knows everything about me." Oliver straddled a chair next to a table.

Kade grimaced. "Why does Jasper know everything about you? You trust him?"

Oliver reddened. "I guess I shouldn't. He isn't a good person. I know that now."

"Why isn't he a good person?"

"I found out lately he's involved in bad things. I didn't know that before."

Kade leaned over and slapped his hands on the table. "Dang-it, Dad. How could you not know before now? Look at the devious things he's done for you." He gritted his teeth. "I guess you're blind to your own malarkey."

David leaned against the wall with his legs crossed and arms folded. "What kind of bad things is Jasper involved in?"

"I found out this morning he is using Island and river people to traffic drugs. And there's another thing, too, but I'm not sure what."

"Is Cosmo involved? It could be why he wants the

casino." David straightened.

"I think so. When I went to confront him this morning, I heard him mention Jasper."

"What were you confronting him about?" Kade asked.

"The moron called me late last night wanting all the keys to the casino. Said he's taking over and needs the keys."

"Dad, what paper did you sign?"

Oliver fidgeted. "A contract for a loan. At least that's what I thought."

"Did you have a lawyer look at it?"

"No. I looked over it, and it seemed all right."

"That goes against everything you know." Kade's voice raised. "You always taught me to sign nothing without a lawyer checking it. You still have a lawyer, right?"

"No. I don't have money to pay a lawyer."

"You do remember your daughter-in-law is a lawyer?"

Oliver sat in silence.

Then the sound of shots shattered the quiet. Doors slamming and pounding feet followed. David whirled around and ran to the window. He could see several men scattered across the lawn and parking lot, running toward the river. He recognized a few of them. Kade and Oliver joined him as he headed for the back of the building.

Cosmo and his cronies stuck heads out doorways and hid behind pillars which supported the structure. Building security ran interference between those shooting and those hiding. Who's shooting? And who started this war?

Oliver pushed aside a window blind to look out. "It's Jasper. He's shooting at the river people." He pulled back and headed for the door. "I've got a gun hidden in the back. I'll get it."

"Good," said Kade. "David, our guns are in the boats. Come on."

They went out a side door and crouched low, moving from one vehicle to another to make their way to the pier. A couple of motorboats pulled up just as they reached their boat.

"It's Josiah." Kade jumped into the boat and handed the rifles to David. "And Ted over there. Looks like the river people are defending themselves."

"You boys here to help or to hinder?" Ted anchored his boat beside them.

"What's going on, Ted? Got a war started?" David stuck his Glock in his belt, checked his rifle, and put a box of ammunition in his pocket.

"If it's what it takes to git things straight 'round here, then it's what we'll do." He pulled a shotgun from under the boat seat and loaded it. "We never wanted a war, but we got rights like anybody else."

Josiah came over with a rifle slung over his shoulder. "We don't want 'ta harm anyone, David, but it's reckonin' time. We gonna put a stop to the crime wave 'round here if it's the last thing we do."

"What are you going to do?" Kade asked.

"Here's what's happening." Brown spit ran down Josiah's chin. "Shepherd hinted that Cosmo Rouge and Jasper Harris are the cause of all our problems. It's them who hire our youngins to carry drugs to and from the city. It's them who steal our little children and sell them."

Kade gasped. "Shepherd said that?"

"Close enough. We aim to stop them dead in their tracks. I mean dead, if that's what it takes."

"Who's there now, shooting?"

"Ah, it's Travis Lynch and his boy Shelton. They're causing a distraction so's the rest of us can get up there to capture the criminals. We got men comin' from all directions. They're surrounded and don't even know it yet."

David gestured toward the men. "But they'll hole-up in the building."

"We got that covered. Shepherd and a few others are there now, making sure the place is empty and locked. When the shootin' starts, we figure the cowards will go outside to find out what's goin' on. Then we'll lock them out so's they caint git back in."

"I sure hope it works."

Ted stroked his long beard. "Iffin it don't, we got another plan. Shepherd will pull the fire alarm. And if that don't work, we'll just go in ablazin'."

Josiah pulled a pocket watch from his overalls. "Well, come on, Ted. It's time for a showdown. You guys comin'?"

They crept over an incline and peered toward the casino. They could hear shouting as the shooting continued. Men were running around the building, jerking on doors and yelling at each other. The doors were all locked, and the men were going berserk. The hotel was too far away for them to run there.

"Careful, David," Ted warned. "They got guns."

They circled around to the side of the casino. It seemed to be clear. Josiah ran toward the building and the others followed. It could be bad if one of Cosmos' men came around and saw them.

They made it without a hitch. Now what? Hiding behind the shrubbery growing along the sides, they crouched low and moved to the back where the men were.

"Look." David pointed. Men with guns of all descriptions were pouring into the area around the casino. They were aimed and ready to fire. Cosmo and his men cowered under the awning that stretched over the back door.

"Put your guns down, men," Cosmo ordered. "It's over." But no, it wasn't.

On the river

Families celebrated and families wept. When agents arrived on piers and boat docks with children rescued from buildings and hideouts, parents rushed to claim their offspring. When their child was not among those found, broken parents turned faces away from the joy of those who embraced their children and each other. The river reverberated with sounds of gladness and sadness.

Thirty-seven

A figure came running over the hill from the river, weaving back and forth, making its way to the crowd gathered at the back of the casino. As it drew closer, a burst of gun fire caused the crowd to scatter. The shooter appeared from behind a tree, firing at the running figure. A battle was happening right before their eyes, and they were helpless to stop it.

David and Kade watched from behind the shrubbery as the runner moved closer. All at once, Kade stood.

"Dad! It's Dad." He slapped his hand to his forehead and called out. "Dad! Watch out!"

"Get down, Kade." David tried to pull him behind the shrub, but he took off running toward the figure. "Kade! Stop. Come back. You'll get shot." They were now close enough to identify Jasper and Oliver. Jasper waved a gun, shooting at Oliver.

Oliver fell, and Kade ran to him. He kneeled and lifted the limp body. He buried his head in Oliver's chest, jerked and collapsed on top of the body.

"No!" The word ripped from David's throat. About fifteen guns went off, and Jasper stumbled and fell. He lay motionless on the ground close to Oliver and Kade.

David tore through the shrubbery and flew to the downed men. He threw himself on the body of Kade, checking for a pulse. None.

"No, no, no." How could his best friend, his soul mate, be lying here on the cold, hard ground, blood running from his body, eyes empty? *Get up, Kade. Get up. We have so much to do. So much to talk about. So much to laugh about. Please, get up.*

Someone pushed him aside and hovered over Kade and Oliver. Sirens wailed, and blue uniforms surrounded him. Stretchers appeared. Kade was placed on one, Oliver on another. David sat on the ground and watched as hands lifted them into the back of emergency vehicles.

They were gone. He knew it as sure as he knew his life would never be the same. His best friend. His soul mate. Gone.

Hands forced him to his feet and pulled him away. He couldn't see or hear or think. He stumbled along between two figures—he had no idea who—into the casino. He fell to the cold floor, chest heaving with heavy sobs that tore at his throat. At one point he lifted his head to stare out the window. Handcuffed men were led away by men in uniforms.

After a while, someone put him into his boat and took him to the mainland. He was led to his truck, and someone drove him to the hospital. Why were they taking him to the hospital? He wasn't hurt. Only his heart.

"David." Someone was calling him. "David!" Jesse was shaking him.

"Dad, he's gone. Kade's gone. What am I going to do without my best friend?"

"David, look at me. He isn't gone. He's bad, but not gone. He's in surgery."

"You mean he's alive?" He stood still a moment, and then jumped into action. "Where is he? I have to see him."

Jesse led him through the double glass doors and into

the elevator. Soon they entered a waiting room where the others were. A tearful Sadie ran to David and led him to a chair where Sophia sat sobbing. He embraced her.

"The doctor said the bullet entered his back and barely missed his heart," she said. "His right lung is damaged, but he said it can be repaired."

Melody joined them. "There were multiple bullet wounds. The doctor says he will be in surgery a while, but he should be okay."

"Thank God." Kathleen rubbed Sophia's back and hugged Melody.

David looked at Melody. "What about Oliver?"

Melody pulled David to sit beside her on a couch. "He isn't good. The doctor said a bullet is lying next to his spine, and another one gazed his head. He's also in surgery. We'll have to wait and see what happens."

The waiting room was abuzz with friends and relatives going in and out, checking on the two men. Food was carried in for the family, and doctors kept them updated on the welfare of the patients. Two agents accompanied Max Shepherd and filled David in on the situation on the Island.

"Cosmo became involved in organized crime while playing pro-football and met Jasper when he came back to the Island," Max said. "Together, they formed what they called The Island Retreat. Agent Sharp has been following Jasper Harris for a while now. Drug trafficking, human trafficking, gun trafficking—there aren't many illegal things he isn't involved in."

Agent Sharp shrugged one shoulder. "At first, we thought he was the crime boss, but he's just an accessory.

Cosmo used him in his human trafficking ring and to find kids to run drugs for him. A while back he led us to a web of traffickers who worked this area and on down the river. Last week we found several children locked in a building and are working to get them back to their parents."

"They used Oliver's casino for a front," Max explained. "He'd become so distraught over his personal and business problems he didn't see what Cosmo was up to. The idea of money and power so blinded him he couldn't see past his nose. Cosmo figured he was home free when he tricked him into signing that contract."

"He and Jasper didn't anticipate the Island people taking charge of things," David said. "Cosmo should have known better. He was raised on the Island."

Agent Newly joined the conversation. "We have plenty of evidence to put those two away for a long time."

David rubbed the back of his neck. "That sure is good to learn. With the corruption cleaned up, maybe the river people can rest easy. They'll be glad to have their lives back."

"Those who can. Some will never get their children back, or if they do, they won't be the same." Max balled his fists.

"True," Agent Sharp said. "And that isn't all. We're having to do a lot of changes in the law enforcement agencies around here. Right, Newly?"

"That's right. At times you gotta dig deep and look hard for the bias and discrimination, especially among those who have been too long in office. When Shepherd brought the complaints of the river and Island people to us, Captain Adams sent us to check it out."

Agent Sharp jerked his thumb toward the city. "Yes,

and there will be a house cleaning in your local sheriff's office."

Hours later, family members were allowed to visit the patients in the ICU. Kade was groggy, but awake. Oliver was in a coma which, the doctors said, could last indefinitely. Nurses escorted the visitors out after a couple of minutes to let Kade rest and encouraged them to go home to get some sleep.

≈≈≈

David shuttled back and forth from home, business, and the hospital every day until Kade was released. Sophia guarded him like a mother hen, making sure he wasn't tired out by too many visitors or too long visits. Melody cooked and cleaned while Sophia attended the patient, who seldom complained. He only fussed about being cooped up day after day.

David answered the phone when he was leaving work one evening. "Please, David, will you come get this man and take him down to the river for a little while? He has cabin fever, bad."

When they reached their favorite spot on the river bank, Kade stretched out at the foot of a large oak tree and sighed.

"Oh, this feels sooooo good! I've been needing this for days."

David plopped down beside him and they sat a moment in silence, watching the river. Some ducks paddled along the edge of the water, and here and there a fish jumped, sending ripples all the way back to the bank.

"Have you ever thought about the affect our lives have on other people?" Kade asked. David remembered his own thoughts about the Ripple Effect.

"Yes, I have. Pretty scary stuff."

Kade picked up a rock and threw it into the water. "My dad has done some bad things, but he's still my dad."

"I know."

"I hope he'll be okay."

"He will. We're all praying for him."

"Yeah. I know."

They were silent again for a while.

"Benjamin's growing so much. I love that little guy."

"He loves you too, Uncle Kade. You spoil him."

"I have something to tell you, but you can't tell anyone." Kade peered at David.

"Okay. No problem."

"Sophia and I are having a baby."

David jumped to his feet. "What? Are you serious?" He pounded Kade on the back. "That's awesome! Now I'll be Uncle David."

Kade laughed. "Now, remember, you can't tell anyone. Not even Sadie. Sophia would kill me if she knew I told."

"Oh, man! It will be hard knowing and not telling Sadie. When are you breaking the news?"

"When I get stronger we're having a dinner. Then we'll tell."

David sat back down on the grass, and his lips curved up. "There's nothing like being a dad. It's one of the best things that ever happened to me."

"I guess it would be somewhat better than just being an uncle." Kade threw another rock into the water. "I hope I'll be a good dad. My dad hasn't been the best role model."

"You will be. The way I see it, you know how not to be

a father. You can borrow my role model. It wouldn't be the first time, you know."

On the river

"Mama!" Blonde curls bounced as little Carlie ran across the yard into her mama's arms. Her mama soothed the frightened girl as they watched a man steer a long, green boat close to the bank.

"It's okay, little one. He won't bother you. He's just fishing."

Up and down the river, children cried and trembled every time a boat drew near the shore close to their homes. Weary and broken parents comforted youngsters who awoke from dreams screaming night after night. Single mothers cringed when their kids left for school, and dads scanned the river for strangers and unfamiliar watercrafts.

Max visited homes where children were still missing. His words were like vapor that vanished with the morning fog that hovered over the water. Their lives would never be the same.

Thirty-eight

"Mom, you sure you want to do this? After what he did?" Kade questioned his mother as she filled out the necessary papers, but she was adamant.

Oliver was paralyzed from the waist and would have to have constant assistance when he was released from the hospital. The doctor recommended an assisted living program, but Melody refused. She would care for him.

"I've already forgiven him, and that's that. No more discussion. I just need help getting him into the car." David pushed the wheelchair outside as Sadie brought the car around. Oliver grimaced as David lifted him into the seat. He patted Oliver on the shoulder and received a half-smile in return.

When Oliver was settled in and rested a few days, Kade and Sophia invited everyone to a dinner party. Even though he objected, Melody convinced Oliver he needed to get out of the house a while. David and Sadie helped her with him.

After a delicious meal of roast beef cooked with potatoes, onions, celery, and carrots, the family gathered in the spacious living room. As they chatted, Melody rocked Benjamin and Sadie smiled as she listened to her mom singing softly to the baby. Her sweet voice rose as she sang the old hymn, "Love Lifted Me". Jesse and Kathleen started humming the tune, and soon the entire family joined to sing the melody.

The song ended, leaving a peaceful silence. Sadie's gentle smile turned into a soft chuckle, then a giggle. Everyone looked at her and the giggle lengthened into a laugh.

"Mom, do you remember the time Mrs. Smalls started singing that song and ended up with the wrong words?"

Melody laughed. "I sure do." She turned to the others. "That lady had a wonderful voice but couldn't remember anything. Pastor Wells asked her to sing in the night service, and she wanted me to play for her. But when she started, she was singing "When we all get to Heaven" to the tune of "Love Lifted Me." I don't know how she did it, but she made the words fit the tune."

"Come to think of it, every song she sang was in the tune of "Love Lifted Me." Sadie chuckled and glanced at Kade. "This gooney bird got such a kick out of her doing that."

Kade laughed. "It was hilarious. I'd ask Pastor Wells before church if he'd let her sing. And he would!"

Melody snickered. "So that's why he always asked her. I wondered. My son can find humor in anything."

"Oh," Kade said, "who wouldn't find humor in that."

"Mom," David said, "remember how Kade always loved to play April fool jokes on you? Didn't matter if it wasn't even April."

Kade slapped his knees and laughed. "Remember the time I told you I accidentally poisoned your flower bed? You kept waiting for the flowers to die. It was hilarious."

Melody put her hand on Oliver's arm. "His dad used to get so mad at him when he'd put a rubber-band on the spray nozzle on the sink."

Sadie covered her mouth and giggled. "Yeah, Dad would spray himself right in the face. He'd get so mad. He threatened to pull the nozzle right out of the sink."

"He got me back though," Kade recalled. "He poured food coloring in my shampoo bottle."

Oliver laughed. "He had pink hair for a week."

"I remember when you had pink hair," David said. "You told me you ate too many cherries. I quit eating cherries for a year."

Laughter filled the room as the memories flowed. They were all together once more.

David caught Kade's eye and raised his eyebrows. Kade nodded and put his arm around Sophia.

"Listen, everyone. Sophia and I have some news."

Sophia smiled and her face glowed. "We're going to have a baby."

Sadie squealed, and everyone surrounded the happy couple. Melody hugged her daughter-in-law.

"Oh, my. I'm going to be Grand Mamá again!"

As Oliver regained his strength, he became agitated about getting his business matters cleaned up. He asked his kids for help.

"Sophia, you're a lawyer. Would you be willing to look over my business and see what needs to be done to get me back on track?"

She agreed, and they went to his office. The first thing to do was get the ownership of the casino cleared up. Kade found a file with the contract Oliver had signed with Cosmo. Sadie looked it over.

"I don't see this will be a problem. I guess when it came to legal matters Cosmo lacked good judgment. Looks like he did this himself instead of hiring a lawyer."

"I think we need Dad here to answer questions about his business," Kade said.

Oliver refused to go to the casino which had been closed since what was now called the Island scandal. They would have to carry everything to him. They carried a large briefcase containing papers from the casino and Crandall Shipping to Melody's home, and together they shuffled through the papers.

"Looks like you went through the profits of the casino pretty quickly," Sophia said as she looked at files and figures. "At least it paid for itself, so there's not really any debt."

Oliver nodded. "Yes, that's one thing I made sure of. I've always paid my debts. Don't like owing anyone." He raised his head and red crept up his neck and face. "Now look at what I owe my family. I can never repay you all for what I've done."

Sadie patted his hand and Kade shook his head. "Dad, that's all over now. From here, we only move forward."

"That's what your mom says. I can't believe she is willing to care for me after what I did to her."

"She's a wonderful person." Sophia said. "You're blessed to have her."

Oliver touched the corner of his eye with one finger. "I am. I will spend the rest of my life making up to my family for what I did. And to you, too, David."

"David is family, too, Dad." Kade picked up another paper. "What's this?" He handed it to Oliver.

"Oh, I forgot about those. When I first started Crandall

Shipping, I did some investing and purchased some bonds. I stuck them in a folder and forgot about them."

Sophia grabbed them and riffled through the file. "Oliver, these are worth a lot of money. I thought you said you were broke."

"I thought I was. You mean those are valuable?"

"Yes, very." Sophia showed them to Kade and David. "Wow! These are from at least forty years ago. Why didn't you ever cash them in?"

"I don't know. Guess I didn't think of them after I put them in that folder."

David pulled out another file and looked inside. "What are these?"

Sophia's eyes widened as she scanned the documents. "You mean you invested in stocks, too? Looks like these may be worth something. I'll have to check them out to make sure."

She did. They were. Crandall Shipping would survive, Crandall Island Casino was free and clear, and Oliver was back. The old Oliver. The good Oliver. He had Melody call a meeting with his family. Jesse and Kathleen were to be there also.

When the family gathered in Melody's large living area, Oliver wheeled his chair to sit beside the rock fireplace facing everyone.

"I want you to know that I'm truly sorry for all the pain I've caused you."

Protests arose, but he held up his hand. "I know I've been forgiven by God and by each of you. But I want to say this before all of you. I know I'm more than blessed." He took Melody's hand as she stood beside him. "Melody has agreed to marry me — again."

Everyone arose to congratulate the couple, then he motioned for them to sit back down. "I have more to say and ask that you please don't interrupt me until I'm through." He cleared his throat. "I want David to take over Crandall Shipping. He can merge it with his own or hire someone to run it. Whatever he wants to do. It's his."

David blushed and nodded his agreement and thanks. Oliver continued. "I want the casino turned into a shelter for abused women and abandoned children." A unified gasp filled the room. "I want Sophia to handle the legal affairs, and Sadie to be over it. It's her baby." Sadie wiped happy tears as Kade hugged her.

"Kade, I want you to take everything else on the Island and make it work for you. The hotels, the businesses, all of it. I know you have a lot of pull with the Island and river folks who work there. I'm sure you'll do right by them. Anyway, it's yours to do as you see fit. You have the finances to take care of it."

He gazed around at the assembled group. "I want to spend the rest of my days with the wife of my youth and playing with my grandkids. I deserve nothing but have been given everything. I love you all." He turned his wheelchair around to leave the room but was halted by family and friends expressing their love, encouragement, and appreciation to him. Then Melody took him to lie down for some much-needed rest.

"You know," Jesse said, "we never know what the river will bring, but wherever it goes, it brings life."

Kathleen nodded. "And what a trip! It has brought life to us all."

Sadie turned to Kade. "I don't know what happened to our dad, but how wonderful for him to give such an unbelievable gift to the Island and river people. Imagine, a place to restore broken people provided by a once-broken person."

"And now it's up to us to bring his legacy to life." David put his arm around Sadie. "Sadie has already found out there are many broken lives on the river. We'll need all of you to help us."

Heads nodded. They would help. They would lay down their lives so others could be healed. Wasn't that what Jesus taught?

ABOUT THE AUTHOR

Martha Rodriguez grew up in rural Arkansas where she attended college and taught high school. She has always enjoyed writing, and as a teacher, she enjoyed teaching her students to write essays and create poetry and stories.

Her work includes children's picture books including the series Life in the Leaves and Life in the Trees, a Middle Grade duo, *Modified* and *Rectified*, and YA novel, *Pepper*, which is based primarily on her life in a large family, and some non-fiction. Visit her at mjwriter.com to check out her work.

Made in the USA
Lexington, KY
21 December 2019